DON'T GO IN THE BASEMENT

She had only seconds to take it all in.

Seconds to see the room with its low ceiling and exposed bulbs.

The others were there, barely visible in the dim light. A woman tied to a chair with a crazy mesh of rope and wire and tape. Her head spun to another, an older man strapped to a wall—she couldn't see clearly, but something had been driven into his hands, pinning him there.

But there was more of this show to be taken in . . .

Now—with one small turn more—she finally looked at the person standing behind her.

"We're all here now, it's time we got started."

She saw the man slide shut a second door, a heavy, hidden door. Any sound would have no chance to escape to the street.

Because despite all the tape, all the gags, all the covering—there would indeed be sound.

In Dreams

Shane Christopher

JOVE BOOKS, NEW YORK

THE BERKLEY PUBLISHING GROUP
Published by the Penguin Group
Penguin Group (USA) Inc.
375 Hudson Street, New York, New York 10014, USA
Penguin Group (Canada), 90 Eglinton Avenue East, Suite 700, Toronto, Ontario M4P 2Y3, Canada
(a division of Pearson Penguin Canada Inc.)
Penguin Books Ltd., 80 Strand, London WC2R 0RL, England
Penguin Group Ireland, 25 St. Stephen's Green, Dublin 2, Ireland
(a division of Penguin Books Ltd.)
Penguin Group (Australia), 250 Camberwell Road, Camberwell, Victoria 3124, Australia
(a division of Pearson Australia Group Pty. Ltd.)
Penguin Books India Pvt. Ltd., 11 Community Centre, Panchsheel Park, New Delhi—110 017, India
Penguin Group (NZ), Cnr. Airborne and Rosedale Roads, Albany, Auckland 1310, New Zealand
(a division of Pearson New Zealand Ltd.)
Penguin Books (South Africa) (Pty.) Ltd., 24 Sturdee Avenue, Rosebank, Johannesburg 2196,
South Africa

Penguin Books Ltd., Registered Offices: 80 Strand, London WC2R 0RL, England

IN DREAMS

A Jove Book / published by arrangement with the author

PRINTING HISTORY
Jove mass-market edition / September 2006

Copyright © 2006 by Matthew J. Costello.
Text design by Kristin del Rosario.

ISBN: 0-515-14128-3

JOVE®
Jove Books are published by The Berkley Publishing Group,
a division of Penguin Group (USA) Inc.,
375 Hudson Street, New York, New York 10014.
JOVE is a registered trademark of Penguin Group (USA) Inc.
The "J" design is a trademark belonging to Penguin Group (USA) Inc.

PRINTED IN THE UNITED STATES OF AMERICA

10 9 8 7 6 5 4 3 2 1

To Tom Hakala—
My good friend and supporter who certainly
knows the *real* Shane . . .

In dreams . . .
you walk alone . . .

Before
the Dreams

Prologue

THE young woman kept walking down Mott Street.

It was Sunday. The street, still wet from the afternoon of rain, empty, deserted.

She fingered the piece of paper in her hand. The street, the address, the location.

The place where all her questions would be answered. Her heart beat fast. Breathing funny as if she had some weight on her chest. She felt nervous, excited. She wouldn't have said she was scared.

Not then. Not yet.

She turned off Mott, then down Pell Street. The sidewalk and pavement glistened with wetness here too—a street lamp midblock was out.

About halfway down the street, she looked at the number of the shuttered fruit market on her right. Her address, the address on the piece of paper, had to be about in the middle of this street.

Yes. Just about where the dead street lamp hung over the dark wet street.

The woman's name was Caroline Brzow. Guys who found her attractive—and there were many of them—would call her Caroline "Wow."

No one ever made the other joke, Caroline Brzow-Wow, as if she might be a dog. Not with her deep, dark blue eyes, sandy blond hair, and gym-trained figure that looked so great on a dance floor bouncing to Outkast.

Later, when the names were revealed, one newspaper would get her name wrong. One sloppy stupid copy editor would screw up her strange last name.

Her one moment . . . of fame . . . ruined by sloppy

editing. In a New York City paper! All of them rags, even the *New York Times* with its mistakes and lies and apologies.

All rags.

How much has been lost?

But now—she stopped. In the darkness. Licking her lip. Perhaps chewing a bit as she held up the paper, trying to see in the darkness, trying to confirm in the darkness that she had the right address.

A building number hung over stone stairs that led down.

She had assumed—who wouldn't?—that the location would be on the ground floor. That the others might already be there, waiting, ready to talk to her, to share *their* story.

She hesitated at those stairs.

She noticed: a railing on the left, and another on the right.

Odd, she thought. *Two railings . . .*

And if she thought it dark on the cracked sidewalk, it looked even darker down those stairs. But anything was better than not knowing. Anything was better than wondering what was happening, whether she was losing her mind.

Anything—even walking down dark stairs to some subterranean New York room.

SHE took one step, then another. She reached out for one of the handrails, and felt the cold, wet metal. Slippery from rain. It didn't offer much in the way of support. Her hand could easily slide off the rail, sending her flying.

More steps, closer to the darkness at the bottom.

But that darkness had one glimmer of light.

One glimmer that glowed in this pool of gloom.

The pale yellow glow of a buzzer. No name visible below it. Just the yellow buzzer awaiting a finger to press it.

Almost there, she must have thought. The end of the rainbow. The quest over. The journey to understand.

Her finger pressed the buzzer.

Strange . . .

She heard nothing. No sound. If the buzzer didn't work, she'd have to knock. She'd have to bang on the heavy metal door. Rap it with her knuckles. Maybe shout out a "Hello!"

Say . . . "I'm here."

She pressed the buzzer again, this time harder, holding it.

Still no sound. Not from the buzzer.

But sounds did come from beyond the door.

Yes, the noise of a dead bolt sliding away. Of tumblers turning, latches freed, a chain undone. The typical overkill for New York City security. So many locks to keep all the bad things out.

Except—as she was only moments from learning—these locks, these latches and chains weren't designed to keep the bad things . . . out.

The door handle in front of her turned, the brasslike metal catching the scant bit of light.

And Caroline Brzow—

That's . . . B, r, z, o, w . . .

—didn't hesitate as the door peeked open.

YOU wonder what would make her do this?

What would drive her to such a dark New York street, a street unknown even to most New Yorkers, to dark stairs, to a strange subterranean room, to do something so scary, so dangerous?

If you were there, you would warn her.

You would grab her arm, feeling the nicely shaped biceps from all her free-weight reps, and tell her, Hold on here a minute.

Let's just wait a second and think about what you are doing. This doesn't look—what?

Cool? Safe?

Okay?

Something's *not* right here.

Let's just back up a minute and think things through.

You might say that. Anyone would. If they were there.

But you aren't Caroline. You haven't seen what she's seen.

The door opened. More darkness beyond.

This surprised her. She expected that once in the room, then there would be light. She'd see—for the first time in the flesh—the others. See them for real. The four others would already be there.

A few thoughts fired in her brain. Disconnected thoughts, or so they seemed. But really all part of what was happening, or what was about to happen.

A thought: This is the wrong address.

She should get to some light and check her address again. Probably some old person's basement hovel.

Then another thought: The others here are scared. Of course, until they knew it was her, they would all be worried. Yes, that made sense. They'd want to see her face, to check that it was *really* her.

But then . . . how could they see her face in all this darkness?

All these thoughts . . . as she took another step into the room. She heard, from her step, that the floor was hard, stone, concrete. No rug here. Some kind of storage room.

The door flew shut. The first noise, a loud *bang* smashing shut. Latches thrown again, tumblers turning. The sound of a chain. All in the terrible darkness.

And then the slow awareness of other sounds.

Movement, rustling, breathing, muffled noises.

All sounds she should have heard right away. Yet somehow she had missed them.

In the darkness, she turned back to the door, the door she knew to be locked again. The door with all those locks to keep the bad things out.

Another thought: Sometimes locks keep the bad things in.

And with that thought, with her breathing even faster, her heart thumping, and feeling dizzy, a light finally came on.

She had only seconds to take it all in.

Seconds to see the room with its low ceiling and exposed bulbs.

I never saw this before, she thought.

She had expected it to look familiar. But instead it was totally unfamiliar.

The others were there, barely visible in the dim light. A

woman tied to a chair with a crazy mesh of rope and wire and tape. Secured to that chair as if about be launched into space. Her head spun to another, an older man strapped to a wall, a web of rope pinning him there. His hands fastened— she couldn't see clearly, but something had been driven into those hands, pinning him to the wall.

"No," she moaned.

But there was more of this show to be taken in. Someone on a medical cot, held there by acres of white tape, endless surgical tape wrapped around the person, so only a head stuck out. A woman, older than her.

And just her head stuck out.

She's dead, Caroline thought. Tears started flowing. Tears for all these prisoners.

But now the chest of the mummy on the cot moved slightly, breathing. Still alive, they're all still alive.

Whipping around, to—

Behind her, a young man on his knees. Caroine knew his name. He was a Wall Street lawyer.

Of course, she had *seen* him . . .

Now he was on his knees, hands tied behind his back, some kind of leather contraption over his mouth as his head bobbed and weaved crazily.

Caroline moaned. Her tears made everything blurry.

So that now—with one small turn more—she finally looked at the person standing behind her; it was the one image that wasn't clear.

She felt him quickly throw something on her wrist. Strips of plastic that tightened into a kind of handcuff.

She started babbling.

Saying all those words that you would say at such a time. Babbling, then screaming, until large gray tape covered her lips.

And then the man finally said some words.

The words beyond horrible in their meaning, and in their intent.

"We're all here now. It's time we got started."

She saw the man slide shut a second door, a hidden, heavy

door. Any sound would have no chance to escape to the street.

Because despite all the tape, all the gags, all the covering—there would indeed be sound.

TIME passes everywhere.

The present inevitably yields to a future.

A future when certain things are over, when they have . . . ended.

A time when you can look back at an event and realize that, yes, it's in the past. Safely neutralizing that event's power, its ability to grip and hold you.

It's not something that's happening anymore.

No. It's something that *happened*.

We have a word for it.

It's called *over.*

Over—as in done, finished. Whatever the event is, there will be no more of it.

And after this event, this moment, weeks passed.

Weeks before the smell was noticed in nearby buildings, even at the Chinese butcher shop filled with its gory hanging rows of ducks. Authorities were called. Complaints lodged. Two young police officers, a Hispanic woman and a burly Irish kid, a throwback, showed up.

The source of the complaint was localized.

There could be no question about it.

Down the stairs.

Down *there.* Behind the big metal door.

Other officers came with special equipment to knock the doors down.

The day? Blazingly beautiful, a perfect New York City blue sky.

Such days can indeed hide and reveal all sorts of horrors.

Though the team of what became now five officers were completely unprepared for what they would see when the door finally flew open, when they finally broke down that other metal door.

The first warning of the surprises that lay beyond?

The way the smell *spiked.* Not a smell as much as an

overwhelming stench. A cloud that erupted from the room. One woman officer gagged. Pedestrians who had gathered around now backed up.

Everyone's nostrils flared with some primal warning about what lay beyond.

The team of officers hesitated.

They looked at one another. Even those with limited experience could guess what that bilious cloud meant. But there was no one of rank there to tell them what to do.

The woman's partner said, "Should we call it in?" He stopped, gagged, choked. "Ask what we should do?"

Another cop, the one who had arrived with the door buster, shook his head, over and over.

"We should"—he also had a hard time speaking—"just go on. We got to see."

On their faces, such terrible pain.

As if each knew how their lives, their minds, their nights and days would be changed forever once they went in.

The street had cleared.

Without anyone saying a word. No yellow tape. No barked order to clear out.

The woman took charge. "We have to go in. Breathe through your mouth." One young cop made a sick face at that thought, as though tasting the smell would be worse than smelling it.

He shook his head. The bright blue sky seemed like a joke. "Jesus . . ."

All five cops jockeyed for the rear position. Each of them put one hand to his or her mouth, while the other hand held a gun. They entered in the standard at-ready position, guns held close, aimed directly at where they'd be looking. Though not one of them expected anything alive on the other side.

When no one took the lead, the woman did.

She gave the second door, a fat slab of now crushed-in metal, a strong push. It fell open.

There was no light inside save for the reflected glow of the brilliant morning outside.

And that was enough.

That was plenty.

And when they were all inside, gagging, choking, turning away—except there was no *away*—one young cop started crying. They had all been seared. Their minds and lives brutally burned by what they saw.

The incomprehensibility of it.

Years of counseling could do nothing to ever make the images fade.

IN the newspaper, Caroline Brzow's name did not appear in the report of the story.

Only later would the papers get a chance to get it wrong.

Down at One Police Plaza it was quickly decided that only a version of what happened could be released. Anything else would be too horrific. In a city that could withstand anything, what occurred in that room had to be sanitized. Details hidden.

All standard procedure. Details hidden so that the police had an advantage.

The papers had a photo of the street. The building completely girded in yellow tape. Local residents kept talking about the smell. No way that could be hidden. The newspapers knew that it had been the scene of a mass murder of five people. Names initially were withheld.

Another detail hidden: no connection seemed to exist among the five people.

No connection except the fate they shared at the end.

The public just knew they'd been killed. The public was not told how they were killed, or, more important, the duration of that process. Or any of the physical details of the space where it happened. Nothing about the markings, symbols, images that filled the stone walls, and the floor and even the ceiling.

The officers said nothing, not even to girlfriends, or spouses, or even priests. Nothing explicit. Partly because that's what they were ordered to do, and partly because maybe—just maybe—if they didn't talk about it, the event could really slip somehow into the past.

Fade into the past.

Letting time make it easier.

But one event leads to another. That is the essence of time.

Some events, even bad ones, are really only a prologue to other, larger occurrences.

Warning signs.

For those who can see the warning . . .

PART ONE

The
Dreamers

1

MARI bounded up the stone steps two at a time, leaving Will in the dust.

"Come on," she yelled, hitting the top step. "You do wanna sweat, don't you?"

Will came close behind her as they ran straight to the promenade of Carl Schurz Park and then cut left, toward Gracie Mansion.

As her good friend came abreast of her, Mari looked at him. And he looked well. She knew he'd had a rough patch months ago, but the meds seemed to be working. He seemed . . . *okay*.

But she imagined that could all disappear so quickly.

"I think it's time for me to take up walking," he said. "Or maybe"—he struck a pose even as he jogged—"Jazzercise."

"Spinning," Mari said. "Crazy women in a dark room with 50 Cent blowing their eardrums out."

"I wonder if there's some kind of exercise that involves cooking and wine tasting? Or maybe checking out men's butts?"

"Hey, then we could still do it together."

They laughed. A tricky thing to do when running, when every breath was necessary just to keep going.

The promenade sloped down to Gracie Mansion, where the mayor stayed infrequently—if at all. Not a bad little shack, but probably not quite to the multimillionaire's tastes. Mari and Will curved around at the bottom of the promenade, where the water ferry docked, and started to head back.

"So, no shoptalk today?" Will said between pants.

Mari looked at Will. "I thought you absolutely hated my shoptalk. I thought you found the newspaper business horribly boring."

"It is. I mean movie times and restaurant reviews can be helpful. The rest? You can have it."

"I do *have* it. It's my life."

"Exactly. And that, my dear, is why I care. You're quiet today. So . . . whassup?"

Mari felt her hair—pulled into a ponytail—bouncing on her back as she jogged. Needs a major cut, she thought. Something short and stylish and not just another fast hack-and-slash job.

Maybe that's why my social life sucks.

Every day's a bad hair day.

Or maybe New York just had too many "Wills." Charming gay guys who, while fun to hang with, were in no way close to date material. And so many of the straight guys were aging frat boy types who thought that a bar wasn't a bar without at least five TVs running distant sport competitions.

Or maybe—Christ—she just worked too hard.

All work, and very little play.

No, scratch that. No play.

That had to change.

"So, things still bad? With your editor?"

"Things are always bad with him. Now only worse."

"Not a happy camper?"

"He hated my last story. Not enough facts, not enough background. Said to me—are you sure you want to hear this? Newspaper shoptalk?"

"You have something else to pass the time with while we pound the pavement?"

"Okay—he said to me, 'Your story is shit and you need to get on the streets.' Meaning I should do some real investigative work."

"Shit? Is that a technical term from journalism school?"

Mari laughed. The park still had some lingering mothers with their strollers, enjoying the later summer light, the incredible river scene. On second thought . . . probably not mothers, but long-suffering nannies from Sweden waiting for one of the family breadwinners to come home.

They passed the small dog run, loaded—as usual—with a bunch of small dogs yapping and chasing one another.

"Five people killed. No details worth a damn from Police Plaza. No photos except for the street. No comments from any of the officers. So how the *hell* do I build a story out of that?"

"Your editor ran it?"

"Had to. He had nothing else. But he said he expected better of me. *I* expect better of me."

"And that's *all* that's bugging you?"

"Yes," Mari said. "Trust me, it's enough."

The lie sat there. Hanging between them as they neared the southern end of the promenade. One Starbucks over-priced latte wasn't too far away.

Will was too good a friend not to know that she had lied.

But the other thing, the thing that really bothered her? Even just thinking about it made her feel crazy.

Talk about it—and she'd have to check herself in some-where.

Probably not a bad option, she thought.

Will stopped at the end of the promenade. He stood at the fence, where one good leap could send a desperate person flying into the river or, with a bad bounce, into the roaring traffic of the FDR below.

"Cutting short our run?"

Will's eyes had shadowy patches below them. She hadn't noticed before. Lack of sleep?

Maybe.

Or maybe something else.

He put a hand on her shoulder.

"I know . . . I mean, I *know* that isn't everything, Mari. It's not just the story that has you upset. And I want you to know . . ." He grinned, and started to sing in an R & B style . . . "I need *you* to know that whatever it is, I will be there for you. *Capiche?*"

Mari grinned. How she loved him. He was worried about her. And how horrible it would be to lose him.

"*Capiche,*" she said. "And now can we finish?"

"Lead on, *girlfren.*"

And they started trotting back, toward the exit from the park, to the darkening streets of the Upper East Side.

* * *

DETECTIVE David Rodriguez stood one step down from the real estate agent, who fiddled with a bunch of keys.

Blond, trim, and wearing spike heels that made her as tall as David.

"I tell you," she said, turning to him. "This place will sell in a heartbeat. *A heartbeat!* Wait till you see it."

David smiled. "Not on the market, though?"

She nodded, with a sharklike smile, David thought, that recognized that every human on the planet was potential victim for a real estate agent.

"Watch this top step," she said as the door popped open. "There's a little half step as you go in."

"Yeah." David was getting used to people who saw him with his cane and immediately went into *watch out* mode.

Like he was a toddler who might go rolling down the stairs.

They entered the small house.

THE agent had left the front door open. Standard procedure.

The man had been a dentist. Lived here, and had his office a block away, a partnership with another dentist—David's next stop on this little tour.

He was here, despite the fact that the place had already been examined carefully by the crime scene unit.

Still, he didn't get to be a detective through a lack of thoroughness.

"Now, Detective . . . Rodriguez, is it?"

"Yes."

"Is there anything special you want to see? The family wants to sell this baby fast . . . so as soon as we have a go-ahead from your department, we want to clean this out. Though you can see—it's pretty damn clean."

That it was.

David looked around. Big plasma screen. No photos anywhere. On a coffee table a few magazines that looked like props. He walked into the bedroom, which also had the look of a hotel room—clean, generic.

Who the hell was this guy?

This Dr. Bernard Kenner, who took a detour to the dark side, a side trip to hell that led to him being hung . . .

. . . *fucking hung* . . .

. . . from a crossbeam.

Back at One Police Plaza they had gathered a pile of personal effects from the guy. He could look at those later.

But for now . . .

"And your office left everything here?"

"Yes. As I said. Very clean."

"I see." David turned to her, facing the radiant smile and ruby red lips.

A hungry real estate lioness.

"Thanks. I can go now."

The woman led him out, and David lagged behind, his cane digging into the plush rug to the door.

"I got a full waiting room, Officer."

"It's Detective, Doctor. I just need a few minutes. From you, and maybe your hygienist."

The waiting room was indeed full—adults, kids, all studying David standing with the dentist, Kenner's partner, Robert Jay, in the waiting room.

David looked around. "Maybe your office would be better?"

The dentist nodded. "And I'll get Marie."

Marie had a massive head of curly black hair, and chewed her gum with an admirable determination.

"I can't tell you much more," Dr. Jay said. "We"—he looked at Marie for confirmation—"were as horrified as could be. Bernie? Bernie killed somehow? It was incredible. And nobody has told us any details."

"Have to do that," David said. "It helps us."

"I'm sure. But we know nothing."

"I understand. But—leading up to the day he didn't show up, when you learned that he had been killed, did you notice anything odd?"

"No, noth—"

The girl popped her gum.

Classy. This is the place I want to come for my root canal, that's for sure, David thought.

But the pop signaled some information about to erupt from that gum-filled mouth.

"Y'know"—one word, of course—"there was somethin', Dr. Jay."

David wondered if Dr. Jay got to sample the hygienist's other skills. . . .

"What was it, Marie?" Jay said tightly.

The woman looked at David.

"For a few weeks before it happened, Dr. Kenner seemed awfully tense. I mean, sometimes he'd just snap at me, and—"

"Marie—" Dr. Jay started. But David reached out and touched the man's forearm.

"Please. Let her continue."

"Like, he'd snap about how slowly I mixed the cement stuff—"

"Fixative. It's called fixative."

"Right, I *know* that, Dr. Jay. Then I saw his hands shake. And his eyes. The guy looked like he didn't sleep at all. It was a little freaky."

"I think that's quite enough. Detective—"

"Hold on a second. Marie, did Dr. Kenner ever say anything, give you any clue what was bothering him?"

"Well, I asked. One morning, when he looked so bad. And he just said . . . 'My sleeping's gone to hell.' He said those exact words."

Dr. Jay let our a giant breath of air.

"Anything more?" David asked.

The dental tech shook her head. "No. And even when he said that, it was like he wished he hadn't said anything, like it embarrassed him. But I can guess one thing."

"What's that?"

"For some reason . . . he wasn't sleeping well."

"Detective—I have a lot of patients waiting. Mine, now Bernard's."

"Fine. All right, I may be back." He looked at the gum chewer. "And thanks. That actually might be of some help."

She smiled, and David walked out of the office.

AS soon as David was on the sun-bleached sidewalk outside the dental offices of Dr. Bernard Kenner and Dr. Robert Jay, his cell phone vibrated with a message.

The office.

Which in this case meant One Police Plaza.

From Captain Hicks.

Simple and to the point.

Come back now. Stuff happening.

David took a breath—the air hot, humid.

Stuff happening. And he imagined . . . not good stuff.

He walked over to his car, his cane now tapping out a rhythm.

DAVID swiped his ID card through the reader. A green light appeared.

Then he shifted his cane to his left hand and pressed down hard with his right hand on the thick metal door handle. Then, with a heavy shove of his shoulder, the door finally moved open.

Christ, he thought, think they could have made it more difficult to get in?

He moved the cane back to his right hand.

This is great, he thought, hobbling into the office. He'd practically had to beg the doctor to sign off on his returning to work. The doctor wanted him to use a wheelchair.

Take a month off.

Christ!

No way, David said. Scootering around didn't go with the image of someone in the Violent Crimes division. Of course, the cane didn't look so great either.

A young woman working at her terminal looked up and gave him a smile. She was new here. Lisa . . . something.

David smiled back.

They had flirted a bit. Before the accident.

Now he was probably *way* off her radar.

He tried to walk as normally as possible to his office.

People went on with their work, some looking up to nod at him, shoot him a quick smile—all of them doing their part.

They all knew it wasn't David's fault that he caught a bullet just above his left knee. So damn lucky—it could have shattered the kneecap. They had said he was all done with operations for now. But he had to wonder if that was true. When he walked around on the leg sometimes, all he could think about was how good it would be to get his weight off it, just lie down on his bed and sleep forever.

Johanna had been great through the whole thing.

For an ex, she couldn't have been better. The visits, the food, the advice . . . *Time to hang it up, David. Unless you want to be dead.*

But Jo knew all too well that he was crap at taking advice.

And the accident—such a fluke thing. He still wasn't sure how it happened.

His long march to Hicks's office was almost done . . . when he noticed that the room was filled.

Fuck.

That didn't look good.

He forced himself to walk straighter. Put a smile on his face. Come on, he thought, *I don't need this.* I took a bullet for the department . . . doesn't that buy me any slack?

But as he walked into the office, the grim faces showed that slack didn't seem to be on offer.

"DAVID, sorry for making you hustle back here."

David kept the smile on his face. "What's the occasion?"

His captain, Ed Hicks, an old-line guy who started out as patrolman in the Bronx, out of Fort Apache, looked pained.

David turned to the other two people in the room. One was the Violent Crimes head, Captain Frank Biondi. More of a political guy than a cop. But he was the five-hundred-pound gorilla in the room.

And standing next to him, a kid.

No, maybe not a kid, but someone . . . what thirty . . . thirty-one? David had seen him around the office. A young detective. Their paths hadn't crossed before—but it looked as if they were crossing now.

"Rodriguez, the leg still hurting?"

David turned to Biondi, still smiling. "Only when I walk on it."

Shit, gotta get that sarcasm under control. Inherited from his Irish mother and not his Cuban dad. David's wiseass mouth always got him into trouble.

Biondi nodded.

"Here. David. Take a seat."

David nodded. No use pretending that standing there— for what looked like a kangaroo court—wasn't fucking painful.

He navigated past Biondi, and past the young detective, to the offered chair. Lowering his body was tricky. It involved positioning his cane in the right place and then trying to land in the seat and then *not* sending the rolling chair flying backward.

He performed it this time with—he thought—a better than average amount of grace.

"We were, um, meeting upstairs, and thought—well— we'd come down, talk to you about the case . . ."

The case.

David knew what that meant. *The case.* As if there was a case. What they really had was a charnel house filled with bodies all arranged in the most disturbing, bizarre way.

One look at that scene, and everyone knew that the department couldn't let any of *that* freaky shit out to the public.

So far, no leaks had sprouted.

And that was good.

But a *case*?

What goddamn case? David had nothing. In his twenty years he had never seen something so devoid of leads, evidence.

"So, Detective," Biondi said, "we're concerned. You know, the press, the mayor's office, all that stuff. Bearing down real hard. And so far, you—the detective in charge—have nothing."

Biondi let his gaze drift down to David's leg.

The implication couldn't be clearer: Maybe if we had a detective with two good legs, then maybe, just maybe we wouldn't be at this dead end.

"Yeah, I know. Been frustrating. For me too. But it's early and—"

Biondi shook his head. "No, Detective Rodriguez. It's not early. Every day is a day too many. We can't let the thing become a black hole."

David let his eyes drift to the window. The NYC Municipal Building with its gold dome blocked his view of the rest of Lower Manhattan. He couldn't glimpse what a lot of cops here called "The Hole." That giant slice of sky made by two fallen buildings, a chunk of sky now open, awaiting a new skyscraper to—slowly, someday—fill it.

Everyone knowing that nothing would ever fill "The Hole."

David looked back at his interrogators.

"Look, I know we don't have much. *Yet.* I have people here looking in other cities, other countries, for similar patterns. And we're not done with the crime scene. No way, not by a long shot. We're still going through everything a second time, and then a goddamn third time."

Easy, he reminded himself.

Sarcasm and language would not be of any help here.

"And the victims. Lot of work to be done there. Their backgrounds, connections—"

"What connections?" Biondi said.

Hicks looked at David. The captain was a big supporter of David. But there would only be so much he could do. His eyes said it all: I'm kinda boxed in here.

Biondi looked to his left. "This is Detective James Corcoran. He's got the background to jump in on this, take over—"

David shook his head and stood up—without the cane.

He didn't even pause to marvel at what a burst of adrenaline could do.

They wanted to replace him with this kid? No fucking way.

"Listen, I'm just getting everything in place. Yank me now and it all goes to hell."

"I think it's already gotten there, Rodriguez. I want someone who can move, hustle. You can't do that. I think—*we* think"—Biondi shot a look at Hicks, David saw Hicks turn away—"you need to be replaced. For your own good. Nothing against you. But you're disabled."

David counted to three.

If Biondi wanted to get him to explode, the D word would do it.

Though Johanna had told him the same thing.

David looked at Hicks for some help. But he could see in the captain's eyes that it was too late for that.

Time for a "Plan B."

He looked at Corcoran. Short, marine-cut hair. Chiseled chin. Probably a gym rat and a babe magnet, maybe ex-military. Blue eyes that were watching all this go down. He hadn't said a word.

And why should he?

The case of his lifetime was about to be dropped into his lap.

My case, David thought.

His three counts over . . . "Okay, you got a point about my mobility. But to waste everything I know about this stuff, my background—"

"You can still do some desk work," Biondi said.

David shook his head. "I need to *see* things, hear people, be out there—"

"Detective Rodriguez can be pretty amazing, Frank. He gets people to remember things; he brings stuff up—it all just leads places."

"Yeah, it's called interrogation," Biondi said. He looked over at Corcoran. "You know how to interrogate, Detective?"

"Yes, sir."

Ex-marine? Formerly of Abu Ghraib?

Could be . . .

David wanted to take his cane and—

He was watching the case slip away. And then he'd be delegated to time off due to a disability or, even worse, desk work. Both of which would drive him totally insane.

"Okay. Listen. You got a point. This guy's legs work just fine, mine don't. I'll grant that. But how about this—we work *together*. You don't lose any of my experience, and we have Detective Corcoran for the wonderful stuff that he can do."

David looked at the young detective.

Thinking: You *can* do things, huh, you gung-ho shit?

David imagined that Corcoran could veto the whole deal.

Hicks spoke first. "You know, that's a great idea. Great training for Detective Corcoran—"

"Corcoran doesn't need *training*," Biondi said.

"Right," Hicks quickly agreed. "But you have to admit that together they could do more . . ."

David stopped there. He wanted to grab his cane, get some pressure off that left leg. But he forced himself to stand there unaided. This was like that ad featuring William Shatner, where he suggests to Nimoy that they *both* be spokespeople.

And Mr. Spock waves a squeak toy at him, declining.

Biondi nodded, thinking.

David weighed whether more words would help or hurt his position. He was about to speak—

"Okay. Done. You two—work together. Share everything. Corcoran, I want you to report to me on progress or lack of same. Rodriguez, you can keep Hicks up to speed. Get whatever resources you need. Anything. Okay?"

Corcoran nodded. He didn't exactly jump for joy. But he didn't make a face.

Though that might come later.

"Great," said David. He looked at Hicks and then Biondi. The guy was maybe a bastard, but he had given him a chance. He didn't have to do that—and he had.

Some pricks . . . aren't all prick.

Will wonders never cease.

David stuck out his hand to Biondi. "Thanks."

"Okay, we'll let you two get acquainted. Do some planning. I got a mayor's meeting in thirty." He turned to leave the office. "Count yourselves lucky that you don't have to sit through *that* shit . . ."

And then Biondi and Hicks left, and David took a big breath and plopped down on his chair, facing his new and unwanted partner.

2

"**YOU** having *another* bad hair day?"

Mari looked up at Julie Fein, a lifestyles reporter and Mari's occasional drinking buddy.

Mari smiled. "My hair looks that bad?"

"Hair's fine—I guess, I mean, for you—but you seem a little distracted."

"Guess I am. To say the least. How about we switch jobs? I'll cover the next movie opening and you—"

Julie laughed and put up her hand. "Sorry, I only do fluff. When I was born, the rabbi pronounced me forever shallow, and I've stayed true to his vision. You on the other hand—"

"Yeah. I'm deep. And in deep shit."

A young male copy editor from across the aisle through the sea of desks looked up from his relentless pecking.

"Careful, you're unsettling the troops." Julie then leaned close. "He is a cute one, hm? Ever let your mind daydream, drift away?"

Mari looked at the young guy with stylish glasses and short hair lacquered into a windswept design that had to take him a good ten minutes.

Men, she thought . . . they're the new women.

She smiled at the guy.

"I wonder," Mari said, "is it sexual harassment to curse in the office?"

"How the fuck would I know," Julie said, and Mari grinned. She needed friends like Julie, and Will. Especially now with the city editor breathing down her neck.

Her reporter's desk didn't come easy, but it could easily just disappear.

"How about drinks after work? Morgan's?"

Mari shook her head. "I need something a bit busier, with

fewer candles unless you're going to put some moves on me."

"Sorry—not my type. Okay, the Campbell Apartment. Pricey but packed."

"Perfect. As long as we don't get any married commuters trying out ten-year-old lines on us."

"So what? Let 'em dream. Good for our egos."

"Yeah. Okay, now can I do some work?"

Julie put her hands up. "Be my guest. I have to do a phoner with Isaac about Fashion Week. And trust me—that's work too."

Mari nodded, as Julie sailed away.

A phone interview with Isaac Mizrahi versus what? Finding out who the five dead people are, how they got killed, why they got killed . . .

All those unanswered goddamn questions.

She looked over at the cute copy editor, now dutifully back on his machine.

And maybe, someday, a candidate for her job?

Dream on, she thought.

Mari opened the file in her folder in the network. She called it "The Five," and it had everything she knew about the killings, and all that she didn't know.

MARI knocked on her editor's door.

The woman inside, in mid-bite of a well-stuffed sandwich, looked up.

"Bad time?" Mari said.

Joann Gully, the ancient editor who had been at the *News* since when it used to be a rabidly conservative tabloid, looked up, mouth full, and shook her head.

"No. Not if you don't mind watching me wolf down my turkey club."

Mari walked in and sat down. She had an instinctive feeling that the woman didn't like her. At times she thought it might be because Mari was—what . . . a good thirty years younger? Still attractive, still hopefully sexy, while Gully had sailed into some gray realm where woman, looks-wise, simply didn't matter anymore.

Or was that just a stupid thought?

Maybe Joann Gully didn't respect Mari's journalism. Respect had to be fought for, *earned*. Up to this story, Mari had been doing well. Now everything sucked.

The editor gestured at a chair filled with a stack of papers.

"You can put them anywhere. I still believe in the paper trail."

Was that a dig, some reference to the old school journalism versus the new Internet Google-ized version of reporting, all of which a warhorse like Gully probably viewed as simply lazy?

Focus, Mari told herself. Stop thinking about anything else but the damn story.

"You have news?" Gully said.

Double-edged question that.

"No. Nothing more. But I spent most of the day going over what we have so far and—"

"Which is hell of a lot of nothing, right?"

"Mostly. But then—I had some ideas."

"Ideas? How refreshing. Tell me a few."

"You can't have five people killed and keep the lid on. Not in this city. They may have strong-armed the families, friends—but that will only go so far."

The editor took another giant bite of the turkey club. What big teeth she has, Mari thought, hurrying on . . .

"If there aren't holes yet, there soon will be. People will talk, leaks pop up."

Gully nodded. "Makes sense. If you don't mind waiting for 'eventually.' "

"If one leak opens, then another will pop open, and the whole net of secrecy will unravel."

"You say that like it's a good thing." The editor took a big slug of Diet Coke from the can.

"Not sure if it's good or bad, but it is our job, right?"

As soon as the words escaped Mari's mouth, she knew that they'd tumbled out all wrong. The editor took a moment to respond, probably enjoying Mari's gaffe.

Probably . . .

Shit, I have to lose this paranoia.

"Our . . . *job* is to find out what happened and, if possible, why. Still, no journalist wants anyone innocent hurt. So what are you looking for?"

"Looking for?"

"You want me to okay something, I imagine?"

Mari leaned close. "Look, I know you haven't been too happy with my coverage—"

"Not just me, Mari. Bill is very, um, disappointed."

"So I want to get out of here. Hit the streets, like they say on TV. See what's happening in the boroughs. Missing people, look for any strange reports, anything odd. Talk to people around the crime scene."

Gully shook her head. "Go get your news the old-fashioned way, hm?"

"Exactly."

The editor locked her eyes on Mari. "You'll need some sensible shoes."

"Got 'em."

A smile.

"Then sure. I'll be more than pleased to see an empty desk for a week or so, okay."

Mari stood up and smiled. "Thanks. I'll do my best."

"I'm sure you will."

And then Joann Gully turned her attention back to her soda and sandwich, the audience over and Mari thinking . . . that her career, at the *News* at least, might be on the line.

3

DERRICK Finney aimed the hose at the stern of the *Flying Marlin III.*

He imagined that, before this fishing boat, there must have been a *Flying Marlin I* and *II,* now gone to whatever graveyard old fishing boats disappeared to.

The blood and guts from the catch of blues fled the on-rush of water, swirling, and finally shooting to the back of the boat and out a wide notch cut in the aft.

A damn good catch today, and Captain Starn sold a lot of fish to the people on the dock, with plenty more left over to sell to the local restaurants.

And about fucking time too.

This whole week had been pretty miserable, with the party boat people in no party mood as all they hooked were spiky sea robins, sand sharks, and a few flounder, and only a handful of the prized bluefish.

Today, that bad luck had changed. The gods of the North Atlantic smiled down on *Marlin III.*

"Gonna need to scrub that down soon, Finney," Starn yelled from his helm seat. Finney knew that the good old captain kept some bourbon stashed up there, and liked to take a few belts when the customers finally left.

Finney, on the other hand, would have to wait until he was finished before he could run over to Spagallos and order a bat and a ball. And maybe, to celebrate the good catch, more than a few bats and balls.

"Right, Captain."

God, calling him "captain." There was just Starn, and Luis, another crew member, who didn't speak much English—and Finney. And still he had to call him "Captain."

Not today, Finney thought. I do not . . . want to scrub the fucking deck today. Shit, let me do a little celebrating too.

"Hit this deck after tomorrow's run, okay?"

Starn looked down at the dock. Most of the other party boats were in and—from the looks of the crowds buying fish right off the boat—all of them had done well.

Going to be a good night in the Sheepshead Bay bars.

Of course, almost any night was a good night.

"Okay," Starn finally answered. "Gonna need a real good job tomorrow, Finney. Gonna have to take your time and do it right."

Finney waited for Starn to add . . . *for once* . . . but he didn't.

He hated the old guy's sarcasm. Every second sentence from his mouth filled with his damn sarcasm.

Still, this paid enough. For now. Though Finney thought he'd better decide sooner or later what he was going to do with his life. Dropping out of college might not have been the smartest move. He knew boats, knew fishing—after all, he had spent his high school summers crewing for a half dozen boats here.

But that wasn't a life.

No future in it.

He'd just get old, drunker—a dead end street.

So what then?

Be nice to own his own boat.

Maybe.

If you ended up like Starn, then that option didn't look too appealing. The old captain didn't seem too happy with his lot in life.

Back to school? And study what?

That was the problem. Finney would rather get down on his knees and scrub the deck than go back to school.

Not my thing . . . , he thought. Books, boring lectures.

So what was?

Cops, FDNY? Do my twenty years, and try not to get killed? A ton of guys from the old neighborhood had done just that.

But when he tried to picture himself in a uniform, well—that was something he just *couldn't* picture.

Finney watched the last sticky slick of fish guts and blood run out the hole in the back of the boat. He walked over and turned off the hose, and then curled it up in a neat circle. Didn't want the bastard making noise about how he left the hose. Everything had to be perfect, as if this was some luxurious cruise ship.

Cruise ship to nowhereville.

He put the hose in the storage bin and then looked up to Starn.

"All set down here, Captain . . . So I'll see you in the morning?"

"Yeah," Starn answered, already a bit of a slur in his voice.

The old fart will probably fall asleep here. Wake up when it's dark wondering what the hell happened.

Finney moved quickly to get off the boat before Starn thought of something, anything else he might tell Finney to do.

A quick jump to the dock, and without a look back, a brisk walk.

As Spagallos beckoned.

PROFESSOR Linda Kyle looked up from her notes.

He was asking questions again.

The young man with curly blond hair who looked like Jim Morrison gone Beach Boy.

Very cute, she thought, and smart, and—

A royal pain in the ass for her class. He challenged her nearly every lecture.

"Yes, Mr. Christian?" She found it funny that the student who led a near daily mutiny bore the name of history's most famous mutineer. Were they related? Not likely a question she'd get a chance to ask.

"Okay, yesterday you ran through the VICAP chart, the seven most successful strategies of America's top serial killers."

Linda rolled her eyes. "Yes, though you'll remember that the chart wasn't called that."

"Right. But today, the people you have talked about . . . they're all over that chart. Some have this characteristic, others this one, and some totally overlap. They're all over the thing . . ."

She looked at the clock, the seminar due to finish by eight P.M. And now at five minutes to, she still had at least two pages of notes to get through.

"And the problem with that?"

She also knew that the other students paid attention to Christian. He was a commanding presence, and—for the girls at least—a very charismatic one.

"Here's the problem . . . no, a question really. Psychology could argue from an Adlerian perspective, that these guys were *made*."

"To a great extent, they—"

"And yet each of these killers is different. Isn't that a problem?"

"There can be many root causes that go into—"

"But couldn't one of them be that they . . . were simply born that way?"

She'd known this was coming—the argument that evil existed, somewhere under the skin. In the cradle, these guys were planning their first taste of torture, cannibals—

"Genetics doesn't give us much to work with, I'm afraid. And we're looking at the psychological issues—"

"I don't buy it."

She smiled. Not much of a response from the mutineer. A rare retreat.

"Good, 'cause I'm not selling anything. This course is called Psychological Issues of Violent Crime. That is what we are exploring."

He nodded, but she also saw a hint of a smile.

God, is he flirting with me? she thought. A sly grin?

Or have I been dateless for too long—dateless, sexless—and starting to let my imagination run away?

Fifteen years older than him; she'd better keep a watch on that one.

"And—sad to say—we are out of time. We'll get to the different profiling standards tomorrow, how they do and don't work."

She turned away, and the class of twenty-plus students, most of them Columbia Psych majors, started filing out.

She turned back to see if the combative Mr. Christian lingered for a post-class word with the prof.

But he didn't.

Steady, she told herself. Don't become another crazy single New York female.

She gathered up her papers.

"PITCH anudder my way, Charlie," Finney said in as exaggerated a Brooklyn accent as he could muster.

"Shit. You must've had a good day, Finney," the Spagallos bartender said, drawing a short draft and pouring a Seagram's 7.

"*Great* fucking day, Charlie. Fish practically jumped into the boat. And Starn stayed off my ass." He took a big swig, killing half the new beer. "Great day."

Charlie grinned and nodded. Most of the non-Latino crewmen of Sheepshead haunted this place, and tonight it was packed. These guys were Finney's friends, as much as he had any. Never any women, though.

They'd stick out in this place as much as they would on a pirate sip.

Finney looked around. He also saw some old-timers, guys who had been doing the party boat thing for thirty years, and looked it.

Is that me? Finney wondered.

It will be—unless I do something about it.

If I don't, I'll turn out just like them.

And then, finishing the beer, gulping the whiskey, he slid off the stool.

Suddenly he felt all the day's work in his aching body, as if somehow the pain he had ignored had to come out now.

"Pushing off?" Charlie said.

"Yeah, I'm beat. Catch you tomorrow."

"Right."

And Finney sailed off to Eammons Avenue, the summer air now turned cool.

LINDA stepped out of Schermerhorn Hall and walked down the giant flight of stone steps to the grounds of the college.

She had hoped it would still be light out when she left. But she'd checked e-mail, looked for some books she needed at home, and now—

The sky had turned a royal blue, the horizon marked by just a hint of orange glow where the sun had been.

She didn't like walking home in the dark.

Though Morningside Heights was certainly safer than it had ever been, with people always on the sidewalks, making it feel almost like Greenwich Village.

Still, with the sky turning darker, she walked off Broadway down 122nd Street, moving away from the university.

The quiet street . . . making her feel the night, feel alone.

Linda kept walking east. She had thought about getting out tonight. No classes the next day—it might be good to have some drinks, some laughs, with a few friends.

But like a lot of things, she let it slide, and now—well, who liked spontaneous things anyway?

No one.

She crossed the street, to her side of the block. Some teenagers stood on a corner, smoking cigarettes. An old woman and old man sat on their stoop, just as they did nearly every summer night. She smiled at them as she passed.

Couldn't be safer.

She wondered, though, if she felt scared because of the class.

It was one thing to talk about John Wayne Gacy and the BLT maniac in a bright room with twenty-somethings.

But quite another to be out on the streets, with the words and images still fresh in her mind—and to be alone.

She picked up her pace.

4

A hurricane was coming.

That's what all the news channels were screaming about. Hurricane Daniel! Heading toward Cuba! The keys getting ready!

That was bad news, Finney thought. Even if the hurricane completely missed the East Coast, it could rattle enough fishermen over the next few days to hurt business.

Good thing the fish didn't watch TV.

Good fucking thing . . .

And with CNN just at an audible level, and a half-finished beer beside his ratty easy chair, Derrick Finney fell asleep.

ON the boat.

Sun. Filled with happy fishermen pulling in blue fish after blue fish, so *many* blue fish that the deck became filled with the flopping fish, nobody caring that they still struggled, that they all still flapped around madly.

Finney thinking:

(In his dream . . .)

I should do something. Something to kill the fish.

You were supposed to do that.

He looked up.

There was no boat.

What had he been thinking? Boat? No boat here. In fact—

He looked down, and he was standing in a pond.

No. He turned around. A *lake*, and he was near the shore, standing in about a foot of water.

The water so cold. Because—

It was night. Right, so dark here, standing in the water, in this place where there were no lights, nothing here.

He looked around, as images of the fishing boat, the panicking fish, the happy day fishermen, became replaced with
this quiet, dark place.

But he could see now that he was wrong. Not completely
dark.

He saw, just ahead, the lights from a house.

He started walking there, and even (in the dream) he
wondered, Is this a place I've been? Have I been here—and
somehow I'm remembering being here?

No, not remembering. Never been here, he knew.

This is just a dream.

Good. That established, he could walk to the lights, pushing through a bramble of bushes, walking under tall pine
trees, the lights closer now, almost as if they were moving.

The lights closer, brighter, warmer. Felt so good to get out
of the cold water, leave the dark gloom of that lake.

To this house.

Just a house. Nothing special or interesting about it. It
was—

He searched for a word.

Yeah . . . *generic.*

Windows, a door, a pathway.

Was there a car?

No car there.

And then—it *was* there. He missed it, a dark shape, impossible to tell what the car could be.

Except definitely a car.

Closer. Until—

Finney saw her. Through the windows of a house. A
woman, someone who looked as old as his mother. Gray hair
pulled back, round face, bustling back and forth, appearing
in one window, then another.

Do I know her? Finney thought.

Is this someone I'm remembering?

Why the lake, the house, this woman?

He hardly realized that he had stopped moving well away
from the pool of light shed by the bright windows. Standing
there, weirdly out of the range of the light, watching the
woman, walking to this window, then another, then—

Movement.

He turned around to the other side of the house, not the side with the mystery car, but the other side of the small house.

To see someone crouched low, low and hugging the side of the house.

And then—*there!*

The person popped up and looked in the window from the outside, then down again.

And inside, the woman appearing at the window from time to time, so busy, so bustling, so *much* to do in her little house, when it was so late.

While someone outside crouched in the shadows, peering in, waiting, sneaking around.

Finney told himself, I know it's just a dream so nothing bad will happen.

Not for real.

The woman sat down in a chair, the light inside showing her sitting down and turning on the TV.

The sound of muffled voices coming from the TV. Laughs, then words, none of it making sense.

The sneaking man started moving. Close to the door.

Then—he turned, and looked out to the darkness.

Out, of course, to where Finney stood.

The man smiled, grinned, teeth catching the light.

Then in the dim light, Finney thought he saw who it was.

It's me.

I'm that man.

Finney thought: I should move.

Yes, I should move, he thought. Do something, even though this wasn't real. I should move.

But—

Movement was an impossibility. His legs might as well have been tree trunks solidly rooted to the ground.

And speak? He tried to open his mouth. But that was as ineffective as the gulping fish on the deck of the ship opening their mouths and shutting them, helplessly, searching for the sea.

Laughter erupted from the TV, crazy insane laughter. It's just so funny!

A click, the door handle turned, the door opening, and a shaft of light cut through the darkness, released by the open door as the woman looked out to the night—and hit Finney in the face squarely.

He blinked.

And—

"—AND hard-hit Cuba is getting ready to take another hit. Barely recovered from Hurricane Clara, the island nation now faces Daniel, an even bigger storm . . ."

Finney opened his eyes. The TV was on, lights. For a moment he sat there as the dream faded.

Shit, he thought. Some dream, a crazy dream. Where the hell did *that* come from?

He breathed heavily, slouched down in his chair. He looked around his one-room apartment. Brightly lit with the crappy lamps he'd picked up.

Nothing scary here.

Then why—do I still feel the hairs on the back of my arm standing up?

He shook his head. Stupid fucking dream. Seeing myself outside that house.

He thought that he should just kill the tube and go to bed.

But that didn't seem like such a good idea.

Go to bed.

Sleep.

He grabbed the remote and changed the channel, stumbling into a rerun of *Friends.*

The people on the laugh track cackling.

But as Finney sat there, he didn't see anything to make him laugh.

He grabbed his now-warm beer and took a slug.

5

THE street at the far end quickly turned more deserted, and Linda felt herself suddenly grow more aware.

She kept the same pace as she walked; but now every step was accompanied by small glances left and right.

That, and she concentrated on the sound . . .

The sound of the steps, the slight wind rustling leaves, but most importantly any new sounds. Sounds that—for the moment—she could not identify.

At night, she always took on a different mind-set as she started down her own quiet block.

The steps, the listening, the small glances.

Usually there would be nothing, and she'd soon be safely inside.

But not tonight.

Not now. Now—there was a noise.

She kept walking, but listening harder.

Definitely a sound that she couldn't identify. A scratchy sound, something dragging over the pavement.

She kept her pace steady.

Partly so that she kept moving forward.

But also because to hesitate now, to pause, to even consider stopping, would acknowledge the possibility—

The idea . . .

That something was wrong.

She heard the sound again, scratching the sidewalk again, but in sequence now.

Just like steps.

The door to her brownstone . . . so very close. But so were those scratching noises.

So she had to stop.

Had to.

Turn, and look. Fists clenched, eyes wide, already running through her options, all the options that depended on what she was about to see.

Turning, looking, then seeing—the rat.

The rat had stopped when she did.

Linda looked right at it, its glistening eyes catching the streetlight, and the rat—a NYC rat the size of a puppy—stared back.

Bold, unshaken.

"Get! Get the hell *away*!" Then—unusual for her—a curse. "You fucking rat—*get*!"

And New York City rats, besides being big, must also pick up a smattering of English . . . because it ambled away, down some inviting sewer.

LINDA took a sip of her sauvignon blanc, and then scrolled down the list of recent e-mails.

Except these weren't regular e-mails, but prospective dates from Loveline.com.

Like shopping for clothes, she thought.

This one's too big, this one's too small, this one looks like a Martian.

And her dates so far?

She had met some nice men and suffered through some interminable cosmos with others.

But no sparks, no fun—and certainly no sex.

Currently she had three men who had been "pulled" by her relatively current online picture and her profile that tried to play up her fun side and downplay the dreary shadow of academia.

One, a film producer, widely traveled, sent a flirty e-mail that caused her to—uncharacteristically—respond in kind.

Now they were setting up a meeting, a quick drink meeting, the obligatory time-limited first date.

Thursday night seemed to be the agreed evening.

She looked at the clock above her TV. Just ten . . . a bit early for bed, but she was tired.

Linda finished her e-mail confirming the date, and then hit enter.

MARI took the mojito from a silver tray held by an amazingly thin waitress whose breasts looked drastically overinflated.

Which they probably were.

She loved the elegant Campbell Apartment, a 1930s lounge hidden inside Grand Central Station.

Louis Armstrong singing—and if you closed your eyes, you were back in the days of Clark Gable and Greta Garbo.

She turned around, and instead of Garbo, Julie Fein gave her a nudge.

"Sorry I'm late. No cabs. Hey, where's my damn mojito?"

Mari grinned and pointed to the bartender. "In the capable hands of that cute and able hunk."

"Ri-i-i-i-ght . . ."

As soon as Julie had her drink, they found two well-stuffed chairs just vacated by two businessmen.

Julie reached out and grabbed her friend's wrist.

"I've been thinking all day about you."

Mari took a sip of her drink. "Glad somebody is."

"No. I'm serious. I'm worried."

"Worried about what?"

"You, and the damned story you're working on. The whole thing is just too damn scary. And now you're going to get closer to it?"

"I'm just going to do what a reporter is supposed to do."

Mari finished her drink. A bit too quickly, she thought.

"Just promise me that you will be careful, that you won't do anything stupid."

Mari looked around for one of the Victoria's Secret–approved waitresses.

"Okay, nothing stupid. My word on it. Just as long as a second mojito doesn't fall into that category."

"Never."

They laughed together, and the cloud that Julie had briefly summoned dissipated.

6

DAVID Rodriguez realized that he couldn't carry his microwaved slice of pizza and his beer . . . as well as his cane.

Two trips required then.

Maybe Captain Biondi had a point. There *were* things that he had trouble doing. And possibly having a young eager-beaver partner might be a good thing.

He can carry my beer.

David sat down, the pizza looking like a gooey science experiment. The Mets game—they were, typically, behind by one run—was on mute.

The papers for the case lay all spread out, covering the coffee table.

He stared at the layout of the room.

The basement room.

The death room. The torture room.

A complete and total horror room for five people who had no connection.

Each killed in a way to maximize both that horror and the pain. All of them taking hours to die.

Hours . . .

Each person with his or her own space in the room. And when the carnage was done, their blood would finally mix on the stone floor.

David took a bite of the cardboard pizza.

Then there were the preparations. Whoever did this—the madman, the killer, the torturer—had to *make* this room.

He had to prepare the room with all the implements needed to torture and kill. And then make it soundproof, with double doors, one-inch-thick steel.

So much preparation.

Yet not a fucking trail worth pursuing. The basement

rooms rented as though he was a phantom, materials arriving for his renovations to the downstairs hovel, no one ever seeing the man.

No one ever saw the man going down there.

Not a single description, not a hair color, not a height—nothing.

David shivered. The AC too high; so damn cold in here.

Cold. Creepy.

Because something here—something beyond the bizarre killings—was wrong.

He moved the map of the room to the side, and now looked at the pictures, the smiling faces of the victims, those happy unaware faces.

What brought them together?

All at the same fucking time.

People who had no connection with one another.

Maybe "wrong" wasn't quite the word.

And David had this thought:

His young partner was damned lucky to have him by his side, bad leg or no.

Because this case . . . was a total fucker.

THE TV still on mute, a new beer at hand, David now forced himself to look at the crime scene photos, when the happy faces—when they still had faces—were gone.

Good thing he had only eaten one shingle-sized piece of pizza. Even after repeated viewing, these pictures were strong, stomach-turning stuff.

His doorbell buzzed, and David jumped in his seat, putting sudden painful pressure on his bad leg.

Another buzz, David got up, grabbed his cane, and started for the door.

"I'm coming, I'm coming."

He opened the door to see his almost ex-wife, Johanna.

"Jo. If I knew you were coming—"

"You would have baked a cake? Mind if I come in?"

"Sure." He moved to the side as she walked in, scanning the room.

"Not bad. I expected you would have attained full single male hovel status by now."

"You never know when someone's going to drop in. Get you a beer?"

She looked down at his cane, the leg.

"I'll get one myself. The fridge, I assume?"

"You should have been a detective."

She walked into the kitchen and grabbed herself a Corona.

"No limes, I'm afraid."

She popped open the beer and took a slug. And yet again, David thought . . . *She's certainly beautiful.*

"Not a problem." She sat down on the couch.

"So why the drop-in?"

"Two reasons. First, the lawyer has the papers ready."

"Goody. Now we can finish this. Fantastic news!"

He made no effort to hide his sarcasm.

As much as he knew that there was no hope of getting her back, he couldn't let that thought go.

Jo made a face then continued: "He'll send them to you. You can sign them."

"Yes I can."

"But there's something else. I know you. You won't let your leg slow you down. But you should. Take some damn time. Get better. Take a leave."

"Did Hicks call you? Second time today I've heard the same message."

"You're working those murders, aren't you?"

"*Those* murders?"

"The five people. Those strange killings. I worry about you."

"Thanks."

"More sarcasm?"

"No, really. I'm glad that—on some level you—still care."

"I do. I will. Will you think about it?"

"I did," he said, grinning. "And I won't. The case is— well, I've never seen anything like it. I can't walk away."

A sad smile from her.

"Not without your cane, you won't."

He smiled back.

"How's the beer? Maybe some food? Frozen pizza's looking good."

She shook her head.

And he knew that this visit from his beautiful soon to be ex-wife was over.

7

HER name is Emma Chappel.

She lives alone, save for her great yellow Labrador, her friend, her confidant, her protector . . . *Rusty.*

Her house sits miles into a scraggly wooded area well north of the Westchester suburbs, out of the reach of commuters, the gray line of men and women who daily trek to Manhattan.

A small lake sits only fifty yards away from Emma's house. Too small to attract fishermen, and nearly completely covered with duckweed and lily pads.

Cetainly not a lake to lure anyone in search of some beautiful waterfront property.

So Emma is—save for Rusty—alone.

But with Rusty, she doesn't feel alone, doesn't feel isolated.

Now the night grows late for her, the TV still on as one mildly amusing sitcom melts into another.

Soon she'll go to bed, Rusty following, to continue reading one of those mysteries set in Africa with a group of ladies.

It will be soon.

Rather—

Should be soon.

Except tonight, in between laughs, Emma hears a noise.

A noise from outside. Not in and of itself a surprising thing.

Animals come near the house all the time. Trying their best to gain access to the impenetrable garbage cans, lured by the smells of her cooking.

Rusty raises his great head up off the ground.

His ears cock. He hears the noise too.

Some hungry raccoon. Maybe a deer browsing his way close to the small house.

The sound again. Something brushing against the house, and now Rusty stands up.

A low growl from the dog.

Emma Chappel picks up the remote and presses the mute button.

But—now there is no sound.

EMMA stops by the door, and waits.

The door is locked, bolted—and Rusty stands beside her. The sound has vanished, and now she is only aware of her heart beating, her shallow breathing. Her fingers—already wracked with small twinges of arthritic pain, a pain that has made her digging in her garden not the joy it once was— reach for the latch, the doorknob, turning it.

And it opens . . .

To the night.

The cool summer night air rushing into the warm room like an invader.

The small overhead light casts a pale yellow pool outside that only reaches a few feet into the woods.

Rusty sniffs the air, but doesn't growl. Sometimes when raccoons come by, or maybe somewhere out there . . . the occasional skunk, or a nosey bear, Rusty will growl, issue a warning bark.

People don't like the bears up here, but Emma thinks that the bears mean that the woods are returning to what they once were . . . bobcats, deer, coyote, and now bear—all sharing this small lake, the dense woods.

She looks left, then right, seeing other small pools of light made by the small house's windows.

"Guess it's just the wind, hm, boy?"

She reaches down and pats the dog's head, and he arches up to get the full weight of her hand as it strokes down to the snout.

Emma then takes a deep breath of the cool air and shuts the door. She latches the lock.

But she doesn't go back to her chair, the TV . . .

Instead she shuts out each light one by one, picking up her mystery novel before the last is turned off.

Book in hand, she sails off to her small, cozy bedroom.

OUTSIDE—

It watches.

Intrigued. Tempted.

But not acting, not now. Not really understanding what draws it to this place. Why it came this close, why it pulls away . . . acting only on the impulse.

It sees the lights go off until now the place is as dark and shadowy as the rest of the woods.

And for now the impulse to stay, to linger, disappears.

8

DAVID opened his eyes, and looked at the clock. 9:10.

The alarm should have gone off a half hour ago, and now he was late. His first day working with his unwanted side-kick, and the guy with a bum leg is late.

"Shit," he whispered, sliding out of bed. The wounded leg had turned out to be clean of any bullet fragments, or at least that's what they told him. Still, every time he moved it hurt, jabbing him with pinpoint pricks of pain.

He did rehab three times a week, learning to ignore that pain as the strength slowly came back to the leg. They said that eventually he'd be okay; he might have a slight limp in his walk, but other than that . . . perfectly normal.

So far, he was having trouble believing that.

He pulled on his pants from the previous night, the wrin-kled white shirt, a tie. Maybe he could grab a few minutes to shave, brush his teeth. Drag a comb across his head . . .

To quote the Beatles.

Stupid clock . . .

Stupid me, he thought. Got lost in all the photos, maps, reports—all revealing nothing—and then screwed up the alarm.

David hobbled around on his cane, getting ready, until he had gotten himself together in what had to be a minimal way.

"**ROUGH** night?" James said.

David looked at his young partner's grin. And just to make a point, he kept staring for a moment, until he saw the edges of the smile begin to crack.

"Yeah. Guess I did. Had a real wild time."

James turned down Houston Street.

"This is not the fastest way to go. You should have—"

"Right," James said. "Still this will get us there."

David nodded. This was shaping up to be a great partner-ship. He knew nothing about the younger detective, and didn't want to know anything. And he knew he'd have a hard time working with him.

I gotta make an effort, David thought.

"So I spent my night looking at all the documents, the photos, the layout."

"Yeah?"

"Guess you've looked at them too?

"That I have."

A cab cut them off.

"Bastard. Maniac cabbie."

"So what did you think?" David said.

There. Proud of himself for acting like a mature profes-sional.

"What did I think? One sick fucker. But smart, almost too smart."

"What do you mean . . . 'too smart'?"

"How did he get that apartment with no paper trail, at least none that means anything?"

"You assume it's a 'he'?"

"I've done my time working with VICAP. Not many fe-male serial killers, and the sheer strength required for what he had to do . . . definitely a male."

"Most likely a male."

God, the kid was cocky. And that could go beyond annoy-ing . . . to turn potentially dangerous.

"What else?"

"And he's never seen, getting all that work done on that place, in that building—and nobody ever sees the maniac? He's smart."

"Too smart for us to get?"

Another grin from James, and David could imagine the girls in the First Avenue bars falling over themselves to hit on him.

"No. Because as smart as he is, he'll do the one thing all serial killers do, the one thing that gives us a chance of catching them."

"And that is?"

"He'll do it again. And again. And he'll keep doing it until, as smart a fucker as he is, we can catch him."

David looked away, as James turned down Ludlow Street, quiet, tree-less, baking in the New York sun, onto Delancey . . . until they reached Pell Street.

He pulled into an empty space.

"Let's hope we don't need a lot of repeat viewings." David grabbed his cane. "And let's hope for the sake of some innocent people walking around now, we get lucky, and fast."

He popped open the door, and the ovenlike heat was everywhere.

MARI couldn't find a parking space near Pell Street, so she was forced to dump the car on a lot on Delancey.

With the heat blazing—and not anywhere near noon yet—she was having second thoughts about doing this story the old-fashioned way.

She walked briskly, catching stares from a few young men in oversized tracksuits who made no secret of looking her up and down, checking her out. She ignored them, and the kissing sounds they made as she walked by.

Farther on, a homeless man with a Brillo beard looked up at her as though watching a parade.

His limbs were—she searched for the word . . .

Akimbo.

Like a marionette with its strings cut, and its legs and arms scattered to the ground. He held a coffee cup, and Mari didn't know whether it was for donations to the lost marionette fund or if it possibly held the dregs of last night's rotgut.

She reached Pell Street.

In this blazing daylight, the street looked innocent. A small bodega, a liquor store, a pizza place on the corner, a hardware store that—even this late—was still closed, a metal gate covering its windows.

Any gentrification invading the Lower East Side hadn't hit this part of the world yet.

She doubted it ever would.

One brownstone, a burnished red stone building, sported an old woman who sat on a folding chair.

Could she be the type of person who might see things, notice things? Mari wondered.

What we'd call . . . a busybody?

Mari crossed the street, now watched sharply by the crone on the stoop.

DAVID stepped under the yellow police tape, nodding to the officer guarding the crime scene. James lagged behind, taking a cell phone call.

Then—carefully down the steps to the subterranean room.

David took out the key and unlocked the main door. The other doors inside would have been left open, the business of hiding the events, the sounds, the screams . . . over.

As soon as the door opened, David could smell it again. The ripe, pungent, metallic smell. He didn't gag this time.

But maybe his new partner would, and David realized he was actually hoping he heard James's voice catch, heard him clear his throat.

Welcome to the big league world of homicide.

Except—homicide wasn't exactly the right word for this. This was something *way* beyond homicide.

"Sorry," James said. "Had to take the call."

David nodded. He imagined James got a *lot* of calls he had to take—young women under the spell of the dashing detective.

Shit, am I jealous? An old jealous fart . . .

For a moment David just stood there. Two overhead bulbs—one that lit this room, and the other an interior room. Still James turned on the flashlight, and started sweeping the room.

He coughed. "Smell's still pretty bad."

"That it is."

The flashlight slid up to the ceiling, revealing cracked plaster.

"What do you think we're going to find here? I mean, you've been down here, before the crime scene team had been over it—"

"Yeah, and they all came up with nothing." David took some steps forward, his cane making a sharp clicking sound on the stone.

He walked into the other room.

The place where it all happened.

"Do you want to know where they were?"

"Sure, I looked at the drawings, but—"

On some twisted level, David realized that he was enjoying this.

"Okay, the dentist from Queens, the bachelor—he was there, wrapped like a mummy with silver duct tape. Over there, tied to the wall, gagged, her body arranged like a crucifixion . . . the teacher. The NYU student sat tied tight to the wooden chair, that very chair . . . right there by you. You can still see the red stain covering the wood."

James let the flashlight move up and down the chair, the light revealing the dark maroon stain.

"The other young kid, from the New School, hung from the roof. They took down the hook, though, took it to forensics. But the guy who did it figured out where a crossbeam was." He turned and grinned at James. "He did his structural homework."

"And the other girl, the—what was she?"

"A CPA, Deloitte and Touche. Pretty, smart, successful. The last to arrive. And he probably did this first"—David dramatically shut the sliding metal door, the steel door that sealed off this tomb—"then grabbed her. She was the last to arrive."

"We know that because—?"

"He didn't do anything special to make her like the others. They were the audience, and she became—I dunno—the show."

"But they found wire wrapped around her wrists, her arms behind her back?"

"Yeah. My guess is he did that fast, then went to work on her, went—"

And just like that David realized he had gone too far with his little game of re-creating the moment for the young detective. Too far, because now he could feel all of them here, their struggles, their screams, some full-out, some muffled; the terrible unimaginable *hours* of horror.

Too far, because now David could *feel* it.

I deserve that, he thought. Fucking with the kid's head.

Now *he* became creeped out.

James cleared his throat, breaking the mood.

"Must have been something," David said.

"Yeah. And—and—" James searched for something to say. "They had no damn connection to each other."

David walked over to the wall where the teacher had been pinned. He reached out and touched the wall. "None whatsoever—though we can talk again to their nearest and dearest. Might be something that's been missed."

"Missed? Like what brought them here? How they all ended up here?" James walked over to David, who now turned to face the room, getting the view that the forty-five-year-old teacher got. "Do you have any ideas?"

David turned to him. "Not yet. But I got tell you something . . . being down here, standing here, I have the feeling that something really big is missing. And until we have a clue about that, we might as well be kids playing cops and killers."

James nodded.

And David said, "Let's just walk through the space, okay? See . . . what we see. If nothing else, we'll get a good feel for what happened that night."

"That's for sure."

MARI started up the steps.

"I'm not buying nothin' from *nobody*," the old woman said.

Mari smiled; the day's heat building, and this porch, this

stoop, seemed like such a hot place for the old lady to hang out.

"Good, because I'm not selling anything."

"Then, what are you? One of those religious nuts? They're even worse."

"No. Not one of those either. I'm a reporter."

The woman nodded, and her tight-lipped expression, which made the wrinkles and cracks of her face seem chiseled onto her face, didn't change.

"Oh, you're here about"—the woman waved at the building down the street girded with yellow tape—"*that.*"

Mari nodded. "For the *Daily News.* There's so much we don't know, and—"

The woman waved a hand at Mari. "I already spoke to people. You understand? I *spoke* to people."

Mari tried hard to keep the smile on her face. "But you didn't speak to *me.* And I'm doing the story. I have to—"

"So you think this is . . . a *story*? That what you think? Some nut, probably some *religious* crazy nut kills five people, and you think it's a story?"

Mari brushed her hair off her face and let out a puff of air.

The old lady wins, she thought. This was going absolutely nowhere. There had to be other neighbors.

"Okay. Thanks for your time. Have a good day."

Mari turned to leave, taking one hot step down.

"Hey, you give up that easy? Some reporter."

She turned back to the lady, who now wore a grin. "I'll talk to you. Hell, but not out here. Too damn hot. Come on inside."

And Mari had to smile back.

The old lady knew how to have her fun.

"YEAH babe—tonight will be good. At seven."

James shut his flip phone.

"Social life all arranged?" David said.

"Appears so."

"Good—and now we can get on with work?"

James looked at him in the darkness, as if considering a response. Then he nodded and smiled.

"Sure. Though I don't think there's a hell of lot we can do

down here. I did want to reread the reports back at Police Plaza. Maybe you want to head home, grab a nap, rest the leg?"

As if in response to the words, David's leg sent a little burst of pain up his thigh. He had purposely not taken the Vicodin today, and now he was paying a price. But that stuff made a lot of things hard to do, including thinking.

"No, I'm fine. But if you want to catch up on your reading, I'll drop you back at the office."

"Why? What are you going to do?"

"I want to speak to one of the victims' families. The CPA."

"That's been done. We have the statements."

"Yeah, in the first twenty-four hours. But read the Q and A again. They don't go deep. Somehow these people all . . . converged here. Has to be a reason. Something we're missing."

"And you think the family might know?"

"I don't think anything. Right now, I'm just revisiting everything that's been done. Starting with seeing this place, then on to them, and just keep going. It's called detective work."

As soon as he said it, David realized he had pushed the plunger too far.

Shit, he thought. Now I'm the asshole.

James took a step toward him, and David guessed that his partner probably played some college ball—big shoulders, tall, strong. Good guy to have if something went south. But maybe not such a good guy to get pissed at you.

"Look, David . . . Captain Biondi was going to give this just to me. And I bet if I tell him that you're making working together . . . not so doable, that he'd reconsider his decision to have us team up. So maybe—for a while—try to ease up on the digs. Okay?"

Yeah, David thought . . . I was definitely the asshole.

"Okay. Deal. So you'll go with me to the family?"

"Sure, when you're grasping at straws, one's as good as another."

9

THE woman, Anne Russell, was eighty-five, she proudly told Mari. And her apartment was as stultifyingly hot as it was outside on her stoop.

A small air conditioner sat in the front window, and Mari had to wonder why the woman didn't turn it on. Saving money? Not hot enough for her?

She had made them both a cup of tea and brought out some crumbly cookies that Mari guessed had been around for a while. To be polite, Mari took a small nibble of one dry cookie and then put it on the edge of her saucer.

She took in the room, shuttered from the brilliant light outside by heavy curtains. A dark red carpet filled most the floor, and the woman's mantel was dotted with a mix of pictures and figurines. Looking around, Mari thought . . . This woman was once young, had a husband, children now gone to different parts of the world, leaving this small old woman in this dark apartment.

Had to be lonely.

"As I said—Mari, is it?"

"Yes."

"I never really *saw* anything. And I told the young policemen that I didn't see anything."

So, Mari thought, is this just a tea party? A way for Anne Russell to grab a few moments of human contact? Like a crab, grabbing at a stray piece of food that drifted its way.

Mari lowered her pen. She wanted to go to the room across the street, talk to the cop outside—not that he'd have much to tell. She had to start somewhere. But was that start here?

"But then"—the woman took a sip of her tea—"I realized that I did see something, a few times . . . something odd."

And like that, Mari was suddenly alert.

The old woman's eyes narrowed, lips grew even more pursed, as if she struggled to remember all the details.

"It didn't seem like anything. But I woke up one night after a dream. One of those wacky dreams. Crazy. Woke up alone; you know how scary that is. A dark room, night, the city sounds. I think I heard a car outside, brakes squealing, a door closing."

"This was before the murders?"

Anne shook her head. "No, dear. The dream happened later, after the murders. But it helped me remember."

Confusing, Mari thought, once again thinking this was probably going nowhere. An old woman's dreams. An apartment like this would give anyone the chills. So dark, cluttered . . .

"No. The dream happened a few days after I spoke to the policemen. The street sounds, and the dream—they made me remember." The old woman leaned close. "I have trouble sleeping. I think old people don't sleep too well. And then I remembered seeing a car."

"Yes . . . ?"

"I mean, a lot of cars go up and down this street. But this car came down the block slowly, too slow. And when I went to the window, I saw the car stop in front of *that* building. You know, where all those poor people died?"

"The car parked there?"

"No. That was the funny thing. It was one of those big, black cars. A limousine, I guess. Well, maybe not *that* fancy. But big, black. It stopped. And someone got out. Of course it was night, so I couldn't see who got out. But somebody got out, and the car pulled away."

Mari wrote words down . . . *limousine . . . town car . . .*

That would explain why no cab companies had any records of someone going to that address, or why no car was ever seen parked out front by any of the neighbors.

The killer arrived at night.

Chauffeured. Probably picked up at night. Did whatever preparations he had to do late at night.

"This happened once?"

"Oh no! As I said, I don't sleep well, so I must have seen that black car three, maybe four times. Funny, how it took a dream to remind me. Old people, you know . . ." The woman took a sip of tea. "And always very late. I just thought it was someone who worked late. But people around here, they usually use the subway, sometimes a taxi." The woman made a small laugh. "Not a big limousine."

'Mrs. Russell, I—"

"Call me Anne, dear. I feel old enough without the 'Mrs.'"

Mari smiled. "I don't suppose you ever saw a license plate, or anything about the person who got out?"

"Oh no. It was *very* dark. But there was one thing. I mean, I'm not sure—"

"Something you saw?"

"I couldn't really see whoever got out of the car, but he seemed to walk funny."

"Funny?"

"Yes, I couldn't see much, but it didn't look—I dunno—normal?"

Mari nodded. "You know, Mrs. Russell"—Mari smiled—"Anne, I will have to tell the police about this. They should know."

"Yes, I imagine you will. That's okay, honey. And anyway, you found it out first . . . and that must be good for you, hm?"

Mari laughed. "Very good . . ."

DAVID let James talk to the policemen guarding the site.

The department had someone stationed here 24/7 to keep everyone from the morbidly curious to the devastated relatives away from the crime scene.

But David imagined that they'd pull that in a few days. The gawkers were all gone.

Nothing to see here, and as far as David could tell, nothing to know.

James walked back over to him, and they looked at the outside of the building.

"What's on the upper floors?"

"Been empty for months. Zoned for apartments. They were last used for some small-time warehousing. Nothing in them now."

"Did our maniac make sure they were empty somehow?"

David shook his head. "Don't think so. He may have known they were empty, but that's it. Probably knew that they were being used for storage. This whole neighborhood had been residential . . . but now who knows what the hell it is."

"Should we talk to the neighbors?" James asked.

"Can do. They've all been talked to. So I guess not much there."

David paused. He looked back at the entrance to the apartment, the steps down.

He stopped, staring.

"Hold on a minute . . ."

And he started back down the steps.

MARI stepped back out to the orange stone steps, the sun even hotter.

I need some AC stat . . .

But she looked at the building down the street, the fence of yellow tape around it—and now saw three men outside.

Detectives.

No one from the NYPD had said anything to the press.

Had they seen her leave this woman's apartment?

Not likely.

She started down the steps, hurrying to the men.

DAVID walked back down the narrow steps.

He noticed a railing on the left and—unusual—another railing on the right.

James stood behind him. The alcove almost completely hidden from the street.

David turned back to James and said, "Notice anything strange?"

David held one of the rails while his cane pressed against the bottom step.

"Besides how dark it is here? How well hidden?"

"Yeah, beyond that."

"The light on the buzzer. Looks goddamn ominous."

"Doesn't it? But not that. Come on, Detective."

David held back the taunt in his voice. Didn't want to get the boy upset again.

James looked around. His eyes landed on the other railing.

"That railing looks new."

"Yes. But there's something else about it."

James let his hand run along the railing, then turned to look at the other railing. "I wonder if there's any way we can find who installed this."

"Could do. But I bet it's as well hidden as everything else that's been done here."

James looked up at David. "Okay, what else?"

"Why have *two* railings?"

"Because he wanted them?"

"Yeah—and that could be important. And you know—for the first time—we may actually know a little something about this sick bastard."

"You think that there's something wrong with him that made this railing necessary?"

"Yup. Not much to go on. Look, we really should hit some of the relatives again, any friends—maybe divide the work and—"

"Detectives!"

David turned back to the voice of the cop out front. He grabbed his cane and climbed out of the sunken alcove.

A woman, dressed in a light summer blouse and skirt, stood on the other side of the tape.

"What is it?"

"This woman—she's a reporter."

David shook his head. "No comment."

"Excuse me—but I was just hoping to get a better look at the building. You guys have told us nothing, so I assume that's what you will continue to do."

Got to give the woman credit for being blunt, David thought.

David walked over to her, aware that her eyes went to his cane. He looked at her. Dark hair, midthirties, pretty—not someone he had seen on other cases.

"What paper are you from?"

James stood beside him, also giving her the once-over.

"The *Daily News*. I've been working with what you have told us—which is nothing. So now I'm doing the story the old-fashioned way."

She was definitely pretty.

Dark eyes, an inviting mouth; she had to be married.

A quick glance to her left hand. No ring. How did someone like her escape?

Probably a slave to her job, that and maybe drowning in the madness that is dating in New York.

"Listen, you do know why we tell you nothing?"

"So the killer doesn't know what you do and don't know."

"That, and to prevent copycats."

"But if I could just ask you a few questions, even look inside—"

James laughed. "You are persistent . . ."

David shook his head. "Sorry. No peeks at the crime scene, no questions; when we have a statement you will get it, along with the rest of the papers."

Then David watched something interesting bloom on her face.

A bit of a smile.

"Okay. I hear you. But here's my card when you can talk."

David took the card and read the name . . . *Mari Kinsella*.

"Yeah, I think I've read articles by you."

"David—we should hit the road." James stepped under the tape.

David nodded, the card in his hand.

"So . . . *David*," Mari said, stepping back, the small grin a bit wider. "I've been working the case, finding out things. So when you're maybe . . . ready to share, give me a call? My cell's on the card."

"Right," he said.

Then she turned and walked away, heading up the street.

David leaned down and awkwardly made his way under the tape.

He said to James, "I wonder what the hell did she mean by that . . . 'ready to share' . . . 'finding out things' . . . ?"

"She's a reporter. Just a trick."

David nodded.

Could be. Could be just a trick.

But with this case, could they take a chance?

He followed his partner to the car.

10

"FINNEY, get up here."

The *Marlin III* could carry up to thirty fishermen, but this morning barely half that number had shown up. The fish were biting, the chubby fishermen busy with their catches and their brewskis.

Good thing, because Finney wasn't having a good day.

He climbed up to the helm, where Starn stood in the shade of the overhang.

"Captain?"

"What the hell is up with you today, Finney?"

"Wh-what do you mean?"

"The boat's nearly full, and you're moving like you're asleep. People need help with catches, Finney; you're leaving 'em cooling their damn heels."

Finney rubbed his eyes. "I had a bad night, Captain. Bad sleep, bad dreams."

"Jesus, Finney. There are a lot of guys who'd love to work on this boat. The fish, the tips . . . it's a good fucking deal."

Finney nodded. Starn made it sound as though Finney had just won the goddamn lottery.

"I know."

"A lot of guys. So you better make sure you get some rest, get some sleep, before you come out on the boat. Be ready to hustle."

"Gotcha, Captain."

Finney turned to go back down, but Starn grabbed his arm.

"What the hell you dreaming about anyway? Pussy?"

Finney grinned, but it faded quickly. He guessed that he should say nothing.

About the nightmare.

But it wasn't just a nightmare.

It seemed too real. So real that even in the morning, it felt as though he had seen it, not dreamed it.

Somehow—he wanted to tell someone.

"No. Something crazy . . . this house, a lady living there, somebody watching her, coming closer . . . like—like—"

He ran his hand through his sun-bleached hair, Needed a cut, but more than that, needed a shower. This job—the smell of the fish—made him just let things go.

"Like what?"

"Something bad's going to happen to her."

"Hey, it's just a damn dream. You should do what I do. Have a shot of Jack just before I turn out the lights. You'll sleep like a baby."

A smile again. "Right. Good idea."

"Now get your ass down there. Keep the yokels happy, got it?"

Finney nodded, and climbed down to the deck, to the fishermen and their full buckets of bluefish.

"Hey, buddy, gimme a hand here."

A fat guy near the bow, whose stomach stretched his T-shirt to the breaking point, yelled for Finney.

"Buddy," or "Pal," or sometimes even "Kid" . . .

Nobody gave a shit that Finney actually had a name.

"Yes, sir?"

"My damn line's all tangled. Snarled. Fucking reel's a mess. And I was pulling 'em in, kid."

Right, thought Finney, as if this tubby didn't have anything to do with getting his line all snarled.

"Let me take a look."

Finney took the rod and brought the reel close. The line had a large bow where the heavy filament had gotten snagged, making the reel useless. Nothing Finney hadn't seen before, usually the result of letting line out too fast then jerking it back, reeling in, yanking the rod.

Sometimes you had to just cut the line and re-rig the rod and reel.

The guy would bitch as if it was Finney's fault.

The man's line still trailed in the water, dangling whatever chunks of bait he had put on the hook, a bit of slimy squid, a porgy fish head. Depending on what you were going for—and what you believed—you selected your bait, and waited to see what it brought up.

Finney reached for the bow of filament that ballooned out from the reel. He grabbed it hard, tugging. If he could free it from the spirals of line that held it prisoner, he might get this guy up and running nice and easy.

Less work for me.

"This gonna take all day, buddy?"

From kid, to buddy. Finney felt like telling the fat fuck that he had a goddamn name, and maybe he should toss his ass into the choppy Atlantic. See what kind of fish *that* brought up.

"Just going to try and free it here, sir."

Sir . . .

Hard to stomach saying that. But Finney knew that this job only made sense with the tips. And to get the tips you needed to smile and kiss as much ass as you could.

Finney grinned at the man, squinting in the sunlight.

"If I can yank this snarl free, you'll be good to go."

"Yeah, good. Don't want to let the fish get away. They're like sitting ducks today."

"Yup." Finney smiled. "It's a good day, that's for sure."

The filament bow didn't seem to want to release, the snarl held fast by two or three tight coils. But then as Finney tugged and grunted, he felt movement. The line gave a bit. Good—maybe just a bit more, he could get it free, and give the guy back his reel.

Another small bit of movement.

The veins on Finney's arm bulged. He gritted his teeth and pulled with all his might. More movement, and in just seconds he'd have the bow free.

His left hand held the butt grip tight, his fingers digging into the sponge covering around the end of the rod, while his right hand pulled tugged.

"This gonna work?"

Finney looked up at the man, smiling. He nodded because if he'd said anything, it wouldn't have been pretty.

Another tug, and then the bow popped free.

Finney's fingers were still inside the bow, now loose, the loose line ready to be reeled in tight.

"Good," the man said.

It happened so fast.

As if it was a trap, and Finney has stepped into it, unaware. Though with all his experience he should have known.

He *should* have seen the possibility of what could happen next.

The line in the water went taut. So fast . . . the weighted line that had trailed down loosely into the churning surf went taut, ripping into those choppy breakers.

Finney had started to pull his hand away from the line that he had only just recently been pulling on so hard. Begun to release it, his fingers loosening, pulling away; but those fingers weren't as fast as whatever now had taken the bait—the piece of squid, the fish head—and started jerking away with all the sleek speed that only a big Atlantic fish can have.

Finney just couldn't move his hand fast enough.

The line and what was once a bow that wouldn't move now sliced down on his hand.

The pain, immense, blinding, made Finney scream.

His left hand still held the butt grip, but his right hand was a prisoner. And though he screamed, it almost felt as if that sound came from somewhere else; that all he was aware of was pain.

Finney looked down at his hand.

The line had cut through the skin, blood gushing now, and he thought he saw the telltale sign of whitish bone.

It seemed like an eternity before someone was there.

Luis appeared next to him.

The other crewman had two heavy gloves on, and he quickly reached out past the blade tip of the rod, grabbed the filament, and yanked it back, grunting.

Only a few inches or so, but enough to create slack, allowing the line to loosen. And finally Finney could remove his hand, the blood now spattering the deck.

"Shit," the fat fisherman said.

Once Finney's hand was free, Luis let the line go and it

snapped into the water. At the same time, he took the butt end of the rod from Finney.

Finney staggered back against the wall of the small boat's cabin.

Starn was there, throwing Finney a towel.

Spotted with god knows what.

"Wrap it, Finney. Christ, you're bleeding all over the goddamn deck."

Not a time to be concerned about hygiene—Finney wrapped his hand, the wound stinging as the terry cloth pressed into the open wound.

He looked up at Luis.

"Thanks."

Luis nodded. He had given the fat man back his rod, and the guy was now fighting the fish that wounded Finney.

Starn came closer. "We better get you inside. See how bad you fucked up."

How bad you fucked up . . .

So this is *my* doing? Great. Good to know that, thought Finney.

How *I* fucked up.

"Goddamn it, I got something big."

They both turned to the man, who struggled to reel in even a few inches of the line.

He sweated, and grunted, and Starn shook his head.

"Luis, take over."

Finney knew that a big fish could cost Starn a rod, and wipe out any profit from the whole day.

Luis, small, compact, but with bronzed, powerful arms, took the rod. The tip bent as he started to fight the fish.

"You better go clean—"

Finney shook his head. "Hold on. I want to see what did this to me."

God knows what kind of infection he'd cook up from the gut-stained towel.

"Luis, shit—you better cut the line. The goddamn rod is going to snap."

And though the tip now turned even more into a hook

shape, Finney knew that the rod, flexible and strong, could take a lot of weight, a lot of pull.

Luis would know if he had to let it go, if he needed to cut the line and let the fish run.

"What the hell is it?" the fat man said.

Not a goddamn blue, Finney knew. No way was it a goddamn bluefish.

He hadn't ever seen a rod look like that.

What the hell was it?

Luis again started cranking the reel, and the tip, though still bent, didn't go that extra inch or so more that would mean that the line had to be cut.

A bunch of people had come up to the railing now to see what the crewman was pulling up.

Finney took a step closer. He looked down at the towel, stained red, but with the bleeding subsiding.

He wanted to see what did it, then he could go soak his whole fist in peroxide, Mercurochrome—whatever crap he could find in the ship's first aid pack.

Still cranking—and the tip eased up its angle. The fish had given up. Almost too easy, Finney thought . . . All that pull, all that fight, and then it just stops?

Another crank.

A line of other fishermen leaning over the side, looking down.

Finney now next to Luis, looking, listening to each click of the reel.

When something broke the surface of the water.

Luis stopped reeling when the fish broke the surface. At first it looked like two fish, a head there, a tail there, but then Finney could see that it was a shark, a small three-foot tiger shark. It thrashed in the water, flapping at the sea with its tail.

Starn looked over the side.

"Can you bring her in, Luis?"

The crewman nodded. The fight seemed to have gone out of the young shark. And though it kicked and flapped in the water, it didn't really struggle, didn't really try to pull away.

"Think the line will hold?" Starn said.

"I *think* so," Luis answered.

Even at three feet, that was one big fish to bring aboard using normal filament.

"Hell, I really caught something," the fat man said.

Finney looked down at his hand and unwrapped it a bit. The worst of the bleeding was over. Luis began to crank the reel, pulling the shark up the last few feet.

Everyone stayed at the railing, watching the show.

The shark came next to the rail, and then with some more cranks, higher, until Luis could swing it into the ship.

"Everyone back. It's small, but it's still a damn shark."

As if to prove the point, the shark's mouth opened and shut as it twisted its head, biting at the air.

Starn took out a knife attached to his belt.

Luis lowered the shark.

Finney, standing just behind Luis, moved away, out of the path of the kicking and flapping body. He hated this goddamn shark that had caused the line to cut right through his skin.

Shark fucked me up, he thought.

Luis lowered it to the deck. Starn took his knife, ready to jab it into the shark's primitive brain.

Finney backed up a bit more, bumping into one of the fishermen.

When the shark turned its head.

As it mouth opened and shut, Finney could see one dark, empty eye. A typical shark eye, single-minded, focused on only one thing . . . eating.

But then, next to it, the other eye socket.

Empty.

A one-eyed shark.

And that one eye seemed to aim itself at Finney, wide as can be, looking right at him.

The tail made a loud flap against the deck.

Starn rammed the knife home.

And then, with one last flap, the shark stopped moving . . . and it was over.

11

DAVID grabbed an arm of the easy chair, worn from years of sitting with arms and hands resting on the curved padded arm.

He placed his cane so it would hook on the side but then—as he sat—the metal cane slipped away, sliding, tumbling to the ground.

"I'll get that for you," the mother said, hurrying up from the chair.

"No, It's okay—" David started to say, but she had quickly hooked the curved end of the cane on the chair.

He looked up. "Thanks."

The father's face was grim, set. One could only imagine the thoughts, the horrors that had to have gone through their minds.

Trouble was—

David could imagine.

"Get that on the job?" the man said.

David nodded. Then—"Yes. Bullet just above the knee. Nothing major."

And David waited. This could be the point where they started asking him questions about what happened—how did he get shot, what happened to the shooter . . . the whole story.

Asking him . . . to avoid their own horror story.

And David didn't want to relive his now.

But instead, the mother, Mrs. Brzow, took her seat. They waited. And David realized why they didn't ask him any questions. They expected David to be telling *them* something, giving them some news, some hope that the nightmare would end.

But that's not why he was here at all.

He was here hoping that anything might emerge from their memories, something that hadn't appeared before.

"I want you to know that the department has your daughter's case on highest priority."

"They damn well better," the father said. The words were bitter, but delivered in a flat, resigned tone.

"And they have put more detectives on it. I'm working with a partner who is revisiting the other victim's families. We will be doing all we can."

"The bastard . . . ," Mr. Brzow said.

Then, from the mother, more quietly . . . "A monster . . ."

David nodded, not sure if "bastard" really described whoever did this.

Even the word *monster* paled.

"What can we do, Detective?" the mother asked. David took a breath.

"Well, we want to talk to all the families again and just review what we know, what we think happened at the time of the murders, and any memories that maybe, somehow could help."

The department already had all the cell phone and landline records, all that data being sifted, people looking at all the calls made, calls received.

All—so far—with no value whatsoever.

"Anything?" Mrs. Brzow said. "I don't know . . . if we . . ." The words trailed off.

David looked at the shredded napkin in the woman's fingers. How many of those did she go through in a day? Turning each paper wad to pulpy fiber.

He began a review of the basic facts. How their daughter, Caroline, left one evening saying she was meeting friends. But no meeting with any friends had been scheduled, no one was expecting her.

And instead of meeting friends, Caroline Brzow had met doom in that basement torture chamber.

What brought her there? There was no sign of a struggle, no sign that she, or any of the victims, had been brought there forcibly. They all seemed to have arrived there willingly.

And with absolutely no reason to be there.

"Your daughter—I'm not sure how to phrase this—but she usually told the truth?"

The man's eyes widened a bit. Best be careful here, David thought. The doors of communication could close so quickly.

"What do you mean?" Brzow said.

"I mean, she didn't say one thing then do another?"

The mother answered. "Caroline was a good girl. She liked to have a good time, but she worked very hard. She always told us what she was doing, where she was going, and never gave us a reason to doubt her."

"Never," Mr. Brzow added for finality.

"So what happened that night was unusual?"

"More than that," Mrs. Brzow said. "It's unbelievable. It wasn't our Caroline. To do something . . . and not tell us."

David looked over to the father to see if he agreed with his wife's assessment. But he just made small nods with his head.

Whatever vision they had of their daughter, they shared. And David guessed it was an accurate one.

Which left him with nothing.

But a word the mother had said stuck; a bit of an open door to more questions.

David looked back to the mother. "Mrs. Brzow, you just said something. The word leapt out a bit."

"What was that?"

"*Unusual.* You said that for Caroline to do this was . . . unusual."

"Why, yes. I mean, she worked hard to get through college, then to become a CPA. We were so proud. She never had secrets, talked to me—us—about *everything.*"

David guessed that there might have been a secret or two Caroline and the mother kept from the stern-faced Dad. But Mom probably did hear everything . . .

"That's what I mean," David said. "Unusual. She did something that she had never done before."

"Yes."

"So, I'm wondering . . . did she do anything else unusual, did anything else happen that didn't fit the Caroline you knew?"

Mrs. Brzow looked at her husband, and David guessed that maybe he might be prompting the revelation of something between Caroline and her mother . . . something not shared with the father.

The room grew quiet.

The noisy AC pumped frigid air into the living room while the afternoon sun sent shafts of light that made the endless swirls of dust look like a universe of tiny flickering planets.

Then—

"Yes. There was something."

Mr. Brzow turned and looked at his wife, eyes still expressionless but staring at her.

About to hear something he didn't know.

"It started . . . about five weeks ago . . ."

MARI knocked on the door to what some of the reporters referred to as "the real morgue."

She opened the door and stuck her head in.

"Anybody home?"

Harvey, the obit editor, looked up from a messy sandwich with lettuce and tomato trying to flee for their lives. A mousy assistant editor, a young girl hired only months ago, sat at another desk dutifully pecking away.

"It's lunch, Mari. That's why the damn door is closed. Lunch, *capiche*? Show some respect, hm?"

Mari grinned, and nodded to the young girl. "New employees exempt from the lunchtime rule?"

Harvey shook his head. "The kid can eat anytime she wants. Not sure"—he looked over at her as the girl pretended to take no notice of the conversation—"she does eat." Then back to Mari. "But I do . . ."

"Okay. I'll go. Hate to see your elegant dining interrupted." She turned back to the door.

"No, wait a second. You're here, you're here, right? So tell me what's up."

Mari grabbed a chair from a vacant desk belonging to a reporter hitting Lexington Avenue for his lunch, daring the Lexington Avenue pushcarts and delis.

"Thanks. I'm trying to figure things out. Sort of go out-side the box working this story."

"You mean the killings? I thought they gave that story to Roberts?"

Mari's eyes widened. "Roberts? Isn't he still on that kick-back scandal?"

Mari felt chilled. Jack Roberts was an award-winning re-porter. A story this big could easily be taken away from her and given to him.

Shit . . .

"Thought he wrapped that up. Maybe not. That was the scuttlebutt." Then Harvey grinned. "But it's only rumors, kiddo. You haven't heard anything, so don't worry, right? This place is one giant rumor mill. Don't worry about it."

Mari nodded, and pushed her dark hair off her forehead.

"Though I got to tell you," Harvey said, "it's one nasty story you're covering." He looked her right in the eyes. "You sure you want to be doing it?"

"It's a story. I'm a reporter. What's the problem?"

"It's not just a normal story, hm? In fact, I'd say it's one of the sickest stories I've ever seen. There's that and—" He took a bite of his sandwich.

"And—? I do like the way you make me wait between chews."

Harvey talked with a half-full mouth. "The cops know nothing. That's the part that would bother me. You're work-ing this thing which makes Son of Sam look like Sunday school, and they know nothing?" He swallowed. "Just be careful. Hate not to have you around this dump."

"I'm always careful. As for the police not knowing any-thing, that's why I came to you."

"Huh?"

"They know something, something that we don't."

"What's that?"

"They know who the five people in there are. They know that, and they haven't told the public."

"Yeah, supposedly to help their investigation. They just revealed the victims' ages, sex . . ."

"Right. But here's where I think we can beat them."

"Really?"

"Anyone who died in the past weeks, you're going to have that here, right? The funeral arrangements, all that information."

"Yeah, unless someone got dumped in a landfill somewhere. All the bodies lead here, even if they don't make it into the obit section."

Mari leaned close. "Precisely. So out of all those deaths, all those funerals, we should be able to create a pool of possible victims. And I bet there are a lot of people—families, friends—just waiting to talk, especially with the police stalled."

"So what do you want me to do?"

"Help me make that list. Help me go through the database, cull all the likely candidates. Look at them carefully, then get the pool of deaths that could be our victims . . ."

" 'Pool of deaths' . . . catchy title for a mystery."

"Yeah, a mystery with a lot of corpses. What do you say?"

Harvey wiped his lips and his bushy goatee with his napkin. "If I say okay, I want a promise that you won't do anything stupid? No brave reporter, Nancy Drew crap. Okay?"

"You got it. I will be very careful."

Harvey rolled up the white deli paper containing the droppings from his sandwich.

"All right, this may take awhile, so we better get going."

He tapped Mari on the shoulder and laughed.

"Gotta tell you—you're lucky that no one important died today."

DAVID watched Mrs. Brzow struggle with the words.

"Caroline was always such a busy girl, working late, dinner with friends. We barely got a word or two with her, right, Jack?" She looked at her husband for confirmation.

"But she told you something?"

"I mean, at first I didn't think much about it. After all, everyone . . . dreams."

"Dreams? She told you a dream?"

The mother nodded. "The first time I saw her in the morning, all dressed for work, a nice suit, looking, looking—" Her voice started to catch. Mr. Brzow slowly reached out and took her hand. David saw the tiny glistening in her eyes.

This was a bad thing to do, he thought.

Bad, unfair—but so damn necessary.

The woman looked to her right, and spotted the nearby tissue box.

She pulled out a single tissue.

She didn't dab her eyes, or brush her nose. She just made the tissue ready.

"She looked . . . You were saying?"

"Tired." Mrs. Brzow nodded. "Circles under her eyes, dark circles. At first, Caroline said . . . it was nothing. Then she told me, as if she had to tell someone. She had a dream about some woman, somebody she never saw before. Nobody from work, not an old neighbor or teacher. A woman in maybe her forties. So I said to her, 'Honey, that's nothing to worry about. We all have dreams, nightmares . . .' "

Now the small pool in her eyes bloomed, and tiny droplets started down her cheek. Mrs. Brzow was quick to dab and catch each, well practiced at this by now.

David resisted the impulse to look at the mantelpiece, to study the line of pictures that documented the high points in their daughter's life.

"But she shook her head. She actually raised her voice to me a bit. And Caroline never raised her voice. And she said, 'No, it's not just the dream. I saw everything about the woman, her street, her apartment—everything. And then—"

Another look at Mr. Brzow, to see if this was okay, if she should even be sharing this.

"She said . . . she could also see in the dream someone *watching* this woman, watching, waiting, and, and—"

The mother stopped talking. Another yanked tissue.

No sound now in the sunlit living room save for her repressed cries, a small blow of her nose.

Then—a few moments of silence—before she started again.

12

"LOOK, Finney—you better take some days off."

Finney stood near the stern of the boat, the day fishermen all gone, the deck still awash with fish guts.

"I'll be okay, Captain. It's all bandaged. I'll be fine."

"I think you better get to the hospital. You know, it might need some stitches. Looks pretty nasty."

"I'll be all right."

"Finney, you can't help people with their lines with a bum hand. And Luis has a friend who can fill in."

Finney shot a glance at Luis up at the bow, hosing the deck down. The bastard was quick to slide one of his amigos into Finney's slot.

"I can—"

"Look, I'm not going to give away your job. I'm not a prick. Freak thing like that could happen to anyone. But come back when it's healed, okay? Get those damn stitches if you need them. All right?"

Finney saw that arguing was useless.

"A few days, okay?"

Starn nodded. "Right. Few days it is."

Finney nodded, then holding his roughly bandaged hand up, he turned and climbed off the boat.

THE afternoon sun made Finney realize what a rat hole he had let his one room on Eammons Avenue become.

Now I got a few days to clean it up, he thought. Get laundry done. Put stuff away.

That was the plan, he thought, taking a big swig from the bottle of Smirnoff vodka. He wished it was cold—cold vodka would be nice, but even at this lukewarm room temperature, it still felt pretty good going down.

He didn't go to the hospital. He'd check his hand tomorrow, take a look at it. Maybe he'd go then. But now the wound was covered with antibiotic and wrapped in gauze.

Probably be just fine.

Probably be okay.

He kicked a small pile of underwear away.

Yeah, gotta pick up.

Another swig, the pint bottle half-gone. He wished he had AC in this room. It was okay in the night, a cool breeze always blowing off Sheepshead Bay even on the worst of nights.

Now the room felt close, the air unbreathable. He pushed aside the blinds, cheap slats of metal that didn't do a very good job of keeping the sun out.

All the morning boats were back by now, and the full day boats not due to return until sunset. Only a few people walked the street, looking at the shimmering water, walking off the fried clams, corn on the cob, or a cold beer from Ummaro's Clam Shack.

That sounded good.

Some fried clams, loaded with tartar sauce. Yeah, and sweet corn, dripping butter. Good days for corn now, nice, sweet succulent. And a cold beer.

Would taste a lot better than the piss-warm vodka.

He looked at his hand.

Throbbed a little.

Could have gotten a little infected. Or maybe it just stings because the damn fishing line cut down to the bone. Could be.

One more slug, and Finney walked over to his perpetually unmade bed.

He lay down.

And that felt good too, with a little bit of a buzz on, to lie back, shut his eyes, trying to ignore the beads of sweat on his brow, the heat, his eyes shut tight against the sunlight that sliced its way into the shaded room.

In seconds he was asleep.

* * *

AND *cold.*

Actually, chilled. He felt the wind blowing, making the leaves rustle, making the tall grass here bend.

And there was the house.

The same house, the small . . . cottage.

Only now it was nighttime.

The same house, and he looked at it, wondering, Do I somehow know this house, have I ever seen this house?

He heard noises, the sound of a muffled TV, unintelligible save for the laughter, the noise.

And he was rather amazed that he knew—all the time— that this was a dream. So clearly a dream. So strange to so clearly know that it was a dream.

Usually something bad would occur in a dream, and only then, like a life preserver tossed out from somewhere in his mind, he'd have the thought.

Hey, Finney, this is only a dream, buddy. It isn't fucking real!

Always such a relief. He hadn't screwed everything up, guys weren't going to kill him, he wasn't falling off a cliff, or bobbing in the water, alone, soon to drown.

Nah, because it's all just a stupid dream.

Such a good moment that.

To realize it was only a dream.

Like this. Crouched down. Looking at the house.

He didn't wonder why he crouched, squatting low to the ground. Looking at the house, hearing the TV sounds, and then . . . moving closer.

And though Finney knew it was a dream, he had to wonder:

Why am I here? Why am I dreaming of this small house stuck by some crappy lake covered by algae?

There must be a reason, right?

He moved closer to the house, still crouching, still not knowing why he was so low to the ground.

13

MRS. Brzow discarded the tissues and then, amazingly, with dignity . . . she apologized.

"Sorry."

"It was just . . . a nightmare?"

The woman shook her head.

"That's what I had hoped, that's what I thought—"

Another quick glance at her husband. He obviously knew this but wasn't happy that his wife now talked about it.

"Then one night I heard her get up in the middle of the night. I came down to the kitchen, and she was sitting with all the lights on; she had been crying."

"The dream again?"

"Yes, but it was different this time, Caroline said. More than just *see* the woman, her street, her apartment; she now saw that she was in danger. She started talking about helping her. I got so scared. I didn't know what to do."

David looked at the woman's face, lined from years of raising a daughter, probably struggling with money, dealing with what looked like a hard husband. All that, and now *this*—

He thought: Does this . . . information have anything to do with what happened? Anything at all?

"Did you ever suggest she see someone?"

The woman nodded. "A psychiatrist? Not that we believe in that stuff, but I didn't know what to do. So I did tell her . . . that maybe—"

She stopped again.

"And did she?"

David tried to imagine what it was like when they came to tell these people the news, the slow crushing wave of . . . *fact* that must have rolled over them.

How their daughter was no more . . . and worse.

Now, weeks later, the horror must be with them every moment.

"She wouldn't go. She said it was all crazy. But she was convinced that this woman was in danger, in her Upper West Side apartment. And somehow Caroline thought she had to warn her."

David felt gooseflesh rise on his arms.

Sitting there . . . hearing what Mrs. Brzow said, as it started to sink in.

"Wait a second. You said Upper West Side?"

She nodded.

"Middle-aged woman who lives alone?"

Another nod. "I can't be sure, of course . . . because Caroline stopped talking to me about it, after all the 'doctor' talk, but—"

David put his pen down. "You think—do you think now she was dreaming about the woman, one of the other victims?"

The mother looked at her husband, hesitating. Then she nodded . . . yes.

Her husband looked away.

"But she never told you the address, or what she looked like, or a name?"

"No. She stopped talking. I could see that she was still haunted, that the dreams continued, that her fear was still so terrible. But now she didn't talk to me about it."

And the mother began sobbing full out now. It took a second, but finally her husband reached out and put an arm around her and pulled her close, hugging her tight as she heaved and shook.

David sat there, waited. Mr. Brzow looked up at him as if signaling . . . Time to go. You've done enough here.

And maybe it was.

But he had one more question to ask.

When the woman stopped heaving, stopped shaking . . . when the tears finally stopped.

"I'm sorry," David said. "Bringing all this up."

Mrs. Brzow shook her head. "No. It might mean something. I mean, it's crazy, but it might."

Now David nodded. "Yes, it might very well. But one more thing, did she tell you anything else about this person, anything before she went off that night?"

"She never told us where she was going that night. Just out, with friends. She had closed herself off to me. I should have—"

Her husband patted her hand.

"But nothing more . . . except, after we talked in the kitchen, I started to feel that this woman, this dream woman of Caroline's, could have been real. And, and that something bad would happen to her."

The woman took a breath, so deep, as if the air itself could somehow give her strength.

David said the words quietly. Whispered them . . .

"And it happened, didn't it . . . ?"

MARI looked through the pages of printout.

"Is this everything?"

"Within the city limits. All deaths get reported to the city coroner. So, even in this bizarre case, the deaths have to be filed, even if they kept the circumstances secret."

"So I can bet that the five people are in here?"

"You sure can. Planning on looking for all five?"

"I'd be happy with just one for now. Mind if I take this?"

Harvey looked at his assistant dutifully pecking away at her keyboard. He took a step closer to Mari and lowered his voice.

"Technically, I'm not supposed to give out that information. Even dead people have rights. But yeah—you can take them. Just keep me posted on what you're doing."

"Deal. If I get anywhere, we'll talk about it over ham sandwiches in the cafeteria."

"Corned beef, and the Carnegie Deli please."

"You got it."

She folded the papers and stuffed them into her oversized purse.

THE afternoon sun turned into golden magical light, still blisteringly hot, the color turned a burnished yellow and orange.

At One Centre Street, David waited in the car for James to show up. They would compare notes, next steps.

If there were any next steps.

He watched other detectives coming in and out of Police Plaza, noticing David, giving him a wave. By now everyone had heard about what happened, and they were probably surprised to see him back on the job.

David smiled, nodded, waved back.

Yeah, I'm still here.

Still here, because the idea of sitting in my apartment, alone, nothing to do, would drive me crazy.

And what if he and his partner got in a situation where his injured leg could slow him down? A situation where his leg could cause someone to get away? Or worse—someone to get hurt?

He shook his head.

Not gonna let that happen . . . he thought.

Someone rapped the passenger window of the car.

James Corcoran, grinning. David reached for the door and popped open the lock. His partner opened the door and slid in.

"So, Detective, how was your afternoon?"

"Interesting," David said. "And you?"

"Not terribly useful. Talked to some of his dentist's neighbors, one cute blonde who lived next door . . ."

"The job has its perks . . ."

"Seemed Bernard Kenner was pretty much a total loner. Tried to jog neighbors' memories about anything he might have been seen doing before he became one of the party of five, strapped to a wooden chair for the ride of his life. But I got nothing."

"Nothing."

"The whole thing more or less as the original report says . . . it happened out of the blue. He just went there, telling no one. You spoke to his partner, Dr . . . ?"

"Dr. Jay. Yeah, yesterday. Nothing there. Wasn't sleeping well apparently. Then out of the blue, he—"

David stopped.

James stopped grinning.

"Hey. You get something?"

David looked at him and wondered if he should just keep his mouth shut. Let the kid make his own breakthroughs. This isn't detective school.

But like it or not, they were a team.

"Maybe. I just . . . flashed on it. Might be something. Hard to tell."

"Share, amigo. Show me how this stuff is really done."

David nodded. Then he told James Mrs. Brzow's strange tale, about her daughter's dreams about someone in danger.

A victim who matched one of the five perfectly.

"Shit," said James. "Sounds like—"

"Precisely. The teacher on the Upper West Side, Susan Hart, high school math teacher—and she dreamed about her."

"And doomed to be tied to a wall and crucified. Maybe Kenner wasn't sleeping—"

"Because of the dreams? Maybe he dreamt about one of the victims too? But that's crazy, I mean how does that make sense?"

"Beats me. All I know is when that woman started talking about her daughter's dreams, it was like Caroline and the teacher were old friends."

David knew that none of the victims' families knew about the other people involved . . . so he could rule out any hysteria or any backward memory creation.

His partner looked out the front of the car.

The sun now hit the dark windows of the Police Plaza building, making them glow a burnished brilliant golden orange.

The building looked wondrous, magical—

Instead of what it really was—the nerve center where everything dirty and deadly that happened in this city ultimately ended.

"Shit," James said again. "That's . . . got to be impossible, right?"

"Right. Impossible. Could never happen."

Another silence. Neither spoke.

And as if with a wave of a wand, the gold vanished from the police headquarters' building and the windows all turned dark again.

PART TWO

The Nightmares

14

THE lecture room in Schemerhorn Hall was dark, the giant windows shaded, with only the outer edges lined with the gold of the setting sun.

"Now, this chart shows the distribution of serial killers by state."

Linda Kyle projected a graphic, a checkerboard of lines, crosses, and shaded areas.

"You can see that California tops the list by far. These are last year's figures. I imagine that it's easily over one hundred serial killers by now. Then it's followed, with a big jump downward, in Texas, Florida, New York, and Illinois."

She flipped to another slide. "One question to think about is . . . do these states have anything—other than population—that creates these figures? Because, as you can see—even adjusted for population density—the distribution of serial killers is radically skewed in these five states."

Linda spotted a hand, a young girl sitting in the front, her hair backlit by the white light from the projector.

"Dr. Kyle, are you saying that there may be environmental factors shaping the numbers . . . and we should think about that?"

"Possibly. Hold on a sec—"

She flipped to another PowerPoint image.

As she did, the gold lining around the window shades vanished, the sunlight now vanishing to the low hills of New Jersey, and the long trek west.

"Okay. The national VICAP center, as well as the local divisions in the big cities, recognizes three types of serial killers. First, you have the place-specific killers. Like John Wayne Gacy right here." She used a penlight to highlight the name. "He murdered twenty-two males in his home. Then there are the local serial killers who do their work within a certain state or urban area. Take a look at Michael D. Terry—he killed six male prostitutes all within a fourteen-square-mile area of downtown Atlanta, Georgia. Then—"

"Dr. Kyle?"

Linda imagined that sitting in the dark, looking at these bloodless facts about bloody murders could be a little unnerving. These students had known what they were getting into. Still, sitting there, summoning the spirits of maniacs—had to be a little strange.

And for a moment, she flashed on her own scare the night before.

Soon she'd be heading home from work again.

Maybe—she quickly thought—she'd do something different. Maybe head downtown to one of the First Avenue watering holes.

A place like Elaine's, always busy, fun.

She had a date with a Mr. Unknown tomorrow. Might be good to get out and practice what remained of her social skills.

"Yes, um, Taylor?"

"That chart talks about site-specific killers. But couldn't that be just where they happened to . . . like to kill?"

"Isn't that what 'site specific' means?" Linda said.

The class laughed at this. Taylor was a smart, funny Psych student. But this laugh . . . she imagined it might be more from nervousness than anything else.

"But we have to look for patterns, reason, anything that let's us predict," she continued. "If we can predict, if we can find a pattern, we can catch these killers. So far, it has worked well. For example, there are—"

The next PowerPoint slide popped onto the screen as Linda tried to move things along.

"The traveling killers—serial killers who travel a regular route and carry out their murders along it. Like Randall B. Woodfield up here, the so-called "I-5 Killer" because he found his thirteen victims all while traveling the same eight-hundred-mile stretch between Washington, Oregon, and California."

"Dr. Kyle—"

She recognized the clear, commanding voice of Elliot Christian. He'd probably make a lousy psychologist, but a damn good trial attorney. Her jousts with Christian were turning into an everyday thing.

"Yes?"

"Isn't this all an attempt to give structure to chaos? These killers do the incomprehensible and we try to reduce it to a system? That I-5 Killer, for example, that was simply the route he took for his sales job? Nothing to do with his killing, nothing to do with a pattern. And Gacy? He spent so much time at home when he wasn't clowning. So that's where he killed."

Another small laugh in the room.

"Not patterns; it's just where they were," Christian said.

"Well, you're getting ahead of us a bit. The real question is where do pattern and ritual meet? And we will be looking at the possible ritual aspect of some of these killings, the importance of ritual and the almost totemistic aspect of them. Some serial killers, we know, plan everything. Others seem to make spontaneous decisions. And understanding that from a psychological perspective can tell us what kind of killer they are."

"I'm not sure," Christian said.

Linda looked out into the backlit darkness.

Not sure . . . The smug kid thinks that his thoughts carry some weight here.

"Well—maybe by the time we're done with this course, you will be. Now, let's look at the target group of these killers—you'll see the targets can also match their pattern . . ."

"SECOND Avenue and Eighty-ninth," Linda said, sliding into the cab, sighing.

The driver nodded, and pulled away from the Columbia campus gates, heading down the west side, and then the Central Park cut-through at Seventy-ninth Street.

She should have picked a place closer to her apartment, but tonight Elaine's was exactly what she needed.

The noise, the people, the possibility.

The streets were still quiet—the benefit of the summer migration to, for one set, the Hamptons, and to the Jersey shore for the other. It was her favorite time in the city. Manhattan turned steamy hot and everyone outside to eat, to sit on front stoops, to just walk around.

And for a few brief humid weeks, getting around the city by cab, by subway, by foot actually became doable.

The driver raced through the streets, daring each yellow light to turn red and stop him. He hit the cut-through off Central Park West with screeching wheels, a turn that sent Linda sliding against the door.

Long ago she learned that you couldn't protest the driving.

No, then you might get a full-blown argument from the driver . . .

What? You don't want to get there fast, huh, lady? Or do you want to be the cabdriver? You telling *me* how to drive . . . ?

This taxi driver—ever the professional—had his cell phone headset on, talking some language that Linda couldn't identify.

Probably planning a new round of explosions somewhere, she thought.

And as soon as she admitted that thought, a good Linda angel popped up in her head and scolded her. Can't label people, can't be suspicious of people just because they speak strange languages and have names with so many u's and m's and the Greek letter omega.

Prejudice is prejudice.

Period.

Right . . .

But she did have to wonder—What kind of cell phone plan were these people on? They can talk all the time? Are they on "forever" minutes?

The cab emerged on the eastern side of the park, the different world of Museum Mile. Here too the streets were deserted—deserted for New York that is . . .

The cab raced uptown ten blocks, then east until it finally

came to a breathless stop in front of that most famous of watering holes . . . Elaine's.

ELAINE'S was packed.

Then again Linda couldn't remember ever coming here and not finding it packed. All the tables filled with diners, both rooms bursting. The dining crowd looking as if they might be film extras, hired to permanently populate the tables as they pushed around the same sad-looking square of ravioli all night.

Funny idea . . .

But they were in fact real. Laughing, talking, eating.

All three things she could use.

And the amazing bar! A wall of people two layers thick protected the bartenders from Linda's order.

She looked for a crack in that wall, a place she might snake into the human wall, a lineman playing cocktail football.

A lady with gray hair and the lined, cracked face of parchment, turned to her friends laughing; her razor-sharp elbows made a momentary opening.

Linda pounced, sliding into the opening sideways, and then—through that first line—looking for another small crack where she could stick in her head and arm and launch her drink order.

But then that wall seemed to close ranks.

A Stoli martini seemed farther away then ever.

"Could you use an assist?"

She turned to the voice, to the tall man standing a few feet away. He wasn't next to her, but at six feet plus, he towered over the crowd.

She quickly took in his vitals: tall, looked fit, maybe over fifty—but that was okay. Had dark hair, great blue eyes, nice smile.

Why the hell not . . .

"Why yes I could."

"What'll it be?"

"Stoli martini, straight up, olive."

"Nice drink," he said, grinning.

The man turned to the bartender, and as if the man's height and his extended arm were enough to command respect, Linda saw the bartender stop and lean close to hear the order over the din.

LINDA insisted the man take the ten dollars for the drink.

She wasn't about to let a perfect stranger buy her drink—at least not her first drink.

"Can be a tough bar to crack," he said with a grin.

The martini lost a few precious sips in the transfer from the bar to her lips, but still it was perfect—cold with tiny floating clear flakes on the surface.

"Mmm," she said.

"I'm Scott," the man said.

Of course, Linda thought. Scott looked like a "Scott." Part of the Central Casting that filled this place.

"Linda."

"Nice to meet you, Linda." The small smile. "Um, come here often?"

And his eyes actually twinkled as he delivered the stock line that, coming from him, didn't seem stock at all.

"When I feel the need. Love the place."

He looked around. "Like this? Not exactly good for a quiet drink."

"A quiet drink I can have at home. I come here for the circus."

A quick thought. Too much information? Linda wasn't at all sure of her dating or relationship instincts anymore. Her last relationship, with another Columbia teacher—Literature of all things!—ended badly. But at least she was the one who ended it.

Eventually even she could recognize the telltale signs of excess baggage.

Such a tricky thing this man-woman-meeting nonsense.

And trickier the older she got.

Scott reached over and tapped her shoulder.

"Don't look now—but do you watch *The Sopranos*?"

"Who doesn't?"

"There's one of Tony's gumbas at table number one, sitting with Elaine herself."

She turned quickly and spotted the faux mobster, highball in hand, holding court.

"Scary," she said.

"Huh?"

"I mean, I know he's *only* an actor. But he still looks like the real deal."

"Maybe he's both."

"What?"

"Both an actor *and* the real deal, *capiche*?"

She laughed again. This . . . Scott was fun, entertaining. A good drink-getter with a nice warm grin.

Suddenly the quiet of the apartment, and the darkness of her quiet street, faded away.

Life is cabaret, old chum . . .

At least tonight, with Scott, at Elaine's.

And she knew that this martini wouldn't be her last of the evening.

15

EMMA Chappel heard the kettle whistling. So did Rusty, whose ears shot straight up as he raised his head off the ground.

The dog eyed Emma, waiting for her to move.

"Don't worry, boy, I'm going to make my tea."

She wanted to wait for the commercial. Though *The King of Queens* wasn't her favorite show—she didn't laugh nearly as much as she did with *Raymond*—still, she liked the wife on the show.

Always with snappy comebacks to everything her husband said.

Only in TV Land could such a smart and beautiful woman be with that fat guy. She knew that's what made it a funny show; still it strained belief. And he'd never be as good as that other supposedly lovable slob to a beauty, Ralph Cramden.

Those shows, when she caught them late at night, could make her laugh so hard she'd have tears.

The commercial came on.

"Okay, *now* I'll make my tea."

Rusty got up to accompany her, walking with Emma to the small kitchen.

Of course she wasn't making real tea, not any kind of tea that would keep her up.

No, this would be one of her herbals, filled with the scent of apple, or cinnamon, or something more exotic. Part of her ritual.

The shows, the tea, later the reading, and a quiet sleep.

It was a life she liked.

The very routine comforting.

She put one of the stringless tea bags in her cup and

poured the boiling water into it. In seconds it deepened to a cherry red. Then she grabbed her honey ladle and let the clear sugary stream flow into the cup.

The smell was wonderful.

She sometimes wished that she wasn't alone. But that dream, along with a few others, had disappeared a long time ago. Emma accepted "alone" now, and felt that the beauty she lived near, the calmness, the *steadiness* of her quiet life was enough.

She started back for her chair, Rusty at her feet.

When she saw . . . something on the floor, midway between her small kitchen and her island of peace, her chair.

SHE stopped, Rusty at her heels. If he had noticed anything—other than her stopping—he gave no sign of it.

She looked at the thing on the floor. There were only two lights on in the small living room—just a waste of money to have more on.

Just one small lamp on the mantelpiece and her lamp by her chair.

And whatever was on the floor sat in the big shadow cast by her chair.

She stopped by instinct, but now she began to think . . . What is that thing on the floor?

It looked blackish and shaped like—what?

A spider? She hated spiders. Though she knew all the good work the hungry spiders did eating insects, their webs trapping so many annoying bugs. But she just couldn't get past how a spider looked, those long arched legs, its speed, and the way it moved . . . as if it was always one step ahead of whatever plan you were cooking up to catch it.

This thing looked like a spider.

Its shape, the outline.

But way too big.

No spider that big.

Even those rain forest spiders, the tarantulas. Even they weren't *that* big.

Could it just be a mouse? She'd had mice inside before, a

few field mice who lost their way from the outside. Her eyes weren't great, but it didn't look like a mouse.

But that would make sense, that would—

It moved.

It moved.

And everything now happened so quickly.

As the thing moved, almost crawled on the floor. One more weird thought flashed in her head watching the way its legs moved, the awkward kind of step, the back legs bigger or shaped different, or—

She thought: It's a big toad. Somehow some really big toad got into the room.

But even as she had that thought she recognized the impossibility of it. How in the world would a toad get into her room? There was no way.

And now—to relieve the silence, the mad guessing, and maybe the aloneness—she spoke, softly, to herself to be sure, but still . . . a sound:

"What . . . is it?"

And the sound spurred the creature to move in an entirely different way.

THE creature leaped into the air, high, then growing twice, maybe three times larger as it unfurled *wings* and flew.

It flew right at Emma, who instinctively brought her arms up to protect herself from the assault, her tea cup crashing to the floor.

But the bat deftly dodged her, swooping around to the side, into the kitchen, then swooping back, madly, back and forth.

Now Rusty began barking; but the bat was way too fast for the dog's eyes. Rusty would bark at one spot, but already the rapid bat had looped behind the dog, back and forth.

Emma cringed and guarded her face with her hands during each narrow circle the bat made.

Until it finally came to a stop in the kitchen.

Landing on one of her curtains over the sink, trimmed with symbols made to recall the Pennsylvania Dutch—

bright red and yellow curlicues, now with the bat holding onto dear life.

Emma realized that she was shaking, rattled by the event.

I've seen enough bats, she thought. Shouldn't have been surprised. Probably it came in through the chimney.

Never happened before—but yes, that's probably what happened.

Rusty barked again, now aiming his snout at the bat resting on the kitchen curtain.

"Shhhh," Emma said.

But Rusty let out one more bark, and the bat leaped off the curtain, tearing into the living room, into Emma's sanctuary . . . once more.

16

FINNEY knew it was a dream.

If he had been awake, he'd have felt the throbbing in his hand, and the throbbing that would have told him that he should get up and coat his wounded hand with more antibiotic, keep fighting the infection that probably already had gained a toehold on his sliced hand.

But knowing it was a dream didn't give Finney any advantage in escaping it.

No, all dreamers have the same rights—or lack of same.

Finney could only be *aware* that he was in a dream, aware but unable to hit some magical button to escape.

But why did this dream—

No, this *nightmare*, trouble him so much?

Was it the fact the he didn't feel like himself, that he crouched low, huddled, waiting outside this lonely house, a house from a nightmare with only a few pale lights, surrounded by so much woodsy darkness?

Crouched . . . outside the house.

Waiting for something to happen.

And though he might think, even plead to—something . . . Let me wake up. Enough of this! It did no good.

He would be there until it was all over.

And, as he was about to discover, it was long from over.

EMMA stood in the kitchen, frozen, thinking, planning—what to do next.

"Shssh," she said again to Rusty, who finally obeyed the order. She couldn't see the bat, now hiding somewhere in her living room. But she knew it was there, waiting.

It wasn't as if Emma had a special fear of bats. On a warm summer's night they were a common enough sight, darting low in the sky doing their best to keep the mosquito population down.

But this was different.

The bat was in the house.

And when she watched them fly overhead, she didn't really think of them as anything more than kind of a bird. But now seeing the thing on the floor, seeing it walk, she realized how strange the rodent—

(And that's what it is, she told herself, a rodent, like a mouse, like a rat . . . a flying rodent . . .)

—looked.

What to do? she thought.

Then she had another worry.

Didn't bats carry rabies? Weren't they big carriers of rabies, worse even than rats? It could bite her, or bite Rusty. And rabies—wasn't that a big problem, painful shots, lots of them?

Good thing Rusty showed no inclination to go into the living room on his own. He stayed right beside Emma.

"Good boy," she said, letting her left hand pat the top of the dog's head.

She knew this: She had to get the bat out.

But how to do that without getting bitten?

The door.

Had to get the door open. Then somehow get the bat to go out the open door. Maybe it would simply fly out the door when it was open. It would see the open door, and—

No. She remembered that bats didn't see very well at all, that they—

A quick sound fluttered from the living room.

She saw the bat circle the living room, once, twice, with its weird erratic flying. Maybe it was getting panicked—and that couldn't be good. Getting panicked, maybe more inclined to land on something, bite something.

She wished the cottage had a back door. Always wanted a back door. An easy way to her small garden.

But there was just the one door. And she wasn't climbing out any of the windows.

What to do . . .

There were gloves below the sink. Yes, they'd be good. Put on the gloves to protect her hands. And then—get the broom from behind the door, the old broom with its splayed bristles going every which way.

And the plan? Go into the living room. As much as she didn't want to. Open the door quickly, stand behind it. Wait and see if the bat just flies out.

But if it doesn't fly out, she'd have to step out from behind that door, find the bat . . . then use her broom, and, and—what was it called?

Shoo it away. Yes, shoo the possibly rabid bat away, guiding it to the door.

That's what she had to do. She was alone here, no one else to ask for help.

She looked at Rusty.

"You be good, hm, boy? You stay right here?"

Though she doubted he would stay here.

She turned and bent down to the cabinet below the sink.

IN moments Emma was ready, heavy gardening gloves on her hands and holding the broom, grabbing it midway down the handle so she'd have some control when she started swinging it.

She took a breath. She walked into the living room.

She didn't look for the bat when she entered the pale light of the room.

No, she didn't want to see the bat, not before she had the door open and the dark night was ready for the bat.

She marched straight to the door, turned the knob, and quickly opened it.

Cool damp air rushed in.

And as she opened it, she stepped close to the wall, and pulled the door tight against her body, wedging herself between the open door and the wall.

And she waited . . .

Rusty had followed her. She knew her command to him had been useless. But he wasn't barking.

Where was the bat? What was it doing?

She looked down to Rusty, and then turned right, to the nearby window, to the rod holding up her simple lace curtains. The bat sat on top of the metal rod as if it had been watching her all the time.

For a moment Emma felt its tiny rodent eyes on her.

But only a moment—because the bat leaped off the rod, and started flying.

Emma turned back to the wall because she was sure that it was coming right at her, diving off the rod, seeing her.

But she didn't feel anything, with Rusty barking again at the bat circling the room.

If Emma was going to use the broom, now was the time.

She turned away from the wall, to face the room. The bat flew in an up-and-down fashion, crazily, as though riding some invisible roller coaster rails. Emma held the end of the broom up to her face. The bat was fast—could she even hit it?

It showed no awareness that it knew the door to the outside, the way to freedom, was open.

She took a deep breath and stepped out from the V-shaped wedge that had been her hiding place.

The bat flew toward her end of the small living room, and she swung at it, missing completely.

Rusty's barking swelled, the sound of the dog making the whole event seem even madder, more crazed.

Another flyby, another missed swing.

But this time the bat stopped at the other end of the living room.

She saw it land right on the headrest of her chair. She saw it land, then—she nearly vomited at the thought—

She saw it leave droppings right *there*.

It was as if the bat wanted to battle her over this room.

But it had stopped flying, it was at rest; and now maybe, at last it was a target she could hit.

EMMA stepped slowly. Rusty maybe thought that the bat was gone, since his barking had stopped.

She guessed that she was three steps away from where she could hit the bat. Swat it . . . and then what?

Another step—without an answer to that question.

One more, and she'd be within striking range.

THEN—she guessed that the broom head could now hit the bat perching on her chair, perching as if taunting her to take a swing. She gripped the handle tightly—and swung.

But as soon as she was into her arc, she saw that she moved much too slowly. While the broom head was still feet away, the bat leaped into the air and flew right at her.

Emma recoiled, and her swing landed uselessly against the back of the chair. But she turned quickly now, spinning back in the direction the bat flew, hoping that she'd see the bat swoop right out the open door.

But no.

Again it landed on her curtains. She looked at it carefully, cursing this thing that had sneaked into her house and wouldn't get out.

Rusty again stopped barking, perhaps now used to the game Emma was playing with the intruder.

But she realized the mistake she had made with her first swing.

It was too big a swing, too big, taking way too long to get there. And she had to figure on the bat leaping at the last minute, so she had to aim up a bit.

She had a plan.

If the bat wouldn't get out voluntarily, then she would treat it like a mosquito, or a fly. She was a human being, and people have dealt with bats for thousands of years.

She'd get it the hell out.

Now she stepped slowly, in a very gentle walking movement, keeping her body straight. She didn't know how echo-location worked, but she imagined that bats sensed quick movements, or a change in movement. By walking slowly, and straight, arms held close, perhaps she wouldn't alarm the bat. Rusty stayed in the center of the room—the best place to watch his mistress battle the small animal.

Step, then another step, and once again she was in range of the bat. She choked up more on the broom, not too much, not to risk missing, but enough so that she had greater control over the handle.

Did bats only rest for a certain amount of time?

Did they land, catch their breath, and then take off again?

Was this one due to take flight again?

She took a deep, slow breath, filling her lungs.

And swung.

This time she aimed slightly above the bat. If it didn't move, then she might send the broom head flying clear over the bat's tiny head.

The bristles flew inches away from the bat . . . and the creature leaped.

Not only that, she heard the bat make a high-pitched squeak, as if it knew it was being attacked. A squeak, answered by a low growl from Rusty, whose ears probably heard the full depth and range of the bat's shrill sound.

But the plan . . .

To aim just above the bat was working!

The bat leaping, springing into the air like a jumping spider. But now the broom head soared inches above it, and Emma watched, and then felt the broom make contact with the bat. And amazingly fast, the creature went careening to the opposite wall, shot near the entrance to the kitchen.

Hitting that wall then falling to the ground.

Stunned. Maybe knocked out; Emma doubted that it was dead.

She moved fast now, quickly debating whether to bring the head down flat to kill the bat, or to use the broom to shoot the bat out the door.

Perhaps it was the thought of having a dead, bloodied, perhaps rabid bat on her hardwood floor that decided the question.

Perhaps that was it.

The small fateful decisions we make.

That can change . . . everything.

Emma extended the broom to its full length and brought the broom head beside the bat like—

A golfer . . . or a hockey player . . . not that she watched either, not that she had ever done either thing.

And she shot the bat toward the door.

Except this time her aim wasn't good enough. The bat, still moving she could see, when she gave it such a big push, thwacked into the wall next to the door, just below the photograph of her sister's family, the three kids, all grown now but forever young in the photograph.

Under the big grinning face of her sister's husband, a man she thought an idiot.

But also paired with this thought: At least she had a husband.

More hurrying. Rusty came close to the bat, sniffing, smelling something.

She yelled at him.

"Rusty, get!"

It would be bad if the dog got bit; then she'd have to get to the veterinarian tonight, for tests. And if he got rabies—were his shots good? She thought they were up to date.

Rusty kept sniffing the air. Smelling something. The bat's blood? The animal dying? Sniffing, but raising his head now.

"Back, boy!"

Emma got to the bat and she had to sweep the bat toward the entrance. The stunned animal tried to unfurl its wings, but something was clearly wrong. It looked like a broken toy, making weird mechanical moves with its limbs.

She moved, almost rolled, the bat to the entrance.

Then she gave it a push, but the bat rolled only a bit, some part of its leather body catching on the wood floor, and the bat now only dribbled to just past the door frame.

Rusty growled.

Emma paid her dog no attention.

To the sniffing, to the growling.

All Emma knew was that she had gotten the bat outside, only not far enough. It was only just at her doorstep.

She'd have to step outside and give it a big kick with the broom, before quickly hurrying back inside, shutting the door, the broom once again returned to its role of something used to clean.

She stepped out. The bat sat amid a pile of leaves on the square piece of flagstone that served as a step that led into the house.

Emma used all her strength this time, and kept the bristles flush and tight against the flagstone, and then swung, and now the bat flew again, probably for the last time, flying into the brush nearby.

Emma stood outside.

Like a baseball slugger finally hitting one out of the park.

She sometimes watched baseball. She liked the poor Mets, always struggling, never getting it right.

The bat flew.

And now—finally hearing her dog, still growling, louder now, sniffing, behind her.

Even though the bat was gone.

The bat was gone . . . and Rusty kept growling.

Strange . . .

But then she felt something grab her leg . . . grab it just below the knee, closing on her calf.

She stood outside, as if she had been lured outside.

Broom in hand, the absurd broom, her mighty weapon— and she looked down.

17

.

THE microwave beeped. Another gourmet masterpiece awaited devouring. David supposed he should really do something to upgrade his cuisine, even get out for a real meal once in a while.

But as he hobbled to the kitchen he thought better of that idea.

As soon as he got out of the hospital, and started walking with a cane, he'd noticed the looks he got. It was just a bit of bullet lodged above his knee. And he wouldn't walk too well for a while.

Maybe, a long while.

Still anything odd, anything strange, and people always looked. They watched his shambling gait, heard the clicking of the cane. People noticed differences.

He opened the door to the microwave and his—tonight—chicken cordon bleu with vegetable medley.

Nothing like a vegetable medley to put a spring into your step and make you realize that life is worth living.

And nobody to stare at him.

David gingerly grabbed the plastic tray at its outer edges so none of the now nuclear-heated material would burn his fingers. But a dollop of the mystery sauce touched a thumb, so he quickly slid the tray to the counter.

He got a plate from the cupboard and pushed the tray onto the plate. Now for a Corona, and his feast would be complete. David grabbed the beer and, to avoid two trips, moved his dinner to the small kitchen table.

This was the life . . .

Not.

He was this close to feeling sorry for himself. Marriage

gone, and he even had his ex feeling sorry for him. Not a good sign.

He started eating.

Wondering . . .

People like to look at the anomalies, those who are different. The freak show effect. Probably been going on ever since man parted ways with the ape.

His thoughts shifted to work.

An idea: people notice freaks.

So, if that's true, how does . . . this killer fly under the radar? The answer to that had to be pretty clear.

All you had to do was look at the thirty-year reign—with some long breaks—of the BTK Killer, Dennis Rader. A pillar of his community and church who just happed to have this little hobby. A hobby that consisted of binding his victims so quickly and effectively that the victims didn't have a chance . . . and then slowly torturing them.

And did Rader ever know how to take his time. The screams, the agony, the tears, the begging—all must have been sweet music to his ears.

Then the K—the kill. Sometimes finished with a sexual act, a bit of masturbatory marking for the finally dead corpse.

Then what? Off to his job, or home, or to a yummy church supper?

Evil . . . can hide.

In fact, David thought that real evil—not the random killing, the stabbing over a drug deal gone south—but the real madness hides so much better than people think it can.

And what about people like him, the detectives, the so-called experts?

We're like kids.

We get them, if we get lucky.

And we're not that damn lucky.

The meal done, time for another beer, and David dug out his wallet.

No matter how many detectives they put on this case, it might still come down to one amazing moment of incredible luck.

Which meant that he should take every chance that he could.

He dug out the reporter's card. Mari Kinsella.

He had read her articles covering a mob trial a while back, and later a series about political scandal involving the deputy mayor (who was quickly and quietly replaced).

A good reporter.

And very pretty, another voice quickly suggested.

Yes, dark hair, dark eyes—what's not to like?

But that wasn't why David had dug the card out.

You can get lucky—but you also had to do whatever you can to make yourself get lucky. And Mari Kinsella said she knew something, and if he was willing to share a bit, so would she.

She was pretty—and, what do you know, she had some information.

He grabbed his cell phone from his shirt pocket and dialed her number.

ON the fourth ring, David started to have second thoughts, sure that the reporter's phone was about to go to answering machine.

But then he heard a voice, breathless, rushed.

"Hello?"

David hesitated. Funny, how hearing her voice made him question this move even more.

But too late now.

"Mari?"

"Yes—" A big breath. "Who is this?"

"David Rodriguez. You know, the—"

"Oh right. The detective today. Which one are you, the kid or—"

David laughed. "The other one. The old guy."

"Not *that* old," she said. "And sorry, was just out of the shower."

"Oh—then I'm sorry. Want me to call back in a bit?"

"No, no—I'm good, got a towel wrapped tight, and—maybe that was too much information." She laughed.

"Detectives love information. Look, I thought about what you said today. That you found something out, and you'd share it. You know . . . we could make you share it. Get a subpoena?"

"Be my guest. I'm just—"

"But look, I didn't call to make a threat. I called to take you up on your offer. There's a lot of stuff I can't tell you. But I can share some, if you tell me what you found out. Sound like a deal?"

Her voice returned to normal.

"Yes. Definitely. When?"

"We could talk now?"

"No. I mean . . . not the phone—let's meet somewhere."

"Now?"

"Why not? I'm all clean and presentable."

David looked at the clock. Only nine P.M. . . . He was turning into such an old man. He'd have to take a few Advil, maybe a Vicodin, but—

"Sure. Where?"

"I'm on the Upper East Side. There's a quiet little place Vespa . . . has a garden area in the back. Probably be empty on a weeknight."

Mari gave him the address and he wrote it down.

"Thirty minutes?" she said.

"Sounds good. You'll know me," David said. "I'll be the older guy with the cane."

Mari laughed again. "Right."

WHEN they walked to the back courtyard of Vespa, tiny, with a few small booths and a scattering of tables, there was one other couple there.

Mari looked at David. "Is this okay? I mean, we could go someplace else."

"No, it's fine. We'll just talk quietly." He looked around. "Cool place."

"Yeah. I love it here. Small bar, all those little alcoves. Very village for the Upper East Side."

Getting to a table, David had to take a step up to a platform. The angle, he saw, could be awkward with the cane.

He felt the other couple look up.

Always the object of interest.

David smiled at Mari. "Just a sec—a little tricky navigation here."

He hooked his cane on the edge of the table, and then grabbed a chair back to steady himself as he made the odd step up, and then slid into the chair. Mission almost accomplished—but then his cane slid off the table and clattered to the stone floor.

Mari recovered it in a flash.

"You are fast."

"In some things," she said, smiling.

David looked at her. Just a bit of banter there, or was that a genuine bona fide flirt?

He was so out of practice; reading a woman's signals wasn't anything he could depend on. After all, she was a reporter. This is all about the story.

The waiter came over.

"Buona sera, signor, signora—"

David turned to Mari. "What would you like?" he said.

Mari turned to the waiter. "A glass of Chianti. Maybe a Pellegrino?"

"Sì. Signor?"

"The same for me I think and"—he turned back to Mari—"a bit of antipasti?"

Mari nodded, and the waiter walked away.

David looked over at the other couple, deeply engrossed in a romantic chat, holding hands on the table, fingers playing.

"I think . . . we can talk here If we're quiet."

Mari leaned close. "I've been practicing my whispering . . ."

David smiled.

Was this a good idea, a bad idea . . . no idea?

He was about to find out.

18

A hand grabbed Emma just below the knee.

Only—as soon as it happened, she knew it wasn't a hand.

Immediately she felt sharp, stinging pain. A moment's reflection and she knew that claws now dug into the skin and muscle of her leg. She moaned into the night; Rusty began barking, *howling*.

The claws did their work, and she tumbled forward, onto the hard ground.

She heard the growl.

Not Rusty's growl, but something so deep, foreign, unknown.

Loud, close.

Her head had narrowly missed hitting the ground squarely. She wasted no time to use her elbow to get up, to raise her head up to see what had knocked her down, what growled at her, what watched her now.

She turned—and saw the bear.

The bear stood closer than Rusty, who had . . . backed away a bit into the house while keeping up a steady stream of barking.

The bear turned and snarled and growled, roared at Rusty—and Emma watched her dog back away even farther.

She used her elbows to crawl forward. A plan forming for dealing with the black bear. Crawl forward, then onto her knees, then *stand*—maybe run to the back of the house, watch, wait—

She had seen bears before. One on its own across the lake, and once another small bear rooting around near the locked garbage bin in the back, digging in the compost.

But this bear was big.

On her elbows, and now, after making a few inches forward, onto her knees, and—

Another growl, sounding strangled, a deep reverberant sound that cut right through her body.

Emma became aware of how she was breathing, the air going in and out fast, in and out, fueling her escape, her getaway.

But with that long, loud growl, the bear stood up, now towering over her, giant, filling the doorway—oh god—and looking down on her, on her pathetic legs as they tried to scurry away, the one calf oozing blood onto the ground.

More rapid breathing. Her knees kicked at the ground.

But the bear moved too . . .

AND . . .

What do we know about bears when they attack a human?

We know a lot more than we used to.

While we may not understand all the things that make a bear attack, make the animal want to kill a fellow mammal, a large mammal, we have learned something.

For example, exactly how big a threat is it?

There are an estimated nearly five thousand black bears in heavily populated New York State, and they brush up against all the suburban and exurban communities, usually with bad results for the bear.

Occasionally . . . with bad results for the human.

And what is the difference between a bear attack and the attack, for example, of that great feared killer of the sea, a great white shark?

There is this:

Most people who are attacked by a great white survive. Usually the shark will hit the person and simply move on. Of course, a person may lose a limb, or get a massive gash in the midsection. But most people who are attacked live.

And bears, those cute, cuddly images from childhood? The teddy bear, Rupert bear, Paddington bear. The list goes on . . .

What happens when a human is attacked by a bear?

While the black bear is not a grizzly, not the famed killer bear of the North American Rockies, if it attacks—

What happens then?

It doesn't just hit the person and move on.

No, when the yelling and running and noise-making all fail to make the amazingly fast bear stop . . .

When it is finally on you . . .

All you can do is curl up, protect what you can. Your head, your vitals, that soft spot in the center of your body that most of us never think about.

Perhaps people should think about it, no?

When that bear is on you, when it bites, when it tears—it doesn't stop.

Committed, it takes its time. Its weight—up to four hundred pounds for a black bear—keeps you pinned, as an ancient battle between human and bear is fought once again, with the bear decidedly winning.

A rare encounter.

Normally . . .

Very rare.

But if it happens, and you are that rare case—

Perhaps . . . you can imagine.

Perhaps you can let yourself . . . imagine.

THE bear fell on Emma.

Two thunderous paws landed as she crawled, and slapped her body flat against the hard ground. Her chin smashed against the stone, and she then knew she was bleeding from her head. She screamed, but only a breathless gasp emerged.

The bear's weight was fully on her. In that mad moment, she had a rush of jumbled thoughts. Someone will come. But there is no one here, no one else out here by this sad, deserted lake.

Or: Rusty will do something, her protector. But she wasn't even sure that the dog was still barking.

He couldn't have run away?

Her beloved dog wouldn't do that and—

Before the next thought, the bear lifted up one paw.

Maybe it would leave. If she lay very still. That was what you were supposed to do. Lie still, let the bear grow bored. She had a brochure where it said just that. "Lie still. Maybe the bear will grow bored."

Holding her down with one paw, so hard for Emma to breathe.

And then the animal roared, its snout so close to her. The other paw slashed at her, cutting deep into her right side, then down and in, and . . . *up*.

She screamed. She begged.

Words.

"No. God, no. No . . ."

Pleading, begging to something. A god she didn't believe in? The bear? To something infinite that might end this.

A sharp pain bloomed in her side. The gash wasn't deep. She bled on the stone, but she knew the bear hadn't dug down deep enough to hurt her, to—

(kill her)

Because she had another thought.

To die now, to die fast, that would be a blessing. She was making deals now with the Infinite, deals with the bear, with God, any god—

(make it fast)

But there was no dealing here.

The snout, the roar came close. She couldn't see the snout, not with eyes shut. But she smelled a sickly sweet smell from the bear's mouth, the roar loud.

Then—just below her neck, on her shoulder—

(it bit)

So many places she felt pain, her mind unable to keep track of it all; the crazy mix of her tears, her screams, never once thinking, *Why . . . ?*

Never once replaying the whole scene from the beginning. The small bat, each fatal step, as if all planned.

A crunch. Bones snapping, a lightning bolt of pain rocketing to her head.

It would not be over for minutes yet.

Those minutes an eternity.

* * *

FINNEY bolted awake, screaming in his dank, humid apartment, the crappy fan sending an inefficient breeze over his sweaty body.

The nightmare was over.

He sat in bed, waiting for the grateful moment when it started to fade.

All so clear . . .

The house by the lake, the woman, the bear pouncing. Like watching a fucking snuff movie.

His entire body covered in sweat. Waiting for reality to wipe away the dream.

He turned on a light.

Just a dream, he told himself. Too much crappy booze. That's all.

But as he stared through the sere curtains of his apartment, he remembered one thing . . .

More disturbing than the horror of the dream.

How he saw it.

How he experienced it.

Through the bear's eyes.

He fell on the woman, he ripped her open, and he—

Finney forced himself to stop thinking about it. He grabbed the remote, and laughter filled the room. The Charlie Sheen sitcom.

Not so freakin' funny.

He had to get the hell out of here.

Yeah, get out. Go get a bite. Some clams. Let real voices make this all go away.

Christ, he thought, what a fucking crazy nightmare.

Finney was just glad that it was over.

19

MARI watched the detective spear a cube of mozzarella with a bit of red pepper curled at the bottom.

"Good idea," she said.

"Hmmm?"

"The antipasti. It's nice. And this is a great place for dinner. You should—" She stopped herself.

Right. This is a business meeting, and though David Rodriguez was attractive, best she put away her New York desperateness.

He smiled, as if catching her drift. "Come for dinner sometime? Maybe I will."

They both drank wine, a dark red Chianti recommended by their waiter.

"Wine's not bad either," David said.

Mari was tempted to ask about his leg. But he radiated such a self-consciousness about it—the slight limp, the cane—that she knew it was no small thing to him.

"Okay. I did make you an offer."

"That you did. And—"

"And you realize that there will be a lot I can't—or won't—tell you. And anything I do tell you, I need you to run by me any story that uses it. Your own stuff you find out . . . well, you can write what you want I guess. Though if you care about catching this guy, it might still be better to show me."

"I got it. Anything you share, I keep to myself. For now."

He smiled. And though his smile was warm, a generous smile, she could tell it was laced with a bit of sadness. Something happened to him, maybe something more, beyond the leg?

The reporter in her wanted to know.

She caught herself—

Bullshit.

She was curious as a female.

"There's this woman who lives across the street. Anne Russell."

"The homicide teams spoke to everyone on the block. They got nothing."

"Yes. She said they spoke to her. But she's a funny bird— I think they asked the wrong questions. Or maybe she was still rattled by the whole thing."

David downed his wine and looked over to the waiter, then to Mari.

"*Two* . . . more?"

Mari nodded.

The waiter went away. "So the woman told you something?"

"Yes, after she nearly scared me off her stoop. She said she saw a car on the street some nights, not the type of car that she'd normally see, but a big dark car, like a limo. And someone coming out, and disappearing . . ."

"Yeah, that basement layout is pretty damn dark. Walk down a few steps, and it's like being swallowed."

"She said the car pulled away; but she did see the man— I mean, she imagined it was a man—walk into the building. And she said he walked funny, as though something was wrong, like he had a limp or—"

David nodded. "Like me . . ." Another small smile. "That's pretty interesting." He took out a spiral pad.

"I didn't even think about that."

The waiter returned with the two glasses of wine and placed them down. He grabbed the now-empty plate of antipasti.

"Anything else, *signor, signorina*?"

"We're good," David said. He looked back to Mari. "So, she said . . . somebody with a wound, or a limp? Somebody with a leg, hip problem, maybe? That's . . . good, real good. Thanks. And the car, that's something too. I can get the computers crunching on car services—though I get the feeling that this is something else."

"Something else?"

"If he used a car service, he'd easily be tracked. But if it was his own car . . ."

"Then if he had a driver—that would be a connection."

"Maybe. Could use a regular driver, an employee. Or change drivers. Those drivers are basically people trying to pick up a few bucks, no questions."

"Wouldn't the driver have seen the story, the news of the murders? God, then he'd have to be as insane as the killer."

David took a sip of the wine. He didn't have to answer, since the thought, the very clear idea came to Mari.

She spoke slowly . . . "Unless he's now dead too."

"Always easy to get another driver. Hire someone who's a loner, someone with no connections. He could disappear easily, no problem. Still something else to check out."

Mari took another sip of the Chianti; generally she avoided reds for their fabled ability to have you wake up in the middle of the night due to a caffeine-like effect. But the Chianti tasted so great.

"So—some useful info?"

"Yes," David said. "Very. Certainly every bit helps. And these . . . are good bits indeed."

"O . . . kay . . ." She saw a sparkle in his eyes.

"Oh, my turn?"

"I do believe that was the deal."

"Right. You understand the ground rules?"

"Totally."

David looked over his shoulder to the remaining couple. As if on cue, they stood up and, hand in hand, walked past them into the main restaurant, and David and Mari were now alone in the courtyard.

"Again, not everything. But I can share some things that, well, I don't understand. Could be helpful."

Mari had removed her steno pad from her oversized purse. David looked at it.

Was he going to tell her no notes? But he went on—

"See—there's this strange thing. We're talking to the people connected to victims. Neighbors, the victims' relatives, etc., and today this strange piece came out of nowhere.

Also like—it was the mother who told me—they didn't want to mention it. Ashamed or something."

"Strange?"

"Caroline Brzow. That's the name of one of the victims."

Mari wrote it down.

"Makes me nervous to see you do that."

Mari's hand went to David's lying on the table, covering it. A gesture of reassurance. "Look, David . . . last year a reporter went to jail rather than reveal a source. I gave my word. I'll keep my word."

She squeezed his hand, and she realized that the gesture had changed. He gave her hand a squeeze back, a strong, powerful hand. She let his fingers release, then pulled away.

"Okay. Caroline Brzow. A beautiful young girl. And the way she died."

"None of those details have been given out."

"I know. Those . . . We keep a tight lid on. But she was the last to arrive. It had to be the worst."

"Worst? Why the worst?"

"She walked in, and saw all the others . . . *arrayed*. Prisoners, maybe some of the torture already begun, their voices muffled. Muffled until he removed the heavy tape from their mouths. She had to see it all, and know."

"God."

His description chilled her. The hot, humid evening turned icy.

"Yeah. Had to be so bad. And the pictures? Worse than anything I've ever seen."

"The mother told you something?"

"So, here's what came out today, like I said—the mother almost embarrassed to mention it. Like we might think she was crazy, or her daughter—"

The waiter popped out to the courtyard dining area. "You folks okay?"

"Yeah," David said.

Again they were alone.

"The girl, this CPA, had dreams . . . nightmares. Before it all happened."

Mari write down the words. *Dream. Nightmare.*

"She dreamed about what would happen to her?"

Mari thinking: Was this something involving precognition, come crazy ESP thing?

"No. She didn't dream about herself. About what was going to happen to her. She had these nightmares about . . . one of the other victims."

"What?"

David nodded. "Caroline Brzow dreamt—in detail—about one of the other victims. Okay—and again forget I said this—but a teacher who lives not too far from here. The girl never met her. Yet she dreamt about her."

"That's incredible."

"Yeah, tell me about it. I don't know what to do with it, what to make of it. Was it a fluke? Just something weird that's useless to us . . . or—"

"The other possibility?"

David leaned close. "It's absolutely key to what happened." He laughed. "In which case I am in *way* over my head."

"So what now?"

David looked down at his empty glass. Mari had also finished. Was he debating another round? But two reds were definitely her limit.

"Let me pay up, and we can walk outside, walk you back to your place."

Mari smiled. "Pretty safe neighborhood."

"Aren't they all these days."

David took out his wallet, and as if by magic the waiter appeared with the check.

20

MARTINI number two always hit Linda hard.

So delicious going down, but then she started to feel like she was drifting, that New York with all its possibilities had suddenly gained the upper hand.

She and Scott sat at a back table. He had ordered some calamari, but when they arrived Linda suddenly didn't want any fried squid.

"They are kind of rubbery," Scott said with a grin.

She had learned that the he was divorced, two kids, a bachelor apartment in the sixties. Some kind of financial planner, traveled a lot.

The basics . . .

"Another . . . martini?"

Linda laughed. "Noooo. I'm already listing. Maybe—a diet Coke?"

Scott called the waiter over and gave the order. Then he looked at the plate of deep-fried squid. "Guess we won't be making much of an inroad with these babies."

"Yes . . . I'm really just not hungry."

"Me either." Scott pushed the plate to the side. "So tell me more about you. You teach psychology at Columbia?"

"Actually assistant department chair."

"*Salut*—I always loved psychology. And you must see some sharp students?"

"Well, I leave the undergrads to others. I do the graduate seminars, the specialty courses. Interesting stuff."

The Cokes arrived. Linda took her glass, filled with ice— nice and cold, just the way she liked it.

The chilly sip.

"Interesting? Like what?"

"I've been, um, specializing lately. In violent crime."

Scott's eyes widened. "Wow. Tell me more."

"A seminar course on the psychology of the serial killer."

A small grin from Scott. "You're making me nervous. A beautiful woman like you . . . and serial killers?"

He's such a flirt, she thought. Still, it was nice being flirted with.

No more than that—she *needed* some flirting.

And a lot more than that.

"So you are an expert?"

"Well, I've done a lot of research, read case histories, did in-depth interviews—"

"Interviews? You mean you have talked to these nuts?"

"Some. A few that were lucid and cooperative; in cases where I saw things that didn't fit any of the molds . . . the patterns."

"Can't believe you sat with them. You weren't scared?"

"Apprehensive. But in a room, inside a facility like Sing Sing, its all very safe. A guard there."

"No Hannibal Lecter leaping over the table to bite you?"

Linda laughed, but then she noticed something. All of a sudden, Scott seemed more interested in her work than her. Interested, and maybe a bit disturbed by it.

Not the best prelude to anything romantic . . .

Shit, she thought—when will I learn to edit my bio for prospective dates?

She wondered: Do I enjoy telling men this, gaining respect—or maybe just giving them a thrill?

But then, as Dr. Phil might ask her . . . *How's that working for you?*

Not too good.

She moved to change the subject. "So, have you already had your vacation this summer? Hamptons—"

Scott had already finished his Coke.

"Hold on, there's more I want to ask you about your work, those interviews—"

"It's shoptalk. I really—"

He leaned close. "But when you are with those guys, knowing what they did . . . I mean, how do you feel?"

How do I feel?

To be in a room with someone who had killed so many people, who reveled in horrible deaths, who planned and plotted
each aspect of their capture, their torture, their end . . .

To be in a room with a monster.

The smile vanished from Linda's face.

"You know, I'm a psychologist. My job is to understand
human behavior. To explain human behavior. But when I
did those interviews, it was like I was in a room with
something . . . not human."

"Like a lion in cage. Or—?"

"No. Not like that. Lions kill to eat; all predators . . . they
kill for survival. These people, as predatory as they are—it's
something else. And all the questions in the world couldn't
help me understand it. I just listen, try to somehow catego-
rize it, add more data to the record."

Scott nodded. The crowd at Elaine's had thinned out; a
sudden quiet fell over the normally boisterous bar. The party-
like atmosphere had ended in a flash, leaving Linda stranded
at the table, with the charming, laughing Scott now serious . . .

And her own mind, back at work, back at a place she so
wanted to get away from.

Back with the monsters.

Scott killed his Coke.

A signal?

Linda looked at her watch.

"It's late. Guess we should go?"

Scott still looked as though he was digesting what Linda
had said, distracted by images of dismembered corpses and
yellow crime scene ribbon.

Great . . .

"Yup. I'll get the check."

And like that, it was over.

HE flagged a cab for Linda and amid assurances that he'd
call for what he termed a "proper" date, Linda guessed that
she had screwed this one up.

Way to go . . .

And why did she do it? Did she enjoy unsettling men?

Was that part of the fun? If that was true, she was not much different than the killers. Getting a thrill out of death.

The drinks made her head spin.

The cab raced to her West Side address, sending her rocking back and forth in the backseat. But the cabbie got her home fast and—for now—that was the only important thing.

SHE ignored the siren call of the computer, and stripped off her clothes, brushed her teeth, and then pulled on her short nightgown. No reading tonight either.

Just the reassuring firmness of mattress, the pillow, and sleep.

Lights off, sleep came quickly, almost instantly.

That moment of a quick fall to sleep felt wonderful.

But the moment didn't last.

BRILLIANT sun; water shimmering, jewel-like.

Overhead, gulls soaring, calling out.

People walking behind her, strolling . . . on what looked like a boardwalk. The air warm, heavy with humidity; she felt the tiny beads of sweat on her upper lip.

Where was she?

She looked around.

Sheepshead Bay.

She wasn't much of a water person. Her brothers always trying to drag their kid sister into the roaring waves of the Jersey Shore. Somehow she connected water with all that bullying, their enjoyment as they scared her with the waves, the bottomless sea.

And there was another factor—she was at the shore the year the shark came to Long Beach Island.

The year people died . . .

That didn't help.

You couldn't see under this water, brownish gray, dense . . . It could hide anything.

And here she was, dreaming about the water, about this oily Brooklyn harbor.

Why? What prompted it?

She heard a boat engine. And there ahead of her, a fishing boat pulling away, sending the shimmering ripples of lights on the surface scattering.

She looked at it.

The name of the boat, the *Marlin III*.

Funny name, she thought. She saw a man steering, holding a big wheel on top. And crewmen moving around, hurrying as though they had important things to do now, racing as the boat turned right, heading out of the harbor.

She watched the boat grow smaller.

Then—there she was—on the boat.

LIKE a ghost, she could watch other people on the boat, not many though. The crew wrapping ropes into big coils, the captain above them, hands on the wheel, the sound of the engine, noisy and loud.

The smell of the exhaust . . . powerful even on this clear blue-sky day.

And someone sitting—

There!

In the back.

A man, his face turned toward the shore, to the setting sun. She could only see the back of his head. Staring at the shore as though that's where he wanted to be.

Linda turned to the front of the boat.

What did they call it? The bow.

To the bow. The crew with big rods, hurrying to wrap the bait on the hooks.

Then, back to the man who still looked away. But now— so fast—the shore disappearing.

And he got up. Twisting, turning, as if it was a difficult thing to do.

He turned.

And Linda saw his face.

21

THE first thing she noticed about the face was how normal, how unremarkable it looked.

The man's thin hair blew in the steady wind, the last patches allowed to grow long, covering a wide stretch of bald scalp.

And the eyes?

Small, dark. Were they brown, black, or maybe a too-deep green? Hard to tell as the man moved past Linda, not seeing her, not noticing her.

Because this was, of course, a dream.

Until she looked down and saw a detail that was remarkable.

The way the man walked, an odd hobble, as if he had been injured, or had an operation. A weird sideways roll, as he made his way slowly to the front.

No . . . the *bow*.

His left hand held the railing, and from time to time his other hand touched the side wall of the boat's cabin to steady himself.

She thought of something then . . .

Something from an old painting, or a fairy tale, a troll-like figure by a campfire, or maybe something stranger, a magical creature plotting evil in the ancient forests.

But then the man reached the bow.

The crewmen had the rods ready. They smiled; the engine slowed.

Linda looked at one of the crew, a dark-skinned man with biceps that barely fit through the armholes of his snug T-shirt.

The other, thinner, wiry, sandy blond hair, long, unkempt . . . blowing in the wind.

The engine stopped.

The captain leaned over the railing to look down.

He spoke, his voice now loud in the odd silence made by the quiet engine.

"Finney, all set down there . . . Finney, all ready?"

Back to the bow.

And the thin crewman with the long hair looked up, squinting.

Finney . . .

"Yes, Captain. All set . . ."

Finney turned back to the man, the troll—

He held a long rod, and at the end an array of hooks, all wrapped with chunks of fish and something stringy, shiny . . .

Squid.

The man with the odd walk gestured at Finney.

Gestured at the water.

Saying: Go cast the line.

Linda saw beads of sweat on Finney's upper lip, his brow. He smiled, a false smile, a smile for a customer.

The strange man took the rod and, extending his arms over the side, began to cast the line out.

And in that moment, the baited hooks seemed to fly by Linda, so many of them! Their sharp tips hidden by squid, a tempting trap for the fish swimming in the dark, opaque water.

So close . . . she could smell them, foul, oily, and—

LINDA opened her eyes. A siren wailed through the night, penetrating even her foam earplugs. She took them out, not liking the dull silence, not being able to hear the real quiet in her apartment.

(And always with that fear that when she took them out, it wouldn't be quiet.)

Not for the first time, Linda thought, in the dark, that maybe she had to change her specialty. She didn't like this waking up, cold, frightened, breathing hard.

Alone . . .

She turned and looked at the clock. 12:10. She had barely

been asleep, and the night still loomed ahead of her. Should she get up and take an Ambien?

She didn't like the thought of getting out of bed and walking into the bathroom. The bright light, the floor chilly from the air-conditioning.

But better that then another dream waking her up in an hour.

She reached out and turned on the light. Her apartment suddenly turned familiar and harmless.

Linda threw her covers off and got out of the bed.

It was the second time this week she had taken a pill.

Yes, something to watch, she thought, as she walked to the bathroom.

MARI looked at David, the cane held in his right hand, opposite his leg. She was curious what had happened to him . . . Was it something on the job?

And she felt guilty that she'd agreed to let him walk her to her Eighty-fifth Street apartment. What seemed like a good idea, a chance for them to talk more, now seemed thoughtless.

She turned to David. "You know, you don't have to walk me back. God knows, I've crawled back from Third Avenue alone often enough."

He smiled at her, and there was something about it laced with a bit of sadness. A smile that said . . . I've seen things.

"Look, it's *fine*. Really. A gorgeous night, and we don't have that many of them left."

"You're sure?"

He laughed. "Yes, I'm sure. Let me enjoy the walk—and the company."

So he is flirting with me, she thought. A man in New York flirting with me. God, he must be married!

But she wouldn't ask the relationship history question.

Always an error.

Best to keep this . . . professional . . .

"Anything else you want to tell me about the murders?"

"Funny." David said. "I don't think of them as murders.

Murder has motive. Someone wants money, or a spouse dead, or both. This—well, I've never seen anything like it. A trap, some kind of sick game, butchery. But not murder. As for more, do you have anything more?"

"No. But I could help. While sitting on what you have told me so far. I have a contact, someone who's an expert on the psychology of serial killers. Dr. Linda Kyle, up at Columbia."

"Yeah, we probably have her in the database. Though I doubt she has ever seen anything like this. So, you've already contacted her?"

Mari thought about lying, then discarded the idea.

"No. But I'm going to call her tomorrow. We could meet tomorrow, maybe afterward—"

Damn, she thought—that was forward. When a phone call would do, she basically suggested a damn date. More antipasti, more wine, more—

He quickly put a hand on her shoulder. "I'd like that. I'll call in the afternoon."

She smiled; the irony of it so strange. Who knew that a mad killer and romance would mix? "Great." She turned around to the first apartment building with a green awning. "And this is me."

"If you say so."

She stuck out her hand.

"Thanks, David."

He shook her hand, and she realized that they both held a moment longer than necessary before releasing.

"There is one other thing. Caroline Brzow left that night without telling her parents; she left to go someplace that—as far as we know—she had never been before. We haven't found anything, any clue, any note . . . anything at all that tells us why. How the hell did she know to go there?" He took a breath. "It's like something drew her there."

"Drew her?"

Another small laugh. "Yeah, I know. Doesn't make much sense."

"And the others?"

"I'll find out more tomorrow. Least, I hope I will."

She nodded. "Thanks for that. It's all so strange."

"That it is."

It's time, thought Mari. She smiled. "Good night again."

"Good night."

And she turned and walked up to the apartment building door, aware that David stood there, watching her until she was in and the door locked behind her.

"HOW'S the fuckin' hand, Finney?"

Finney held up his still-bandaged hand. "Healing well, Lou. Going to get back to work tomorrow."

"Too bad." The bartender put down another bat and ball, a short beer and a shot. "Could use some of your business during your recovery. Gets kinda slow here during the day."

"You get too much of my damn money already."

Lou laughed, and then sailed down to the other end of the bar.

Though it was late, the bar still had a bunch of regulars hanging around, people Finney didn't know but always saw. A middle-aged couple who came here a lot, working together to kill their livers. A retired cop who read the paper and never talked to anyone. A few young guys who played pool and put on the jukebox—though the place felt better with just the blare of the TV.

A baseball game, basketball—that's all a joint like this needed.

Finney downed the shot. He thought of the dream.

Not that he wanted to. It was like that thing . . . *Try not to think of a pink elephant.* And there would sit a giant pink elephant right in your head, grinning and blowing bubbles from its trunk.

What the fuck was that dream about?

He'd never dreamed like that before. Like he was inside the fucking bear. Too fuckin' weird.

And then killing that lady—that dream lady—so detailed, he could almost smell it.

He took a deep breath through his nose now, the smell of

booze heavy in the air. Used to be smoke too, smoke and booze, the perfect atmosphere . . .

No, he did smell it.

In his dream. He smelled . . . and felt everything.

Maybe it had something to do with his hand?

That was it. Like shock. He hurt himself, and had a weird dream.

He drank half the beer, and the bartender came over with the bottle of Seagram's 7.

"Another?"

Finney shook his head. "Nah, Lou—going back to bed. Got to convince Starn I'm okay tomorrow."

"Okay, Finney. You take care now."

Finney slid off the stool. He heard the crack of another rack of balls being broken on the half-sized pool table in back.

"Always, Lou. Watching out for number one."

Then Finney sailed out of the bar, and into the still-warm night air.

22

MARI sat at her desk and listened to the zombie-like recitation of options, navigating Columbia University's phone tree.

The bigger the institution, the bigger the maze.

Eventually there will be a phone maze that, like Theseus and his Cretan labyrinth, will be completely inescapable.

The guy who invented this bit of progress should be shot, she thought.

Julie Fein planted herself in front of Mari's desk.

"You talking to a human?"

Mari shook her head.

"Working on the story?"

"I'm trying."

"Uh-huh. Want to do lunch today?"

"Maybe, If I ever get through this—" Mari hit another button, and then miraculously, she got to the phone directory for the university.

She hit the keys for . . . K . . . Y . . . L . . . E.

Then a woman's voice: "Dr. Linda Kyle."

She hit star to get connected.

The line ringing.

"I think I just got through. I'll let you know about lunch."

"Sure. There's nothing happening in my little day. . . ."

Mari nodded, then heard a woman's voice, answering the phone.

LINDA Kyle sat in front of her desk, which overlooked a grassy mall surrounded by university buildings, a pile of essays in front of her, all awaiting correction. She should have hit some last night, and now she was way behind.

She picked up her phone.

"Hello?"

"Dr. Kyle?"

"Yes?"

"I'm Mari Kinsella with the *Daily News*. A reporter."

The morning sun seemed to be fading, the last summer grass now darkening as clouds moved in. Supposed to rain tonight, thunder.

And again she was going out.

"Yes, how can I help you?"

Not the first time that a reporter had called her. When you're an expert in the psychology of serial killers, you get calls.

"Dr. Kyle, you've read about the killings on the Lower East Side?"

Right, Linda thought. She had read about them—and wasn't surprised that sooner or later, a member of the press would call.

"I read what little that's been published. Not much there."

"I know. They have kept details under wraps. But Dr. Kyle—"

"Please, *Linda*. I get enough 'Dr. Kyles' all day."

The reporter laughed. "Okay . . . Linda, I have found out more. And I thought that maybe you might have some insight, some ideas—"

"For an article?"

"No. I mean, not immediately. I've found out a few things, and I shared them with a detective working the case. And he also told me some things; my deal . . . is I publish nothing until I get his approval."

"Okay. So what I tell you—I mean, if I can tell you anything—you will share with him?"

"Yes."

"And I won't see it plastered over the front page of the paper?"

"You got it—not without your approval."

"I have to tell you, I may have nothing to say, no matter what you tell me."

"That's okay. It's only a lunch, on the *Daily News*."

"Will have to be a late lunch, I have some students coming in for a few hours of seminars and need to at least take a look at their essays."

"No problem. Name the time and place."

"One thirty. There's a salad place on Broadway. Called TossUp. Meet there?"

"Perfect. And thanks."

"See you then . . . ," Linda said, hanging up the phone.

Back to the pile of papers. She looked at the title . . .

"Fetish and Ritual in Serial Murder."

Written by Elliot Christian. She wondered if Christian was as challenging on paper as he was—constantly—in class.

She started reading.

DAVID parked his car in the underground garage below One Police Plaza.

Once this was a public lot; anybody could have parked there. They ramped up security after the first World Trade Center attacks. Cement barriers, making people pop open their trunks for inspections.

But after the buildings fell . . . its days as a public lot were over.

Sitting under both the Centre Street Municipal Building, with all of NYC's administrative offices, and the heart of the police department—it was just too rich a target.

Left plenty of space for the cops and workers now.

David grabbed his cane and swung out of the driver's seat.

A sharp spike of pain ran up his leg.

Going to get better, the doctor said.

But when?

He shut the door, the slam echoing eerily in the cavernous lot, and headed for the elevators up to the plaza, and police headquarters.

JAMES was already there, sleeves rolled up, pouring over papers.

Such an eager beaver.

"What did you do? Sleep here?"

James looked up. "Morning. I tried calling you last night. Wanted to plan for today."

"I was out. Should have given you my cell."

"Yeah." He looked down at the file on his desk. "I think we should look at these two today."

"Who you have there?"

"The report on the teacher, and the kid from NYU."

David walked around to the side so he could peer over James's shoulder. He'd needed to grab another coffee and wake up. But Jimmy Neutron here was already at full speed.

Probably started the day with a three-mile run at dawn.

David grabbed a chair, hooked his cane on the back, and sat down.

"The interviews seemed pretty thorough to me."

In truth, David had planned on looking at both of those people again, seeing where they lived, talking to friends, finding out everything they did that led up to their slaughter.

His comment was simply fishing to see what James could be thinking.

"Not so sure." James picked up one report, the file on the NYU student, Parker Kamen. "Like this kid—wealthy parents in Boston, well liked though no tight friends; good grades. So what makes him go to that apartment? There's got to be something we don't know."

"Duh, as they say. Yeah . . . big pieces missing, huge chunks of . . . who the hell knows what."

James turned and looked at him.

"Where were you last night, Detective? Called your apartment. Something to do with the case?"

David considered lying. But there was one thing he knew about working with a partner. Tell them everything. No secrets, no lies. All the bad stuff. Your life may depend upon it. The success of the case certainly did.

"I called the reporter."

"What? *Shit.* You called that reporter?"

That information didn't seem to be going over so well with his eager beaver partner.

"Yes. She said she knew something. I thought we'd better find out what it was."

"You could have told me."

David grinned. "We hadn't exchanged cell numbers. Next time I will."

"Next time? Did you tell her something?"

"I made a deal. No publication till I say so. She told me what she found out, I told her a little about Caroline, the dreams, the sneaking off."

James looked away. "Christ. Wish you had spoken to me."

"Look, I'll be honest with you. What do we have here?" David leaned forward and tapped the pile of reports, all the background for the five pathetic, butchered victims. "What the hell do we have here?"

"Not much."

"Not *anything*. And the trail, whatever it might have been, grows colder by the hour. So if I can get something"— he took a breath—"if *we* can get something, I'll take it. I'll make a deal, I'll do what I can, if I think it'll help us stop other people from getting killed."

David caught himself.

Lecturing a fellow detective, even a young one . . . not a good thing to do.

"But you're right. Should have spoken to you first."

"Damn right."

David took a breath.

"But don't you want to know what she had to say?"

A small grin on David's face. James turned to him, and grinned back.

"Yeah, I do."

David nodded, and told him what the reporter found out from the old lady on Pell Street, about the black limousine and the strange night visitor . . .

23

FINNEY woke up to the sound of scratching, a low hiss that blended in with the pathetic sound of his puny fan attempting to move the air in his stifling room.

The radio alarm—set to some nonexistent station.

He stood up. He wanted to get down to the *Marlin III* and Starn, show him that he was all right, all set to get back to work.

And—fuck—now he had overslept.

It's because of those stupid dreams, and the heat, and too many boilermakers.

Eleven A.M.

Starn would bring the *Marlin III* back around one. He could catch him then, tell him . . . "Look, Cap'n, I'm okay. All set to go back to work."

Because if Starn said no, then Finney would be out of a job, and out of money in less than a week.

Great fucking life, he thought.

He got out of bed and started pulling on his jeans and a tropical T-shirt where all the bright fish and coral had faded to near invisibility.

He grabbed his socks, strewn across the floor as though escaping his sneakers.

Gotta do a damn laundry soon, he thought.

Gotta get my life together.

Finney once had a plan.

For something better, something more.

He thought he might get a degree in oceanography. Loved the water, loved the sea—and after a course at Nassau Community College, it all seemed possible.

But that one course turned hard, impossible, and then

Finney didn't do the reading, and he didn't write the essays, and then—

He stopped going completely.

Screwed that one up too, he thought.

He pushed aside his curtain. A gray day outside. Supposedly only one day away from getting hit by what was left of Hurricane George. Probably no big deal—still, a hurricane of any size made the boat owners nervous.

He went into his closet-sized bathroom and squeezed out whatever toothpaste he could. Just a smear to add a little flavoring to the splayed bristles, now bent every which way, long past fighting to keep Finney's teeth really clean.

He scooped up some water and rubbed it on his hair, smoothing the askew blond haystack so that—for now at least—all the hairs went mostly in the same direction.

He looked in the mirror.

Ready.

To grab some coffee, a bagel, then go meet Captain Starn.

Reporting for duty, sir. Good as new.

Hand's just fine, and I'm all set to help the yokels with their bait and hooks and line.

He walked out of his apartment.

FINNEY sat at a corner stool of the Atlantic Diner. Always packed before the boats set out in the morning, but now—too early for lunch—the place was quiet, the waitresses, like exiles from some fun house gone wrong, tiredly clearing tables and getting ready for the lunch crowd.

A TV over the coffee urns tuned to ABC.

Some stupid talk show ending, and the news coming soon. More about Hurricane George, maybe.

He took a bite of his bagel. A sip of the coffee, too strong, probably from sitting at the bottom of the urn.

Strong—but already the coffee had chilled making the bitter taste even worse. Still, he took another gulp; the caffeine would help him wake up, clear the alcohol fog from the night before. Make it easier for Finney to plant a big smile on his face.

The news started.

Finney expected that the hurricane would be the lead story.

That's what he expected.

But it wasn't.

HE looked at the screen, and in a moment he felt a chill run over his skin. As if someone had opened the door to a meat freezer, and a gust of icy air escaped.

The diner itself—so brightly lit, with its stools, and silverware, and napkin holders, guarded by the waitresses—all of a sudden turned even weirder.

The news came on . . .

The first story.

Finney saw the face, a woman's face. Smiling on the photograph, but a face he knew he remembered.

From last night . . .

And then the house.

Finney thought to himself . . .

(the thought itself crazy)

I was . . . there.

There, outside the house.

The TV picture was live, police milling around the small house by a lake. A yellow-brown dog, leashed and held by a trooper, turned left and right, looking, confused.

The reporter, grimly holding the microphone with the Channel 7 logo, talked about what happened.

"Police and wildlife authorities are unsure about what drew the woman out of her house, and how the bear attacked. We have no details about the woman's death except the fact that they are keeping our cameras well away from the scene. This attack, a rarity in New York State, has sent a shock wave through the small neighboring community of Ellenville—"

Then the screen cut to the same reporter interviewing people on the street, asking them what they thought.

How terrible it was, and did they ever see Emma Chappel in town?

And do you think bears are becoming a danger?

Should something be done?

"You okay, Finney?"

Pete, the owner of the Atlantic Diner, came opposite Finney.

Finney turned and looked at him, nodded. "Yeah. I'm—okay."

He immediately heard how hollow his voice sounded, empty, thin, the air sucked out of his lungs.

He turned back to the screen. Another shot of the small cottage, grim and dull under the morning's gray skies.

Then they went to the weather guy.

"Another refill? You look a little pale."

Finney shook his head.

He had to get the hell out of here. He had to think, and he couldn't think here, under the bright lights of the fun house diner.

FINNEY leaned over the metal railing by the dock, near where the *Marlin III* berthed. Large rainbow-colored oil slicks swirled in the water . . . all the water here covered with the sheen of oil from so many boats, all their engines spewing smoke into the air and oil into the water.

What the hell had happened . . . ?

He dreamed about that woman.

No doubt, *that* woman. Dreamed about her, two nights in a row. And then more . . . he dreamed about her death, the bear attacking, and—

He rubbed his arms.

More than that. In the dream—

(the fucking nightmare)

—he was the bear. He killed the woman, cut her open, and—Christ!

Finney turned away from the water, and looked left and right, to check—could anyone see the crazy thoughts going through his head? Crazy, because if anyone could tell, they'd lock him up.

He took a berth.

The air growing more humid by the hour. Thick, wet air, getting pumped up on humidity, ready to start unleashing the rain, the swollen tides, the surges that would slap against the stone walkway.

But then he had a thought. An idea that offered something else.

Something that didn't scream *crazy*.

Something almost rational.

There were people . . . who could see things. Yeah, people could see how people got killed, or where it happened, or who did it. *There were people like that!* He had read somewhere that police used them.

That's what this was. That's what happened to him.

Had to be.

Somehow he saw something that happened.

(Or—maybe . . . he even saw it as it happened.)

He shook his head. All his life he was nothing, and now, all of a sudden . . . he sees something important.

That had to be it.

There were even TV shows about these people who helped the police.

He had another thought then, a merciful thought that brought him back from the strange and scary world his mind had taken him to.

I'm not crazy, he thought.

No. Things like this happened.

Not crazy.

But then . . . a question. What to do about it?

Tell someone? The guys at the bar would love that, wouldn't they? Finney the psychic. More likely, Finney the nutcase. Alcohol getting to you, Finney? Going from your liver to what's left of your brain?

No, he couldn't tell anyone here.

But he knew he had to tell someone.

(And why did he have to tell someone? But he knew the answer to that one. What if it . . . happened again? Another dream, someone else dying? What if the dreams kept coming, and he hadn't told . . . anyone?)

They might laugh, whoever he told. Think he was some

nutcase. But at least he would have *told* them, and the next time—

The next time he had one of those dreams, he could let them know.

He'd call the police. Tell them what happened. Give his name. Sure, they'd think he was crazy.

Didn't matter. Didn't fucking matter. Because if it did happen again, they'd take his call, his name—and in the middle of the night, he'd have someone to tell.

Someone . . . to warn.

He looked at his watch.

Close to one P.M. Starn would be back soon. Finney couldn't go call now. He might miss the boat. He wanted to be here, waiting for Starn, waiting to show the captain that he was okay.

But as he stood there by the dock, even Finney had to admit . . .

He certainly wasn't okay.

24

MARI walked into the Morningside Drive salad restaurant TossUp.

She walked past a long counter holding every type of green known to humankind, along with every possible thing one could throw into a salad.

She looked for Linda Kyle—but outside of a pair of students deep in conversation, the place was empty.

Mari looked at her watch. Just past one thirty. Did she get the time wrong, or the place?

But then the door opened behind her and a stylish woman walked in, definitely no student. She also wore that searching look, hunting for whoever she was supposed to meet.

"Linda?"

Mari remembered to can the "doctor" stuff.

The professor smiled. "Yes, Mari Kinsella?"

"So they say." Mari smiled, and then turned to the rows of empty tables.

"Shall we grab one?"

But Linda turned to the salad counter. "Let's order first? I'm starved."

"Right. Me too."

Linda ordered a mix of spinach and arugula, with pine nuts, goat cheese, and sliced pears.

"That sounds delicious. I'm usually an iceberg and vinaigrette person." Mari looked at the man behind the counter, grim faced, with the expression of someone who didn't exactly love the fact that he ended up making salads all day. "I'll have the same . . ."

The man put more of the identical ingredients in a large metal bowl and began mixing their salads. In a few moments they had their plates of greens, topped with dollops of goat cheese and nuts. They both grabbed Diet Cokes.

"Okay . . . how about here?"

Mari noticed that Linda walked all the way to the back of the place, well away from the lone couple, and far enough away that anyone arriving wouldn't bother walking back.

She sat opposite the psychology professor.

"Come here a lot?"

"Actually, no. I usually grab a sandwich in my office. But that place is a mess. I'm sinking under thesis papers. Good to get out."

"I do appreciate it."

The woman nodded, and speared a forkful of greens.

"No problem. I had read about the killings. But there was so little information."

"I know. Almost nothing. Guess they hope that will give them an advantage."

The woman shook her head.

"I don't think so."

Mari's turn for a mouthful of lettuce.

"No?"

Linda Kyle looked up, as if checking to see if anyone could be listening. "No. And here's why. Most serial killers plan their activities. I just had a student do a paper on the fetish aspects of their hunt. And then there's execution. It's all amazingly complicated. The ritual, the observation, and, as I said, the execution."

Mari nodded. She realized she was getting a one-on-one seminar on serial murders with an authority.

And from what she'd Googled, *the* authority. Could be no one knew more about serial murderers than the woman having lunch with her.

"But those patterns—the way they plan their killing—that's what lets police have a chance of capturing them, right?"

"Another myth. People think that most serial murderers are eventually caught. Nice fantasy, but it just isn't true."

"They're not? News to me."

"The open logs of unsolved cases? Mammoth. And that's only including the murders clearly being carried out by an identified serial killer. There are hundreds of other killings which—I'd guess—are the work of repetitive killers. But without enough evidence, enough links, they just don't get connected."

"Leaves the police a bit hamstrung?"

"A bit? Completely. The police, and the FBI. In the VI-CAP department they know they have scores of killings that have to be somehow connected. But no way for them to find the linking tissue."

"You do help them though, right? I mean, it is your area of expertise."

"I can help to the extent I can see the fingerprints on a killing, the signs that connect one part to another. Then, working backward, I start thinking about the psychology of the killer. Looking at their mobility pattern . . . How far do they travel, for example? Is it seasonal? Do they have some kind of inner 'alarm clock'? If so, when is it? What is the exact nature of their ritual, at least the part we know about, the part we can see. But I can only do all that when the killings can be connected."

Linda looked away, as if embarrassed with the way she rattled on.

"Sorry," she said quickly. "What I'm saying is, a lot of times, the police don't have much and my expertise is pretty damn useless."

"But before you said that the police don't get an advantage by withholding information?"

"Right. Normally, holding back information is a way they can screen copycats, so that as they learn the killer's style, his secrets, they can keep that hidden. Gives them a better chance of trapping the real murderer."

"But not in this case?"

Mari watched Linda take the last forkful of salad then wipe her lips with the napkin. Funny, though the professor made eye contact from time to time, it was as if she was lecturing. More than that, she looked as if she wandered some corridors of her mind filled with reams of data, theories, profiles—all dealing with the act and art of serial murder.

Had to get creepy sometimes.

And she had to wonder: Did something personal bring Linda Kyle to this expertise?

A question to ask when she knew her better.

"I doubt that holding back information gives the detectives a huge advantage. This person synchronized five murders, five different people who, I imagine, never heard of each other."

"That's right. How—"

"Easy. If they knew each other, they would have spoken. Some kind of alarm, alert would have gone off. Five strangers, and each travels to this destination? It would be a nice connection to have. But it's not there. And was everyone looking for the same thing, or something different? I'd say the same thing. And then there's the trap."

"When they walked in . . . ?"

Linda nodded. "So carefully planned. It makes the planning of most serial murderers look amateurish." She took a sip of the Diet Coke right from the can. "Can I ask you something?" She looked Mari right in the eyes. "Do you know more than what's been published?"

Mari nodded.

"How did you find that out?" A small smile. "Whatever it is you know."

"I did some old-fashioned Q and A with the neighbors. But—" She wondered if she should hold back what she was about to say.

She didn't.

"I've been talking to a detective on the case."

"Sharing information?"

A nod.

"Good. My guess: that can only help. And if he'd ever like to share that information with me, I'd be glad to tell him what I think about it."

"I'll tell him."

Linda held the stare. Did she suspect that Mari was interested in the detective as more than just a source?

Reminded her of her own psych professor at Albany State. Guy would look at her like he saw every little secret in her head.

"Good. But there's something else. My guess—based on

how this killer operates—is that he knows about him, knows about you." Another laugh. "Maybe knows about me now. So be careful. Five people lured to a coordinated killing? I'd be very careful."

Mari looked down at her plate, her half-eaten salad looking weighed down now by the dressing, suddenly not appetizing.

She wanted to tell Kyle about the dreams, how Caroline had these nightmares about one of the other victims.

But she had promised David—

"You're not done with your salad, Mari—but I got to go. Another eager student at my door arrives in fifteen. One other thought—"

"Yes?"

"Not sure you should look at those five killings as a pattern. It's too big, too coordinated. Could be the killing is about something else."

" 'About'? What do you—"

"Could be those killings are only a prelude to something else."

"What could that be?"

Linda laughed. "Don't we wish we knew, hm?"

She took out a pen and—on the paper mat under Mari's plate—wrote down a number.

"You have my office number. This is my cell. If you want to talk. If the *detective* wants to talk. And I have your number—"

"That's my cell too."

"I figured. I'll call if I wake up in the middle of the night with any great revelation."

"Please do."

"So then—gotta run."

"Bye—and thanks." And then Mari watched the psychologist walk out of TossUp, back to the soothing and safe world of books, classrooms, and students.

While she sat there.

And for the first time since she'd started covering this story, in a way that was suddenly so personal, she felt scared.

25

"MUST have been a good student," James said, looking around the neat and spare dorm room. "Are you sure Parker Kamen's parents didn't come and clean this room up?"

"No," David said. "Been left the way it was the night he got killed."

"Where are all the rock posters, beer bottles, scraps of paper, underwear on the floor? You'd think he was at some Bible belt school and not NYU."

David opened drawers, filled with neatly folded piles of clothes, shirts, pants, shorts, a half dozen pairs of socks in tight, neat balls. Weird . . . Someone dies and all this becomes irrelevant.

Clothes never to be worn again.

Parker came from Ohio.

Never been to Ohio, David thought, and it seemed unlikely that he'd ever go there. He looked at James, flipping through the official report on Kamen. "Nothing here, really no close friends in the school. No girlfriend. I wonder—maybe he was gay?"

David laughed. "Just because he's so neat?"

"Well, and no girl in the picture. A good-looking kid."

David went to the desk and turned on the computer.

"Says in the report that someone from IT went through his e-mail, word documents . . . and found nothing."

"That's okay; I'd still like to look myself."

The machine booted quickly.

David sat down and started sorting through Kamen's recent Word documents and e-mails, not having an idea what he hoped to find.

* * *

"WE should move on," James said.

"Yeah. Almost done. Nothing here but essays, e-mails from home, the usual spam."

"No secret meetings?"

David turned around. "What?"

"No secret meetings scheduled?"

"How would we see that?"

"Well, I'm sure he has some kind of calendar program, fires off little reminders. Good for stuff like the dentist, girl-friend's birthday . . . that sort of thing. IT probably checked."

"Where would that be?"

"Let me take a look. Could be I'm a bit more computer savvy. You old-timers, you know."

David laughed. Though he didn't exactly love having a partner foisted on him, James was smart and kept his sense of humor.

A good thing to have when you dealt in corpses.

David took his cane and stood up.

"It's all yours."

James slid into the seat and began hitting the keys fast.

"Okay, he's got Microsoft Calendar on here. Let's see—"

More tapping, moving the mouse back and forth—and—

"There we go . . ."

David leaned forward. "Got something?"

"Why, yes I do. A regular Wednesday appointment four P.M. with a Dr. Bergstein, at some place called the SSB. Know what that is?"

David opened the brochure he had picked up from the administration office, with a small map showing NYU's far-flung buildings.

He scanned it.

"Nothing here. No SS—wait. This might be it."

"What?"

"Student Services Building?"

"SSB. Has to be. Let's go, and see if they have a Dr. Bergstein."

* * *

DAVID asked for "Dr. Bergstein," and the guard at the front desk of the building pointed at a directory behind him.

Room 251.

James suggested taking the stairs.

But David raised his cane. "Stairs are still a bit tough for me . . . so if we could wait for the elevator."

"Oh, okay. Sorry. Forgot about that."

They took the elevator up to the second floor, then figured out which way the numbers ran.

"What if he's not here?"

"At least we can learn what kind of doctor he is."

They got to the room, and saw the man's name on the door. *Dr. Richard Bergstein, Counselor.*

David knocked, and a muffled voice told them to come in . . .

"I was just about to leave . . ."

David explained who they were and the counselor seemed agitated.

"You're here about Parker?"

David looked at James.

Like the guy was expecting a visit from the police. Why didn't he come forward?

"Yes. And we'd like to talk to you a bit."

"As I said, I was about to leave. Getting out to the Hamptons early; the traffic's so bad these dog days of summer. Doesn't matter what day of the week you leave."

James sat down in a chair. "We'll try to be fast."

Another troubled look from Dr. Bergstein, obviously concerned with the growing traffic on the LIE, as opposed to helping them with Parker Kamen.

David took the other chair. There was no place to hook his cane, so he placed it on the floor.

Trapped, Bergstein went behind his desk and sat down.

James began the questioning. David guessed that having pulled out the lead, James felt entitled to the "kill."

"If we could start. You saw Parker Kamen regularly?"

Bergstein cleared his throat. "Only recently. We've had three, maybe four sessions. I'd have to check."

David leaned forward. "Is that why you didn't tell anyone?"

"I would have, if I had anything to say. And I figured the police would find out that Parker saw me. They'd come talk to me if they wanted to, if it was relevant. Like, well, what you're doing now."

"We had to dig a bit, Dr. Bergstein," James said.

The guy looked nervous, and he clearly had nothing to be nervous about.

Or did he?

Maybe there was something here.

"What were the sessions about, Dr. Bergstein? What was Parker's problem?"

Bergstein sat back. "I'm afraid that is confidential. There are rules—"

"Doctor, we can get the necessary orders that will help you violate those rules. There are times that confidentiality has to be broken, and this is one of them. And while we got that necessary paperwork, you'd have to stay here."

David nodded. "No Hamptons, I'm afraid."

The trapped look came back to Bergstein's face. David thought: Not sure I'd want this guy for my shrink.

"Okay. I understand. Parker came to me about sexual issues. He was clearly gay, but hadn't stopped fighting it. No support from home, and now in the city. It was causing him a lot of anxiety."

"So you counseled him about 'coming out'?" James asked.

"I counseled him in general. 'Coming out' is a personal decision, and an important one. I tried to help Parker think through things. So you see, I didn't think his . . . concerns, his attempts to deal with his sexuality were really at all relevant to his murder."

"Pertty big assumption," David said.

Bergstein's eyes widened. "You mean his being gay may have something to with his getting killed?"

James looked over at David, then back to the counselor.

"There's a lot we don't know. So anything, *everything* can be relevant."

Bergstein nodded.

"You mentioned Parker's anxiety?" David said. "What exactly do you mean?"

"It's not uncommon for a young man—struggling with those feelings—to experience extreme anxiety."

"I'm sure. But what specifically did you see?"

"The symptoms? Well, he had the classic symptoms of panic attacks. Bouts of obsessive behavior; times when he'd feel like he was losing control; trying to force the orderliness onto all aspects of his life." Bergstein cleared his throat. "Oh, and trouble sleeping."

James fired David another look. "In what way?"

"Parker was having very troubling nights. Waking up, often tired. He kept having these disturbing dreams. That's not—"

"Doctor," David said, "did you take notes about these dreams?"

"Of course. Though nightmares don't really tell you much. I mean, some psychologists have given them credibility. But I don't really. Dealing with real-world problems is difficult enough without adding the confusing symbols of dreams."

"I'm sure," David said. "Still, your notes . . . ?"

Bergstein pulled open a file cabinet and yanked out a file folder.

"I can give you these. But there's not a lot here. He had these upsetting nightmares, involving a girl. A young girl, beautiful. Parker said she seemed so real to him. One could say it possibly represented his fear of feminine sexuality, but—"

This time James interrupted. "He dreamt about her a number of times?"

"Yes."

"What kind of dreams, doctor?"

"I mentioned he had traces of an obsessive disorder? Well, that began to play a role with his dreams too. He saw her in danger, that danger growing, and he became anxious because of that. Somebody wanted to hurt her. I tried to get Parker to focus on his real-life problems. But in the last session all he kept talking about was this dream girl . . ."

Dream girl . . .

"As I said, I didn't give a lot weight to the dreams. I tried to get him to move past them. I mean, that's what I'm supposed to do . . ."

DAVID looked around at the room.

Diplomas on the wall, a wooden bookshelf, a small black leather couch by the window.

Pale light filling the room with a yellow glow while an air-conditioning vent in the ceiling pushed out cool, dry air.

And as he scanned the room, David tried to think quietly about the words he'd just heard.

Dreams.

What the hell did they mean?

What they were hearing, what they had found out . . . made no sense at all.

In fact, if he and James were to describe what they knew—Captain Biondi would tell them they needed a break.

They'd be kicked off the case.

The cool air tumbled out the vents above.

Too cool. Chilly.

Or was something else making him feel so cold?

He listened to the questions James asked Bergstein; the answers coming slowly after a few moments.

David realized that not only was he confused.

Not only did he not understand this at all.

Add something else, he thought. Something new.

I'm scared.

And with that bit of information, he rejoined the conversation . . .

OUTSIDE the school, David turned to James.

"Want to see where the other student lived?"

David grinned as he said the word . . . *student.*

"What? Something funny about that? We got two students, right? Am I missing something?"

"You read the reports?"

"Yeah. Didn't seem like much of a "student." Some probation problems, drinking, drugs, a wild party . . . right?"

David kept his smile on. "Right. It's worth a look. Might tell you something. I've only seen the kid's room once. But—I wouldn't mind seeing it again."

"Let's go then."

And David turned and walked out to the street, with James following.

DAVID rapped on the door again. The music blared, filling the hallway.

"Guess the other neighbors don't mind the noise"

"Unless they're dead," David said. He had started to knock on the door again, when the door popped open, followed by pungent smoke billowing out to the hallway.

The bleary-eyed kid who opened the door tried to quickly shut it. But David leaned on his cane and moved his right foot into the opening, stopping the door.

"Police, son—open up."

Stupid kid, David thought. Living in the apartment of a victim and blowing weed. Did he think that the cops were done with the place?

The door slowly opened, and the kid, now coughing— whether from his last toke or nervousness—backed up.

"Um, we were just—"

James walked past David, into the living room. A few other stoned bodies lay sprawled on the couch and the floor, a sleeping jumble.

"Cramming for the big test?"

The kid shook his head. "Shit, we were just—"

David put up his hand. "Easy kid, We're not here to bust you for smoking dope. Though note to self: it is still illegal . . . so you may want to take it down a notch."

The kid rubbed his mouth. "Right. Sure."

David turned to James. "It's back here."

They walked through the smoke-filled hallway, the entire apartment like one big bong, back to a door still crisscrossed with the yellow police tape sealing it.

"Least they haven't raided the kid's room for his CDs, drugs, whatever . . ."

David opened the padlock on the door and turned the handle.

"Brace yourself."

He walked inside.

DAVID stood there while James walked around, taking the room in.

"Bit different from preppy Parker Kamen, hm?"

"You can say that again."

The room, painted black from floor to ceiling, was dotted with paintings done with phosphorescent paint, glowing even with the black window shades tight.

And the images . . .

Bodies sprawled, open wounds, severed body parts.

Carnage, David thought.

"Jesus, looks like a fun kid."

David picked up a stack of empty CD cases, the CDs probably passed on, their contents dumped onto an iPod that had probably vanished into someone else's hands.

"Had classic taste in music too . . ."

Most of the goth-looking CD covers featured gruesome-sounding bands that David never heard of . . . Ozzie was obviously a bit too mainstream for this sick puppy.

"So this is Jack Finch's room?"

"A bit of a contrast, hm? And I heard that Finch's parents went nuts when they saw it—though I'm sure they must have seen his pierced and tattooed body whenever they got him home for the holidays."

"If he was my kid, I think I'd run away to Cabo, and let the service staff take care of him at Christmas."

"And yet—he died like the others, drawn to that place. Butchered with people he didn't know."

"Yeah—but there's one thing . . ."

"What's that?"

"This kid kinda fits in."

David nodded. "Well, this is all playacting. That was real." He sniffed the pot-laden air. Outside, they had turned down the music, and now probably stopped smoking in the giant bong that was the living room.

James walked around the room, studying the glowing drawings of dismembered bodies and gory mayhem.

"Still, he looked like he was one sick—"

David saw him stop.

"Shit. David, come here."

David walked over. Having already explored this room, he was in no mood for an extended visit.

"Look at this. You got to bend down."

David nodded, leaning down and holding onto the side of the desk, covered with dried wax, carved names, and paint droppings.

James's finger pointed at a single severed head, glowing red erupting from a pinkish-blue face.

David grabbed the bumpy edge of the desk.

He looked at the head.

"So—another severed head."

"Yeah," James said. "Now tilt yours, so you can look at it . . . straight."

David tilted his head.

And finally saw it.

The face was that of Parker Kamen.

"Wow," David said.

"Right. *Wow* indeed. It's the other kid. And there's no way they knew each other."

"Though I imagine that Kamen might have fantasized about someone like this."

"Yeah—in his nightmares."

Nightmares . . .

He looked at James.

"Somehow they're connected, and they didn't even know each other."

"And the only thing they have in common is that room, their slaughter."

Did David feel a slight buzz from the secondhand smoke? For a moment the room felt airless, the glowing colors brighter.

"Good eyes, James."

"Twenty-twenty," he said.

"And—hell—I need some air. You're welcome to stay and look some more."

But James stood up from his crouch.

"No. I think seeing this . . . was the prize. A link of some kind we didn't know about."

David nodded. "Like Caroline's dreams. And now that we know about it, we get to wonder what the hell it means."

And with that, they walked out to the cannabis-saturated hallway . . .

26

FINNEY watched Captain Starn guide the boat into its slip.

He waved, and Starn, both hands on the wheel, nodded back.

As soon as the boat was close enough, Luis jumped off with a rope and began tying up the bow.

"Need a hand?" Finney said, now moving close to the fishing boat. But Luis had already jumped back onto the boat, racing to the stern. He grabbed that rope and soon the *Marlin III* was tied up.

Finney tried to plaster a smile on his face, trying to keep away any crazy thoughts about his dream and the woman he'd watched die.

Got to keep my focus, he thought.

Starn killed the engine and then Luis helped the customers, five fishermen holding heavy plastic bags of fish, get off.

"Good catch, Captain?"

"The *Marlin III* always does good, right, Finney?" Starn said, lying for the benefit of the men walking off. Captains liked to perpetuate the myth that there were lucky boats and unlucky boats.

And you wanted everyone to believe that your boat was *definitely* one of the lucky ones.

Finney worked to keep the smile on his face.

He wanted to tell someone what had happened.

But Starn was definitely not that someone. Finney had to convince him that he was all set to come back to work, all A-OK . . .

"Thought you'd be in the rack and nursing your hand, eh, Finney?"

Luis dealt with the rope—but looked up and grinned. More tips for him if I'm not here, Finney knew.

He held up his hand. "What this? It's not anything. A little ointment, wrapped it all up, and it's fine."

"Yeah? Well, good for you."

Finney waited a moment, hopping Starn would make the offer.

Come on back to work, Finney. The boat isn't the same without you.

But Starn left the wheel and walked down to the deck.

Finney moved onto the dock so he was opposite Starn.

"So . . . I can come back to work, Captain?"

Did it sound too much like begging?

The sun was in Finney's eyes, and Starn stood backlit, in the shadows, so Finney couldn't see his face.

"You wanna come back already, hm? What do you think, Luis, should we let old Finney back on the boat?"

Another grin from Luis.

The bastard . . .

Starn stepped closer to the boat's railing.

"So you're good to go, eh, Finney?"

Finney broadened his false smile. "I sure am. You know me. One day off, and I want to get out on the water."

"Get a little buggy, eh? Maybe hit the sauce too much."

Come on, you old crock, Finney thought. *Either let me back or tell me to fuck off.*

But stop jerking me around.

Finney lowered his voice. "I'm ready."

"Yeah. Well, it's your lucky fucking day, Finney. We have a special charter. Night fishing tonight. Could use both you and Luis."

Night fishing.

Finney didn't like night fishing.

Another myth said that you got the big fish at night, that you could find the big schools at night. Boats in Sheepshead Bay trumpeted that they offered special "Night Fishing" trips.

Starn didn't do that; he thought the whole night fishing thing was bullshit.

"Some guys want to go out at night?"

"Not some guys. One guy. Wants the boat all to himself. Full crew, he said. Told him I'd have two guys help him." Starn laughed. "And he's paying through the nose. So you kiss his ass real good and you'll probably get a great tip."

Night fucking fishing.

Bobbing around the Atlantic in pitch dark, miles from the shore, miles from anything.

"What about the storm?"

Finney had heard that the remnants of the hurricane were due to roll in by nightfall.

"Look up. Lot of blue sky and sunlight. I think we're going to dodge it. Besides, if it turns bad, I bet the guy won't want to sit out there. If it gets choppy, we'll head in."

Finney nodded, and Starn turned to Luis.

"Luis—after you're done hosing the deck down, check baits and reels for tonight?"

"Yes, Captain."

Starn turned back to Finney. "So are you in?"

"Sure. Definitely. What time you sailing?"

"Told him we'll shove off around eight. So be here seven thirty, okay? And Finney—"

Starn stepped off his boat and put a hand on Finney's shoulder. "Make sure you arrive completely sober, okay? Not even a beer."

"Oh sure. I'd never have a drink before heading out."

Starn laughed again, a massive guffaw filled with skepticism.

"Oh, right. That's a good one, Finney. Real good . . . See you later."

And Finney grinned while the captain walked off the dock and headed across Eammons Avenue.

FINNEY had to search for a pay phone.

Everyone had cell phones these days; even snot-nosed kids had cell phones.

But he didn't want the sixty-, seventy-dollar expense hitting him each month.

Besides—who would he call? Who'd call him?

I don't need any damn cell phone . . .

A local call was still a quarter, right? Maybe he could even use the 911 number.

No, he better not do that. This wasn't an emergency.

But how would he get the number for the police? Information? But that's not free anymore, was it?

Shit, he'd call 911.

And he knew they'd think he was crazy. But he had to tell someone. Then—screw 'em—they could ignore what he told them.

I might be the real deal, Finney thought.

One of these guys, these psychics who can see things before they happen.

He picked up the receiver and listened for a dial tone. Nothing for a second, then he heard the tone. He hit the keys for 911.

"Police Emergency. What's the problem?"

"Oh, this isn't an emergency, I just needed to reach the police and—"

"Sir, this number is for emergencies only."

"But I have to reach the police."

"Hang up and call 212-555-2134."

Shit, nothing to write the number down with . . .

"Could you tell me the number again?"

The operator repeated the number, and Finney kept repeating it in his mind, repeating the sequence in his mind, over and over.

The police operator hung up, and Finney quickly put another coin in the phone, and hit the keys for the phone number, hoping that he hadn't messed up, switching the numbers . . .

But the number worked.

Finney heard ringing, and then someone answered.

IT took him a while to explain that he had something to tell an officer, something really important, and that the receptionist should switch him to a detective.

Where was this? he wondered. Where had he called?

Some local precinct, or the main department in New York?
It was going to sound crazy.

"Sir, Detective Brown here. Could I have your full name, please?"

"You need my name?"

"Yes, sir."

Right—they wouldn't just take an anonymous call. "Derrick Finney."

"Address please?"

All of a sudden this seemed like a bad idea. The detective was writing done information about him. "1250 Eammons Avenue . . ."

"Brooklyn, right?"

"Yes."

"Phone number?"

"I—I don't have a phone."

"I see you're on a pay phone now. No cell phone?"

"No."

Who the hell doesn't have a cell phone? I must seem like such a loser already.

"Okay, Mr. Finney. What's the problem?"

He took a breath.

27

THE teacher's name was Susan Hart.

She lived in the shadow of Lincoln Center and one local subway stop on the 1 or the 9 to her school.

She still had two weeks of vacation left before opening day, before facing yet another sea of shining fifth graders.

Retirement for Susan was still a good fifteen years away.

A retirement that would never arrive for her because Susan Hart, who lived alone, who had no family within five hundred miles, had been crucified in the company of four strangers, all of whom also met their own unique deaths.

All this Mari discovered with surprising ease.

Knowing the date of the killing, and the few facts that the police revealed, proved to be enough. Only a few deaths reported within that period met the key criteria—the women who could have been the unnamed teacher.

One died after a long bout with lung cancer, another was in a car accident. And of the third, Susan Hart, there was no information other than her death reported to the coroner's office.

No reason given.

At the police department's order, Mari imagined.

She was confident that this Susan Hart had to be one of the five. And knowing that, finding where the teacher lived was easy.

And all that left . . . was getting into the apartment.

THE Upper West Side building, one of those prewar beauties that everyone wanted, had no doorman.

Good thing. Doormen could act like imperial guards. They took their mission in life seriously, in their seedy uniforms with shiny buttons and caps with braid.

Like they were some lost division of the armed forces.

No doorman meant that Mari could deal directly with the superintendent.

His name, as posted just inside the entrance, was Teddy Rubio.

And according to the official posting, said superintendent could be found residing in apartment 1-G.

Mari took a breath, reapplied her lipstick, and practiced in her head what she would say.

This had all gone so smoothly, it would be a shame if Teddy Rubio became the final hurdle she couldn't get over.

But she needn't have worried.

"YAH, you know, I think I read your stuff."

"Good. Always good to meet a reader."

Teddy stood with the door open.

"I'd just love to take a quick look in the apartment. You know, get a feel for the woman. Has anyone taken her stuff yet?"

"No. In fact, I told them it has to be this week. I mean, I feel bad that she died somehow. I mean, that's all they told me. She's dead, right? But we're gonna have to get the damn apartment ready. The owners told me that—"

"She has relatives?"

"Some sister, somewhere out west. Not close. Miss Hart didn't have nobody here. I always saw her alone." Teddy smiled. "Though she did have a cat. Was against the rules. No pets. But she kept one and I didn't know. I had to get it a few days ago. Little white snowball. Cute. But had to take it to the shelter."

Teddy's smile faded, probably conjuring up the cat's fate.

"So everything is pretty much as she left it?"

"I guess so. The cops came and looked around. But they didn't tell me nothin'. Seemed like something was up, but they didn't tell me nothin'."

"That's why I'd like to take a look. I'm writing about her, what happened."

Teddy sniffed deeply, as if capturing errant nose material about to fall to freedom.

"Something bad happened to her?"

Tricky moment this, Mari thought. She could tell Teddy what the police obviously didn't, and hope that her confidence in him won her entry to the apartment.

Or she could lie.

She flipped a virtual coin in her head, and decided to lie.

"That's precisely it. There's a mystery surrounding Susan; that's why I'm writing about it. If I could see the apartment for a bit . . . it might help."

"Not much in it. Just her paints and stuff. She liked to paint."

Mari smiled, nodded . . .

Come on, Teddy.

Another thought: Would a rolled-up twenty grease the wheels?

But that could easily backfire. There were times to bribe people such as Teddy, and times not to.

"I won't touch a thing. Just like to see if the apartment tells me something more about who she is . . . what might have happened to her."

Teddy's upper teeth released his lower lip; a decision point reached.

"Yeah, okay. Guess that's okay. I mean, if someone wanted to rent the place, I'd be showing it, right? So why not you?"

Mari let her grin broaden.

"Right."

Teddy nodded. "I'll get the keys."

TWO locks kept the apartment sealed, and Mari watched Teddy fumble through a ring overloaded with dozens of keys.

"Ah, here we go—"

A click, and the door popped open.

"After you," he said.

Mari walked into the one-bedroom apartment. A musty

smell filled the place, the result of windows being shut for weeks. The air smelled bad, even unhealthy to breathe.

"Been shut up tight ever since she died. Dunno when her relatives will show up, or even if they will. If not, Salvation Army gets all this stuff." He laughed. "Except maybe for that TV."

Mari turned and nodded. She wondered if Teddy was going to dog her steps as she explored the apartment.

"I'm just going to look around. Get a feel for who she was."

"A teacher. That's what she was. And—whaddya call 'em?—a spinster."

She hadn't heard that one in a while. So damn sexist. A spinster. A loser in the grab-a-man game.

She quickly realized that she fell into the same class.

Not doing too well in that game myself.

Teddy hung here a bit while Mari took another step or two into the apartment. It suddenly felt creepy to have him there with her, lurking in the shadows.

But then he cleared his throat and spoke.

"Guess I'll just leave you. Maybe come down, knock on my door when you leave. So I know it's all shut nice and tight, okay?"

"Sure. I won't take long."

"And you best not touch stuff. Don't move anything. The cops may come back, might want another look. Though they spent hours here. And I doubt that they found whatever the hell it was they were looking for."

Mari looked right at Teddy. "I'll let you know . . . when I'm done."

He nodded.

"Okay. See ya."

And he turned and walked out of the apartment.

FIRST thing, she wanted to open a window.

Had to get some air in here.

That, and light. The whole apartment was shrouded in a gloomy shade. Open some blinds, throw on some lights, pop open a window.

She walked straight into the living room looking for a light switch on the wall, but seeing none. Probably had to be one in the kitchen, but here in the living room, the only lights were two lamps.

She walked over to an old-fashioned floor lamp and turned it on.

Now she could see the living room.

Unadorned, with a TV, a few magazines placed on a coffee table, art prints on the wall.

But there was one unusual thing.

A big easel, with paintings clipped to the wood backing. Susan Hart's paints sat beside the easel, all watercolors.

Mari walked over to the easel and sat down in the hard-backed chair that faced it.

She stared at the first painting on top of the pile.

At first, it looked like an abstract, but then she could make out a swirl of blond hair, blue eyes, lips, surrounded by a smoky swirl of gray.

Something done quickly, she imagined, the face edgy where it should be smooth, the hair strands just blotches of blond.

But one thing was quite clear.

The face was scared.

The painting captured that quite clearly. But it wasn't Susan Hart's face. No, from a photo on the wall showing her holding some kind of award, the teacher had rather mousy brown hair and dark eyes.

Who was this terrified person, and why did Susan paint her?

Mari reached up and undid the clip, sliding the top painting down and revealing the next.

Again, something done quickly, broad details, all with that smeary forgiving look of watercolor.

Mari sat back.

It came into focus.

Stairs leading down. Railings.

Two railings.

A bit of a door, paint chipped, forbidding and grim.

And despite the sealed room, she felt gooseflesh rise on her arms.

It's the door to the room.

She painted the door to the room . . . before she ever went there.

And the gooseflesh remained as her fingers went again to the clip.

She remembered that she hadn't opened a window.

She was sealed tight in the airless room.

Could do it now, she thought. Could get up, open the window, come back, and look at the next painting.

But she knew that she wouldn't be moving. Not yet, anyway.

Her thumb pressed the clip again, and she slid the painting of the door away and revealed the next image.

Mari let the clip slap shut with a loud click.

She started breathing fast, sucking in that foul air.

(Air which now seemed to have a smell to it, something odd, something *wrong*.)

Breathing in and out, and looking at the same blond girl, but now—

Hands tied to a beam, eyes wide. Red watercolor slashes crisscrossed her body. But despite those slices, her eyes, her lips said that she was very much alive.

And though the image still had the appearance of something being done fast, looking at the girl Mari figured out something.

It had to be the girl from Queens, the last to arrive, the CPA David told her about.

Susan Hart had seen her death. Before it happened.

Had seen her death, had seen the place.

Did she just paint them or did she dream them too, dreaming about someone she never met, someone to be brutally murdered, and, and—

Another twisted thought.

She'd go there. She couldn't tell anyone. She'd have to go there.

To see if she was mad. If the dreams were crazy. And when she walked down the steps, and saw those twin railings—would she hear something?

Why didn't she recoil, run away?

Unless . . .

She thought the girl was in there.

Mari imagined the conversation Susan would think of having with the police: I dreamed about this girl.

No, I don't know her. But I saw where she was going, I saw her tied up, and—

And would the teacher think that there was any time for that? Any time left at all? If she really believed in her dreams, her visions, then the answer was clear.

No. No time.

She'd have to act. Especially after a last dream, a dream that didn't get painted.

Mari's hand went to the clip. She quickly slid the painting off the easel, and—as she had guessed—the next sheet was blank.

The last nightmare never recorded.

Susan Hart's own grisly death.

She had to tell David about this. The police could have easily missed these, thinking they were just paintings.

She stood up from the easel and pushed the chair back.

She'd take a quick look in the bedroom and then it was probably time for her to leave.

MORE darkness in the small bedroom.

The shadows even heavier in this room with a window facing east . . . There'd be little light here even if the shades weren't drawn.

As she entered the gloom . . . again her hand went to the wall, sliding her hand up and down looking for a light switch and then finding one on the wall.

These old apartments. She thought.

Old wiring, old lighting setups.

Lots of charm, but mired in a time when one lamp was all the lighting anyone wanted or could afford.

Mari liked a lot of light.

Make sure every corner was visible.

She took a breath, and noted that the stuffy smell was stronger here. But again . . . something besides stuffiness.

She spotted a bedside lamp on an end table. She walked over to it and turned it on.

The bed was made.

A violet coverlet on a queen bed. Big pillows trimmed in lace. The bed perfectly made.

By the police, or is this how Susan Hart left it every morning? A perfect but empty bed for her to return to every night?

She turned to a chest of drawers, now able to make out a row of pictures.

Mari walked over to them. One showed a family.

Maybe the distant relatives. A guy with a crew cut and tortoiseshell glasses, a blond woman with a locked-on grin. Three kids.

Then a picture from school, a group picture from Susan Hart's school. Mari picked it up and searched for Susan.

There . . .

Standing in row three.

A bland smiling face among a sea of bland smiling faces.

Mari found herself hoping that Susan Hart had a richer life at school than what the apartment appeared to show.

But she doubted that.

Another picture, vintage, a wedding. A sepia-toned picture of two people, a bride and a groom.

Her parents, Mari guessed. Long dead, but forever trapped as a young couple with a full life ahead of them.

Then the last picture.

Susan Hart standing with another woman under a palm tree. A beautiful tropical sunset in the back, the sky a deep indigo above them, but still a light blue flecked with orange at the horizon.

Was Susan Hart gay?

Mari doubted that. Just because she did a tropical trip with another woman meant nothing. And Mari guessed that if she was gay, she would have had an easier time finding a partner, since—

A noise.

Holding the picture, Mari froze.

There was a sound in the room.

It wasn't a creak. No floorboard from a tenant above. No little rattle of pipes.

It was a sound in this room.

Coming from somewhere in this room.

Mari's mind raced to search for an explanation. She remembered Teddy mentioning Susan Hart's pet cat.

But he took that away, right?

Unless she had another. And if she did, it had been here for . . . weeks.

The sound again, a faint, scratching sound.

Mari looked around the room.

Where was the sound coming form?

Silence.

Then again.

She realized that she still held the tropical vacation photo in her hands. She put it back on the chest of drawers.

She took a step closer to the nearby wall. Then another.

Maybe from under the bed? Should she crouch down to take a look?

She saw another lamp on a second end table, a matching lamp. She could walk over there, turn it on and have more light.

A few steps, and the sound again.

From her left, from behind a door.

A closet.

These apartments had small closets, hardly enough for a few dresses, a few pairs of shoes.

But that's where the sound was coming from. She grabbed the doorknob, and opened the closet slowly.

Thinking . . . Don't want anything jumping out at me . . . even if it is a kitty.

Not thinking: What kind of cat could last two weeks in an empty apartment?

The door open, then the musty smell of clothes, and now the other smell, ripe, full, released. Mari felt her throat catch, a bit of bile rising.

But she couldn't see anything.

The noise . . . there.

Then not there.

Was there a light in here? She stuck her hand into the narrow rack of clothes, feeling for a pull-string, the only kind of light Mari could imagine being in here.

Her eyes even adjusted a bit to the blackness.

She felt the wispy string, slipping away as her hand first brushed it, and then returning for her to close her fingers on it, clench tight, pull—and—

A lightbulb on the ceiling of the closet came on. The row of clothes, a sea of browns and grays, revealed their drab colors.

Mari looked down, to where the noise had to be coming from. But the clothes blocked her view of the closet floor.

So without thinking, she crouched, lowering herself down, bending down to get a clear view of what might be on the floor, making a noise.

And as soon as she could see it, she stopped moving.

A pink food bowl, filled with some dried, brown rotting material. Probably the source of the smell.

And everywhere, filling the floor, skittering back and forth, panicking now under the light, under her . . . inspection.

Roaches.

And with the benevolence of the free meal on the floor, these roaches had grown from small, thumbnail things, to nearly finger-sized creatures, now crawling over one another, crawling off the bowl.

Mari made a gulping noise, as if trying to squelch her disgust.

But when a few of the bigger ones crawled over her feet, dragging their ancient insect bodies over her shoes, perhaps even pieces of the rotten food still held in their chewing mouths . . .

She shot straight up.

Standing, then kicking her feet forward to send the roaches flying into the closet, one flying high, landing on a brown skirt, and holding on for a moment, before dropping to the floor to join the madness of the other roaches doing whatever they could to escape the light.

Then—at what could not have been a worse moment—a hand landed on Mari's shoulder, and she screamed.

28

MARI whipped around, and the hand flew off her shoulder.

And Mari saw David, standing in the room.

"Jesus, what the hell is wrong with you?"

"I thought you heard us. The super said you were here; I even said your name when we came in."

"I—I didn't hear. I guess—"

She looked behind her. By now most of the roaches had dispersed, and only a few stragglers still performed their aimless scrambling.

"Man, that smells ripe."

"She had a cat. Kept it hidden."

"And the food too, apparently."

"David, those pictures, the paintings outside, they—"

The other detective came into the room. Mari looked over as he stopped and shook his head. "You seem to be following in our footsteps."

David turned to him. "Or in this case ahead of them." Back to Mari. "How'd you find her?"

Mari took a step away from the closet. "If you don't mind, I'd like to move away from the smell."

David moved to the side, and then she saw him take a look into the closet.

She walked over to the other detective. "It wasn't hard. Only so many people fit the profile. Process of elimination."

"I see," James said. "I know my partner here has talked to you, and you've promised to keep the lid on things for now. But I gotta tell you—I don't think it's cool that we bumped into you here." He took a breath and looked over at David. "I don't think it should happen again."

Mari thought of debating him. But he seemed like a by-the-numbers kind of guy.

So lying might be the best solution.

"Okay. It won't."

"Good." Then to David: "When you get a second, look at the paintings outside."

"Okay," he said.

But as David started out, Mari grabbed his arm, holding him there till they were alone.

"Look, there's something else I think we should talk about."

She spoke just above a whisper.

"Something you found here?"

"Yes. But I don't want to get Robin the Boy Wonder mad."

David smiled. "He's not that young. And I'm certainly no Batman."

"Can we talk later?"

"Yeah. I got some paperwork to do. Don't have much to show for the day. So if you have anything . . ."

"I do. But I have to tell you. It's crazy."

"What about this thing isn't?"

She thought of suggesting Vespa again . . . but would that seem like a date? America has its Desperate Housewives. New York just has desperate women. And lots of them.

"So can we talk?"

"Sure." He fired a look at the doorway. "Where . . . when?"

"You know Carl Schurz Park?"

"Yup."

"How about seven P.M.? There are benches on the prome-nade near the large dog run."

"The large dog run? Guess that means they have—"

James called from the living room: "David, can you take a look here?"

"Gotta go. See you there."

Mari nodded. Then: "Thanks . . ."

She followed him out to the living room, but kept going, leaving them in the apartment as she left, her racing heart finally slowing . . .

* * *

FINNEY shot up in his bed.

He had planned to nap so that he could stay awake during the night fishing.

How long had he slept?

He looked at the clock.

Near five. Time to shower, get a bite, and head down to the docks. Starn would like it if he got there early, got the rods and reels all ready as they waited for the sun to set.

He pushed open the curtains.

But instead of bright golden sunset, he saw only the gray glow of an overcast day.

Which would lead to an overcast night.

The coming storm . . . but not due till tomorrow. So they should be okay tonight. Should be. Might be a little bumpy, but that didn't matter to Finney.

The customer might get rocked and rolled some, sending whatever seashore dinner he just ate flying right back into the sea.

But Finney was way past that.

He slid out of bed.

He had a thought; he remembered something . . . from his sleep.

No dreams.

No fucking dreams.

No old lady, no bear, nothing.

Maybe it was just a crazy coincidence.

Yeah, that's what it had to be. A crazy fucking coincidence.

Another thought . . .

Can't believe I actually *called* the police and told them that I knew that lady was going to die.

Such an asshole.

He started walking to the shower, and then laughed.

Least they won't think I did it. Can't pin a bear attack on me!

He stepped into his squalid bathroom, months overdue, he well realized, for even the most cursory cleaning. The toilet bowl had taken on a deep rust-colored hue that was probably permanent.

He stripped out of his underwear, stepped into the shower, and turned on the water.

At least the water—shooting from the ancient round nozzle—was clean.

He tested the spray for temperature, and then moved under it.

DR. Linda Kyle opened her apartment door. She put down her briefcase and keys on an end table and walked to the small table with her computer.

She always left the computer on, and just a tap of the space bar made it jump to life.

She went to the Loveline dating site to check her messages. She had tentatively arranged to meet a guy for drinks tonight, a guy who descried himself as being "in television."

Linda entered her password and then checked her messages. A bright yellow glow indicated that she had a new message. She clicked on it, and a message from "Adventurous Spirit Sought" popped up.

Yes, drinks tonight would be great! How about Morgan's Bar on Madison at 7? Here's my cell if you cannot make it, otherwise . . . look forward to seeing you there.

Linda smiled.

Such a game, this online dating thing. The searching of profiles, the first few e-mails back and forth, the proposed meeting. The anticipation, usually followed by incredible disappointment.

Still, now, she felt excited.

She looked at the clock. Plenty of time to get ready and get to Morgan's.

And as for her briefcase filled with papers with such grim titles . . . they could wait until tomorrow.

MARI knocked on Will's door.

Dance music blasting in the background, Will opened it wearing only what looked like bicycle pants.

She grinned. "Got company?"

He laughed. "I wish. I love sex in the afternoon. Got any young men in tow?"

"No, but I was going to squeeze a run in. Want to come along?"

He nodded. "Ran this morning, but can never have too much of a good thing, eh, kiddo? You go get dressed and I'll meet you in the lobby in ten?"

"Great," she said. "See you there."

Will shut the door.

Mari headed for her apartment. A run would be good to shake off the creepy feeling from the apartment, maybe to shake everything off.

Until it all had to come to life again when she met David.

JAMES didn't start the car.

"I don't know what the hell you think you're doing."

David guessed that he deserved whatever crap James was about to dish out.

He decided to play dumb.

"What do you mean?"

"There's no way in hell that reporter should have been in that apartment."

"She found it herself."

James banged the steering wheel.

"After talking to you, after whatever the hell you told her. And you know it's not just that she's circling whatever bits of information we're trying to get . . . You're doing something *even* more stupid."

David winced as he felt a spike of pain move up his thigh to his hip. If he was honest with himself, he'd admit that maybe he should take a day, get some X-rays, see how the damn leg was heeling.

Or not, as seemed the case.

Instead of hobbling around and pretending that this didn't hurt.

He turned and looked at James. Yes, there was shit he should take from him.

But the word *stupid* . . .

David knew that—under his Anglo veneer—he could sometimes be very much a Latino. Maybe he should let James know that.

He started right at him.

"Stupid?"

"Exactly. You know that we don't have a clue about what we're dealing with. So you are putting that woman at risk. If something happened to her, it would be our fault. Actually, yours!"

David took a breath, and turned away.

Not exactly the place for any machismo bullshit.

"You've got a point. Hadn't thought about it."

"Well, think about it, partner. Look, I have some paperwork to do. Want to call it a day?"

David wondered if he should cancel his meeting with Mari.

"Yeah. My leg isn't feeling so hot."

"Good then."

And James finally started the car and pulled away from the apartment, heading into the flurry of Lincoln Center traffic.

MARI and Will jogged in place on the corner of First Avenue and Eighty-fifth, beside women in business suits and men with their collars open, ties partially undone.

The signal turned to walk, and they bolted ahead of the workers strolling home.

"So want to tell me what you've been up to?"

Hitting the next corner, and then flying up York, she turned to him. "Sure you want to hear?"

"Why not? Then I can tell you about my boring day."

Mari had to work to keep up with Will.

How much should she tell him? she thought. About the dreams, the paintings, the impossibility of it all?

Or maybe about David?

Easy choice.

"I think I like this detective that's been helping me."

"Ooh, nice. You have to love cops, with their handcuffs and uniforms."

She laughed.

"He's a detective, Will. He doesn't wear a uniform."

"Bet he has one in his closet."

"Dream on. Anyway, he's been helping. Not sure if it's just . . . what he's doing for the case, or maybe he's interested too."

"If he's a hetero male, then why wouldn't he be interested? Single? Some of those cops like to play on the side. Or so I heard."

Midway up York to Eighty-sixth, with the entrance to the park across the street.

More jogging in place.

"Single, so it seems. And I get a vibe that he's interested. I just don't want to think anything dumb."

"Baby, you can think all the 'dumb' you want—it's the doing 'dumb' that you have to be careful of . . ."

Again the signal turned to walk, and they raced across the broad avenue and into the park.

As soon as they entered the grounds, Mari felt a chill. A breeze off the water. She looked up, noting the clouds, now darker.

Might rain later, she guessed.

Might not be a great evening to meet by the water.

Then they hit the stone steps up to the promenade, and Mari focused on taking the steps two at time . . . and keeping up with Will.

DAVID looked at the clock. Time to get moving soon.

For what—a meeting with a reporter? Or was it about something else?

He wrote the five names down on his yellow pad. But he didn't put them in a list, one after the other.

No . . . for some reason, he arranged the names in a circle, almost mimicking the way the bodies were arrayed in the basement room.

He looked at the circle of five names.

No connections between any of them.

Nothing he knew about at least.

He drew a line from one name to another. Then, from another name a new line across to a different name.

Then more lines, crisscrossing, almost as if in the act of making lines, the connections would make *something* appear.

When—it did.

He stopped.

The lines, the crisscrossing hatch marks.

Made it all look like a web.

Just an image, an accident? Or had David stumbled onto a secret, something somehow revealed by his unconscious drawing?

It looked like a web. The five people, the five tortured bodies, making a web.

A thought: Maybe solving these murders wasn't about finding a pattern—

Maybe it never had been.

There hadn't been murders staged like this before, so whoever did it—shit—couldn't have really been about patterns.

Yet—the theatrical display of the bodies, the bizarre staging of their horrible deaths—

Would make someone look for the connecting tissue, search for a pattern, the traditional path for hunting the serial killer.

Except—looking at this image—there was this new thought.

If it's not about connections, not about patterns, could it be what in fact it looked like?

A web.

A web with the five innocent people at its center as bait. The killings a trap for something else, something bigger, something more important to whoever did this . . .

Detectives lived or died based on instinct.

It was lesson number one once you got your shield. Trust that unconscious part of yourself that works hard even when you're tired, even when you're not even paying attention, even when . . . you're sleeping.

David looked down at his arms. Little pin pricks of gooseflesh.

And with a sudden sense of sureness, he felt as if he had stumbled onto an important bit of truth in the dim maze that was this case.

But a new question: If it was a trap, what exactly was it intended to trap?

And—what were the other parts of the trap?

He left the pad on the table and got up to go meet Mari Kinsella.

PART THREE

Him

29

WHAT is evil?

Don't laugh.

Consider it a question worthy of an answer.

We think—*you* think—you can recognize it when you see it. That event, that thing that occurred . . . *that's* evil.

Or *that* person, that group of people . . . they too are evil. And usually it's because we can say: look at all the evil things they did. Evil things are done by evil people.

Such a safe, sane logic.

Which anyone trained in philosophy could tell you has no real logic at all. You cannot define something by using the thing itself in the definition.

And yet we all feel we know what it is.

Like the old joke . . . I know it when I see it.

But that's just it.

Maybe it is a joke. We don't really understand evil.

So let's for now, remove this word that has no real definition.

Let's take "evil" away for a bit.

Ready?

Now.

Gone . . .

AND what are we left with?

Well, unlike our ancestors from so many centuries ago who seemed so secure in their knowledge that there was evil, that they could easily recognize it and even deal with it, we now, today . . . have something new.

Yes, back then the recognition of evil was an accepted part of the human perception.

And not only that, what to do about it.

In some places, the evil people were tortured, brutally and horribly tortured with devices made—not by evil people, no but by the more creative souls representing good.

Oh yes, good is evil's opposite.

But you knew that!

Devices to inflict pain and terror, implements of agony to make evil people scream and swear to things they did . . . and even the things they did not do.

Screaming, howling under torches and flickering lights.

The evil people brought low by the use of these devices that—surely—any evil people themselves might imagine using.

Yet other times, evil could be dealt with quickly.

A trial declaring someone a witch. Done! A quick hanging. A bolt of electricity for the bad man. A syringe filled with something designed to remove life quickly and quietly and neatly.

Always we ponder . . . how to deal with evil.

But what happens when the word loses meaning, loses its power?

What is evil replaced by?

Do you know what that is, what it could be?

WHEN the doors to psychology opened up, when the human brain turned into this great playground for theories and ideas and suggestions and suppositions, suddenly—a possibility loomed.

Humans could *understand* why certain things were done.

Why certain people turned into deranged and methodical killers.

It could be *grasped*, yes, and understood.

And if understood, perhaps we could change it. Or if not change the person, at the very least the modern human could understand such a person.

The person did what he or she did because this *thing* happened to the person.

That's all! That's the only reason. Like a plant moved from the sunny window to the dark shadows of a closet.

The leaves turning and twisting looking for light, struggling for light where there is none.

The soil turning dry.

The plant slowly withering, dying, in a void of old clothes and unwanted shoes.

Just like that.

A cause and effect for everything.

How pat. How *sane*.

But there is this dirty secret. Those who have done some exploration into the subject will know what it is.

When one begins looking into the mad, twisting corridors of human behavior, looking at all the killers, the planners, those who have taken their obsession to truly mammoth stages, there is no closet.

Meaning . . . often nothing can be found to have made them what they are.

Nothing has shaped their peculiar obsession.

Nothing has helped them develop their own peculiar fetish.

They spring from the bosom of humanity, perfectly formed, secretly dedicated to their work, as industrious and dedicated as any artist who has felt the infinite and now tries to convey it to the waiting, stumbling horde of humanity.

Except—

You'll guess this, I'm sure—

It is not the infinite that these killers have seen, that they have touched, that has touched them . . .

Oh, they have been touched, they have been embraced . . . by something completely different.

And all the theories and explanations, the closets and histories, blow away like the ephemeral puffy seeds of the dandelion that turns from a pretty yellow flower into an insistent, powerful weed.

THE Canadian Rockies.

Stand there, on a mountain peak.

To see: what start as the most impressive mountains in

North America, turn even more majestic, more powerful as the range spreads up to the rough, icy wilderness of Alberta, heading to a frozen north.

Here the mountains stand like rows of jagged teeth, like frozen creatures arching so high up to take bites out of the deep blue sky, to cut a tear in the underbelly of the puffy white clouds that sometimes sink lower than the peaks.

People go to these mountains.

They go to appreciate their grandeur. They go to experience wonder. But perhaps other things happen. When they are there, they touch what is ancient. They touch something borne of a violence that dwarfs anything in human history, a snapshot of a chaotic earth, a violent earth where life is irrelevant, where deeper and sublimely more powerful forces are at work.

Some may turn away, get back in their cars, almost hurrying from the alien landscape. The pictures sitting in their cameras do little to capture what their eyes have seen.

And more—their cameras do nothing to capture the odd emotions, the uneasy feeling that possesses them as they look at the snowy peaks, watching the mountains bumping into each other, the lumbering stone mastodons.

They will remember that.

Some of them.

For most it will fade.

For others, what they saw will emerge in dreams, part of strange nightmares, disturbing nightmares, and they don't know where they come from.

One last point . . .

Before resuming—

Because there is much to . . . resume. So many people . . . *good* people . . . so unaware.

They will not stay in that state for long.

For that last point, look now at the top of one mountain, one peak, that looms over the touristy town of Banff, Canada.

Sulphur Mountain.

At 7,500 feet, this mountain is it not one of the most impressive mountains in the world.

Still it towers over the other mountains that guard the Bow Valley. In the middle of summer you can still get a snow shower planting a foot of snow at its top.

Big horn sheep prance around, eking out a living from the tough mountain shrubs and plants . . . while dodging the mountain lions that also share this harsh terrain.

But they also share the mountain with so many human visitors.

A dramatic gondola ride, lines of wires that go from the base to the peak, runs all year, ferrying people to a world most never see.

And at that top, they can spin around and take in the dizzying view.

So ancient, the mountain range now a stone picture of violence and upheaval.

A walkway guarded by a fence produces the necessary illusion of safety.

An illusion.

Safety is *always* an illusion.

But they can walk from the visitor's center and its restaurants and gift shop, on a boardwalk trail to the highest part of the mountain.

To a stone cabin, to the weather station.

Decades ago, people would climb here, taking a full day to hike to the peak, to check instruments, then sleep in the stone building. Some nights, the sound of the wind, the roaring gales of snow and ice, must have made it seem as if the mountain wanted to throw the human invaders right off the top.

The scientists must have huddled there.

Wind screaming. The attack of the climate personal, directed right at them.

Did they sleep at all?

Or were the hours of wakefulness one long night of horror?

And—years later, something was added to the small weather station.

Off to the corner, by the side of the twisting boardwalk that leads from the gondola to the stone hut.

A yellow metal box, with a funnel at one end and instruments inside.

The cube, a little under a meter on each edge, is suspended on a pivot that lets it turn.

Today it looks neglected. Today it looks as though it's not functional.

Because it has done its job.

It told us what we needed to know.

(And yes. It is nearly seven P.M. It is nearly time to return, to resume . . .)

But first, a look at this odd metal box, atop a lonely peak.

IN 1956, they put the box on the peak attached to Sulphur Mountain.

Its purpose: to measure and gather the stream of gamma rays that bombarded the earth, especially at these higher elevations. . . . especially before being deflected by the atmosphere.

The knowledge of the existence of gamma rays was relatively new; and in what was called the National Geophysical Years of 1957–1958, they had become important.

Not so important that headlines screamed about them in the papers.

No, the papers still dealt with mob killings and political infighting, the random plane crash—

But scientists knew . . .

About the gamma rays, streaming from other galaxies, traveling millions, billions of years.

Rays consisting of protons, alpha particles, and other high energy electrons—all producing radiation.

See, not terribly interesting.

But wait! That radiation, bathing every inch of the planet, the pions, muons, and electrons hitting each and every living thing on the planet.

Scientists understood something by that sleepy and safe mid-century year . . . They knew this:

Evolution had been triggered by that radiation.

And not only that.

Another word was mentioned. Mutation.

Luck of the draw.

A spin of the wheel.

The right combination of particles, the wrong stream hitting a living object, and anything could happen.

That's right.

Anything.

The genetic code could be changed by something far more ancient than those mountains.

So little understood.

These chance mutations.

Proving what caused them, or how they occurred.

So difficult.

And to think they have been going on from the dawn of time.

If time ever did have a dawn.

A sea of particles covering our planet, reaching from across the darkness of the universe.

Implicated—in ways we still don't understand—in the creation of lightning, triggering the spears of electricity that shoot their bolts of massive energy down to the planet.

That doesn't make the papers either.

Guess what causes lightning?

And now we can mention the word again.

(Before we resume.)

Evil.

IMAGINE a mutation that feeds off the pain.

Imagine: the twisting of a normal mind so that it thrives on the horror.

Then—imagine that . . . *that* is not the only mutation.

Imagine that it is not even the *half* of it.

And, best of all—the good part as they say—no one has the faintest idea.

And with that all imagined, lives and their destinies can continue.

It is . . . seven P.M.

PART FOUR

Dream a Little Dream of Me . . .

30

"FINNEY? Nice and early!" Starn yelled from the wheel. "I like it."

Finney grinned as a strong wind blew from the east. He looked at the water in the harbor, and already it had developed the telltale bumps that preceded any serious swells.

And the thick clouds overhead meant that things weren't going to get better.

But Starn would never jeopardize a big payday over weather.

Finney hopped down to the boat.

"Where's the customer?"

"Not here yet. Told him we'll get going around seven thirty or so. He said that suited him. Be nice and dark when we got out to sea. Told him we'll catch the schools of blues just as darkness fell. Good fishing."

Did that make good fishing or was it just more charter boat captain's bullshit?

And was there a line dividing one from the other?

"Take a look at the rods, Finney. Let's make this as smooth a deal for the guy as possible, okay?"

Finney started for the stern, where the rods, reels, and bait were stored. And as he walked there, he heard Starn's voice behind him, louder:

"No fuckups tonight, okay?"

Finney nodded, but thought . . . *Fuck you.*

MARI pulled her thin jacket close.

Maybe not the best idea suggesting meeting here. The weather said that the storm was not due till after midnight.

But now, at the promenade that ran along the elevated park, already the wind felt cold, wet, and threatening.

Usually on a summer night, this stone walkway would be filled with couples strolling, enjoying the fading light. Now only a few people dotted the promenade, the few with dogs forced to hurry out before the bad weather arrived.

All the benches beside the railing opposite what they called the "large dog run" were empty.

She thought of the line from *Psycho*.

When Janet Leigh asks for a room, and Norman, smiling, goofy, says, "Twelve rooms, twelve vacancies."

She sat down and looked at her watch.

Five after seven. Could David's partner have gotten to him and convinced him to stop seeing Mari?

Would make sense. But she really wanted to talk to him about the paintings.

A burst of wind, pushing her hair back, the wind strong enough that she felt chilled.

She hoped he showed up.

Because she knew it wasn't just about a story anymore.

THE door to Morgan's Bar stood a little north of the entrance to the Morgan Hotel itself.

A heavy metal door that took all Linda's strength to pull open. She had been here late, when a burly doorman, flanked by two small bits of velvet chain, would pull open the door . . .

Or not, as the case might be if someone looked like he or she didn't belong in the inner sanctum.

She walked down dark stairs with scant light showing the steps.

One could do a nice fall here.

Still, this was one of Midtown's more interesting places. The subterranean bar felt as if you had to be in Soho, the Village, or the funky bars and lounges below Houston. Not here, in the shadows of the big buildings and power corridors of New York.

She pushed open a heavy velvet curtain and entered the lounge.

* * *

DAVID looked at his watch. Never a cab when you wanted one. Should have been a piece of cake, but now he was trying to get uptown and every yellow cab that went by was occupied.

He debated taking his car. But that was blocks away—another delay.

He had become preoccupied talking to the data department down at One Police Plaza. He had assumed James had put an inquiry in when he got back—and then was surprised to learn that he hadn't.

So David had asked them to run a check.

Anything pop up in the past few weeks about dreams? Try dreams and murder, dreams and crimes.

The woman taking the call laughed.

Said she'd do a search, so amused by the strange request. *One dream hunt, coming up.*

In minutes she called back.

"This is weird," she said. "I'm still searching the records for the past three weeks. But, well, I tell you, Detective, this is *really* weird."

"Tell me," David said.

"Got this in today, Detective. Someone named Derrick Finney called. From Sheepshead Bay."

David wrote the name down. *Derrick Finney.* He had an aversion to new names. New names meant information that he didn't have, people he didn't know. New names were surprises.

And being surprised was never a good thing.

"Okay. Derrick Finney called and—?"

"Yeah. He first called 911. We got that. Then they directed him to call here. The guy said he had a dream about a killing that occurred."

David had turned away then, from his computer monitor, looking at his apartment, the neglected living room with papers scattered, random coffee cups, his life growing progressively messier.

Just like this case.

"A murder?"

"No. Like I said . . . really weird. He said he *dreamt* about this woman on the news, Emma Chappel. Saw her getting killed by a bear." The woman on the phone laughed. But the laugh sounded hollow.

No, David had known that laugh before.

People, as different as they were, all responded the same. A little laugh to hopefully signal . . . *This isn't anything. Nothing to fear here.*

When a little voice in your head might be whispering, real close to your ear . . . *Be afraid.*

"What does this Finney do?"

"Works a charter boat at Sheepshead Bay. He wanted police to know 'that maybe he could see things.' And that's all it really says here."

"Phone number?"

"No. He has no phone. Pretty amazing this day and age when toddlers have picture phones, hm? But I do have his address. Want that?"

"Sure. Give it to me."

Though David imagined that this could be nothing. Calling after it happens. Saying you saw the bear attack. Nothing at all there.

That's what he'd thought then.

But now, waiting for a cab, another thought:

If there is a web, if something is happening here, where does one strand lead to another . . . how does this fit? This Finney character imagines the killing of a woman and—who does he lead to?

David didn't have a clue.

In this city of stone and sidewalks, cars and commerce . . . An island of pragmatics and money, New York was starting to feel—

What word fit?

Medieval.

Finally—a cab pulled up. David hopped in and gave the driver instructions to the Upper East Side park.

Then he called Mari, saying he was on his way.

* * *

THE rods were prepared, two main rods, both of which would be used.

And two backups, all in good condition. So in case of a tangle, they'd have another rod to put into the hands of the customer.

Sometimes Starn called them . . . *the client.*

Like he was some freakin' shrink or something.

The wind blew steady now, blowing Finney's thin hair off his forehead. His hand ached as he worked, but he made sure no one saw him wince. It would be so easy for Starn to replace him. So many guys who knew enough about boats and fishing that he'd be so damn easy to replace.

A car pulled into an empty space near the boat.

Finney saw that it had those new types of headlights, brilliant lights that blinded you. Damn things should be illegal.

A black car. A driver in the front.

Some kind of town car. Didn't exactly look like a limo, except it was black.

Finney took a few steps toward the middle of the fishing boat.

The back door popped open.

And he watched someone get out.

31

LINDA Kyle was halfway though with her martini.

She had been waiting for her date to arrive before eating the first of the two olives safely submerged in their sea of vodka.

But now she took out the plastic spear and pulled off olive number one with her teeth. Saturated with the Grey Goose, it tasted yummy.

She resisted looking at her watch. Three sips ago, it had been ten after seven. So now what was it? Another ten minutes?

At least.

There's a rule in this online dating thing.

After twenty minutes, begin to consider that you've been stood up.

Stood up by some prick I never met, she thought.

She took another sip. The music, electronic with a beat, chantlike singing below it . . . sounded soothing. Dozens of candles flickered behind her, casting an equal number of shadows moving into the room's floor. Other couples sat close together, talking, flirting, while Linda sat alone, waiting.

"SORRY. Cabs a bit tricky tonight."

Mari turned and smiled. "Just glad you came. Thought maybe your partner would have—"

"Talked me into *not* coming? He told me to stop talking to you. For all I know he may complain to my boss. In which case—"

"You're in trouble?"

David smiled, realizing that they were playing a little game of finishing each other's sentences.

"Trouble? As much as I can get in trouble. I don't really care."

He sat down on the bench, shifting his cane to his other hand and then grabbing the back of the bench to carefully lower himself down. Mari saw his face tighten with the pain as he did so.

"Hurting today?"

"Worse when it gets humid. Least that's my theory."

"So you don't care about getting into trouble?"

He turned to her. She wondered if he felt chilly, if the wet wind made this a pretty dumb meeting place. Still, they had it all to themselves.

"All I care about is catching whoever killed those people. Catch him, stop him so it doesn't happen again. And if talking to you—helping you as you help me—makes that happen, then give me all the trouble you want."

"Glad you think I can be of some help."

She realized that her comment sounded plaintive. As if she was asking for something more.

She wished she could retract the statement—do a quick erase, like editing an e-mail written too hastily.

David smiled. "I've enjoyed—if that's the word—talking with you about it. James is okay. But he's young. Don't think he dwells on things too deeply." David took a breath, sharing something. "I, on the other hand, do . . ."

Mari laughed. "So you think I'm deep?"

An old man walked by with a dog the size of a New York rat. He pulled the hairless animal away from the bench.

David grinned back. "I didn't exactly say that."

He looked at her then, and then both of them turned away.

David watched the old man steer his tiny dog.

"Guess that one doesn't get to 'run' with the big boys here."

Mari laughed. "I think he's even too small for the small dog run."

David turned back.

"So—my instinct tells me you saw something today more than old pet food and roaches. Want to tell me about it?"

Mari took a breath. And as she spoke, the isolation, the chilliness of this spot, seemed perfect.

"ANOTHER," the waitress said.

Linda nodded. And only then did she look at her watch. Near seven thirty. The room half-filled, the music turned a bit louder. And still no date. No TV producer.

Shit, she thought, realizing that she had wasted an evening getting ready coming here, now with a second martini on its way, chasing a phantom date.

The martini returned with breathtaking speed.

"Keep it on the tab?" the waitress said. All of twenty-two maybe, with every part of her body looking in about as good a shape as it ever would be. No fat, great curves, flowing blond hair pulled back.

Ah . . . youth.

Doesn't it suck? she thought.

Linda nodded.

And this time, she took the spear and pulled off the two olives at the same time.

FINNEY stopped in the middle of the ship. He knew that Starn would want to walk out and greet the customer himself.

But for now—Finney watched the man get out of the car.

Not quite believing what he saw.

First two legs swung out, taking so much time. First one, then the other. The legs looking short, not quite midget legs, but something about them looked *wrong*.

The man in the car pushed himself forward, the feet touching the ground.

Shoes, Finney thought. The man wore shoes, not sneakers . . . like he was going to dinner somewhere. Then, finally, he saw the man's torso, a head, his arms reaching for a bar on the door, and then reaching up for a strap hanging down from the car roof.

Shit, Finney thought. Why didn't Starn tell me we were taking out some kind of freak?

The man in the car turned, and looked at the boat.
Looked right at Finney.

AT first Finney felt an incredible urge to look away.

The man getting out of the car looked like he might be a midget or dwarf. But then as the man shut the car door with a powerful thud, Finney could see that he was more . . . bent over than short. His torso hunched over, twisted somehow— and the rest of his body also looked bent in odd ways.

And the man walked in such a strange way . . .

Nearly a crablike walk, shuffling left and right, his whole body tilting with each step.

"Finney, put your tongue back in your goddamn mouth and get busy," Starn hissed at him.

One last look—the man had thick arms, and his giant hands fluttered by his side as if seeking to grab something for better balance. As Finney turned away, the man reached the railing.

Starn hopped down to the rail while Finney turned away, thinking:

This is the guy we're taking night fishing?

No fucking way.

"Give you a hand here, Mr. Owen. Coming aboard can be a bit tricky."

Finney heard Starn helping the guy into the *Marlin III,* but he went back to the bow, and the fishing rods. They were all set, but as for now, Finney didn't know what to do with himself.

"COLD?" David asked.

Mari shook her head. Then she smiled. "A little. But it's okay here."

"Bet this little park is real nice on a warm day."

He looked at her eyes.

David believed that the eyes said it all. The truth, the lies, the love, the loss—it was all there if you looked.

"I jog it all the time. I love it here even in winter."

"So—today?"

"The paintings, you know the ones your partner grabbed?"

"Yeah—guess the teacher liked to paint."

"Look at them again."

"Why?"

"They show it all, David. Everything that was going to happen in that room. The place, that girl from Queens. Susan Hart painted it all *before* it happened."

"More dreams?"

"Yes. Or fantasies. "

"This gets harder to explain."

He looked out at the water. Every few minutes the scene changed as different ships passed the promenade. Now a classic tug with a single giant smokestack chugged by pushing a barge.

Probably moving garbage, David thought.

Taking New York's trash somewhere else.

He'd read that the city was running out of *somewheres* . . .

"I don't think you can," Mari said.

"Hmm?"

"Explain it. Look, we both know that what's happening here is—"

"Impossible?"

Her eyes seemed to flash in the gray light. Was she scared, excited, or—

"Yes—and yet it happened. People seeing things in dreams, then something bringing them together until they could all be killed together."

"Exactly as planned."

"Except—and this sounds crazier than all—those plans include dreams."

"As I said, a real hard sell to the brass."

He looked up, the clouds thickening as the late summer light began to fade.

"I know," Mari said, "I couldn't write it even if you said okay. Who'd believe it?"

"And I haven't said okay, by the way," he said, smiling.

"I know. You have my word. But what are you going to do?"

That was the amazing thing, David thought. The one bit of information they had about the killings was nearly useless. Each victim dreamed some part of his or her own ritual killing, seeing the others, seeing the place.

But what do we know of who did it?

"We don't have much. A car, those railings. No—scratch the 'not much' part; we have almost nothing. You know, most killers do not get caught. Big secret for the general population. They go free, staying out here, practicing their trade."

She reached out and touched his wrist. "I can still help. If you let me."

He shook his head, and he saw Mari pull back as if stung.

"No. And I'll tell you why. But if you're not cold, I am. Let's walk."

He grabbed his cane.

Put his hand on the back of the park bench. He noticed that Mari remained seated.

Let the guy with the bum leg get up first.

He pushed himself up.

"I do believe it's going to rain."

Mari stood up beside him, and together they started walking off the riverfront promenade.

32

LINDA Kyle stood up, and Morgan's Bar seemed to wobble before her eyes. Two martinis, as big as these, packed a mighty wallop.

She smiled as the barmaid brought back her credit card and receipt, wearing an insipid smile.

She wondered if they often had women stranded at Morgan's, stood up by a phantom rendezvous.

Either way, the evening was wasted, and all she could think of was getting home, getting into bed, and forgetting about it all.

She took the dark stairs carefully, her hand locked on the railing. Wouldn't do for a respected Columbia professor to tumble down the stairs.

Oops . . .

She safely reached the door to the street, where, by now, the bouncer/gatekeeper was in position to open it for her.

She stepped out, the air surprisingly cool, the street already nearly dark.

She hated when summer started to fade.

The light receding from the nine o'clock hour, to eight . . . in an inexorable march to the dark, icy gloom of winter.

She stepped to the curb and raised her hand for cab, and miraculously one appeared.

And an early bed beckoned . . .

THE boat pulled away, and Finney looked at the man standing near the back.

Already the swells made the fishing vessel bob as it moved out of the harbor.

"Get a look at our customer?" he asked Luis.

But Luis kept his head down, cutting long, thin strips of squid.

Normally Finney would go back, say hi, see if there was anything the customer wanted. A cold beer. A bag of Cheetos. Pack of smokes. For a charter, Starn also had a bottle of Jack Daniel's he could whip out.

That way, if no fish emerged, still there would be a few blasts of bourbon to accompany the lost fish story.

Finney turned back to see the man, Mr. Owen, heading toward him.

The man walked slowly, holding the railing. Walking in that weird tilted way he had, his body leaning this way and that. Finney had only glanced, but he could tell that the man's eyes now were on him, his eyes and a freaky smile.

He wants to talk to me, Finney thought.

So he waited.

DAVID and Mari left the park, and she kept the pace slow, a gentle amble so that David didn't have to work too hard with his cane.

But the detective—so aware—seemed to have noticed.

"Hope this isn't too slow for you."

"No. Not in a hurry, are we?"

"Leg's acting up tonight. Must be the dampness."

She nodded.

Then: "Can I ask . . . How did it happen?"

They were stopped at the intersection crossing York.

David laughed. "You know, for a reporter, took you long enough to ask."

"It's none of my business."

"No, it isn't. But I don't mind telling you."

The light changed. She watched David put his cane down to steady his walk across the street.

"Was such a strange thing. Just two weeks before the murders. I got a call from someone about this minor boss we were watching. We were pretty sure he was responsible for some missing contractors that had suddenly popped up in the fields of Jersey."

"A mob guy?"

"Oh yeah. Did I need to say that?" He stepped up the curb to stand opposite Molly Malone's bar. "Shall we? Then I will finish . . . my tale."

"Sure."

David pushed open the door, and they went into the bar.

LINDA gave the driver a ten and a five, and then squirmed out of the cab. New York cabs were so damned uncomfortable.

London—now *they* had cabs.

She fumbled for her keys even as she went up the steps, taking a quick glance down the block. The few scrawny trees swayed in the building wind.

Good thing I'm home early, she thought. Going to rain, thunder.

Yes, good thing I got stood up.

She shook her head, and opened the first door to the small lobby, and then opened the second, as always checking that the front door had closed tightly behind her.

In a city, there were rules.

Never open the inner door until the outer one was closed.

Because otherwise someone could slip in.

She started up the stairs to her apartment; her bed only minutes away.

AND then—the man, Mr. Owen, was there.

Finney turned and looked at him. The man still smiled, and close up his head seemed oversized, with thick eyebrows and a square, clean-shaven chin. But Finney also noticed the man's hands—supporting himself with one resting on the railing and the other holding onto a bar on the outside wall of the cabin.

They were massive.

Thick, powerful looking—way too big, considering the size of the man.

And up close, Finney could tell that the man wasn't

anything like a dwarf or a midget. No, something had made this man's body twist and turn in ways that gave it the appearance of being small.

But it wasn't small.

No. Not small.

More like coiled.

The ship hit a big wave.

"Going to be bumpy, tonight, hm?"

"Yes, sir." Finney plastered a big smile on his face. "But hopefully not too bad."

"Yes, hopefully not too bad," the man repeated.

Almost mocking . . .

Finney shrugged the thought away.

The man looked up at the sky, the cloudy sky now nearly dark, night having finally arrived.

"If it gets too bad, Cap'n will bring us in."

Another turn toward the man, and Finney watched Mr. Owen's hands open and close on the railing, reacting to Finney's words.

"I do hope that doesn't happen. I really do hope we get to fish."

Finney nodded.

Luis had finished slicing the squid and had moved to the stern, away from the man.

Great, thought Finney. Leave me with the freak.

"Won't take us long to get out there, sir. Get the lines in the water, get you some fish."

And then—in a moment that made Finney's skin crawl more than any fish belly exploding from the heat or some fat slob tossing his cookies after inhaling a bunch of salty hot dogs—

The man touched Finney's wrist with one of those hands.

It looked so fucking big on his forearm—and those arms weren't exactly small.

The hand closed.

No, not closed.

Tightened.

"That would be so good. To catch fish. It's why I'm here, no?"

That tone again . . .

Then as suddenly as it had grasped him . . . the hand popped free.

"I've heard that night fishing can be so good."

Finney felt the urge to back up, but the railing at the bow had him pinned. There was nowhere to go.

"Can be, sir."

Usually the customers told Finney . . . *Call me Mac,* or *Call me Tom . . . I'm not in the goddamn office.*

And everyone got on a chummy first-name basis.

But not here.

"Some fish come up at night; they come up to feed, when the light is gone. And they school big-time, moving from one feeding area to another."

"A lot of fish all together, hm?"

"Sometimes. Sometimes the sea can be alive with blues and big black bass. You can't pull the fish out of the water fast enough. They swim like underwater bullets. Can be amazing."

"I do hope that happens—"

Another bump, the ship momentarily careening into the air, then slapping down.

Finney felt himself come off his feet.

But the man? As if he'd known that chop was coming, his hands held tight.

He didn't move.

Solid little bastard, Finney thought.

Finney looked up. The lights of Sheepshead Bay, and farther away . . . Coney, began to shrink.

Civilization disappearing as the fishing boat plowed its way into the ever bumpier Atlantic.

"SO I got this call. This punk, who had turned into a one-man stop for removing people, was meeting some 'executives' from the trash business, if you know what I mean."

"You went there alone?"

"Yeah, usually they get pretty polite when a detective crashes their party. They're all about lawyers and covering their asses. It's never dangerous."

"But this time it was?"

The bartender put down two dark Guinesses, each with a half inch of creamy foam on the top.

They each took a big pint and clinked.

"Mmm," she said. "Yummy."

"Not many female Guinness drinkers. I'm impressed."

The jukebox played some Celtic aria, a female voice soothing, mixing in with the laughs and talk of the other customers.

"I come here sometimes . . . just for this. So—you went to the meeting?"

She saw David look away, as if remembering. She had to wonder if this was a mistake, getting him to relive that moment.

Or maybe she should feel good that he trusted her.

"I had an address. I figured I'd bust up the party, get names, see who was there."

He took a breath.

"But it was all wrong—"

33

LINDA Kyle kicked off her shoes and for a moment thought she might just kill the lights and fall into bed.

But she took a moment to peel out of her clothes and grab her short nightgown curled up in the middle of the bed.

In moments she had her head on the pillow, earplugs in, lights out—and the alcohol haze quickly sped her to a fast sleep.

WATER.

Gray water. Choppy water. For a moment that's all she could see. The nearly black water snapping left then right, watery teeth with foamy white fangs.

The dream came from nowhere.

She thought that immediately.

Nothing familiar here at all. Didn't dreams always have something familiar? A face, some person you knew, if only slightly? Or a place you'd been to—even if the dream would change it, adding colors, mixing places together.

This all felt strange and unknown.

Linda didn't like the sea. Never had. She lived on an island surrounded by water, in a city on the edge of a great ocean, but for Linda the sea did not exist.

The splashing, slashing together of the waves grew.

And with that the light seemed to fade even more.

Until she looked up.

And saw she was on a boat, a fishing boat.

At night.

Somehow in this dream she started to move, to see who else might be here.

* * *

"FINNEY!" Starn yelled at him, his red face glowing from the reflected light.

Nearly night, and the heavy cloud cover only made it turn dark faster.

Finney ran up to Starn.

"Captain?"

"It's crappy out here, Finney. This is just bad." The boat hit another swell, and the bow flew up and then smacked down hard.

"You gonna go back?"

Starn shook his head. "And throw away all the money for the charter? No fucking way. But I don't want to stay out here any longer than I have to, got it?"

"Yeah. So—?"

"So soon as we get a bit further out, I want you to get Mr. Owen's lines in the damn water, okay? Get two, three lines. If we get lucky, we'll start pulling in fish fast. Once he's got ten, twenty big-ass blues, and the water is still nasty . . . then we can say we better head back pronto. But we got to load him up with a ton of fish, more fish then he could eat at in a year."

Finney nodded. Then:

"But what if we don't hit any fish? What if—"

"We'll get fish. Don't even *think* we won't get fish. Got it?"

"One thing, Captain . . . Wasn't this storm supposed to come tomorrow?"

"Fucking weathermen."

"Yeah," Finney said. He hustled down to the deck.

"THE caller, a regular snitch, had given the names of key mob guys due to meet. No bosses, but still people of interest. Just their meeting up would be enough to bring them in. They all would have outstanding warrants for minor stuff. And at least we'd know who was working together. That was the plan."

Mari took a sip. David didn't seem to mind talking about what had happened. But maybe, she thought, he was good at keeping things hidden.

"But that wasn't the plan?"

He grinned. "Someone had a plan."

"Meaning?"

"When I showed up, the building was quiet. I walked in, went up to the apartment. I had one cop with me—just an extra body. We like to throw scares into mob guys like this. But this one backfired."

"They were waiting for you?"

"No. It wasn't a mob party. Just a crystal meth operation, low-level, with cookers and buyers and crazy speed demons. And guns. We kicked in the door, and most of them ran like rats. The apartment was filled with that oily smoke you get from a meth cook operation, boiling down cold medicine to produce the cheapest and fastest high on earth."

"No mob?"

"No. But one guy didn't run. One guy thought he wanted to use his gun. I told him to put it down, that it was all *okay*. All your buddies split, so why don't you? His eyes like bull's-eyes, big white circles with dark dots in the center. The guy was *gone*."

Mari watched David take a sip. Though he was speaking low, the bar was quiet enough that the bartender could come close and could probably hear if he wanted to.

"The Rime of the Ancient Detective," Mari thought.

"Tried to calm him." David laughed. "As if that was possible. The cop with me was good. Kept his hand ready, but his gun holstered. But then the guy moved, raised his gun fast, some Russian piece of shit. Oops, sorry."

"I've heard the word before."

"I imagine you have. The guy got off one shot. Hit my thigh, nicked the bone. The cop was quicker than me, and hit the guy in the shoulder, which left him writhing."

"Sounds scary."

"The guy could have gotten lucky. Could have hit my chest, head, in which case you'd be buying your own Guinness tonight. As it was, the nick wasn't much. A direct hit on my knee, and I could have been in rehab for months."

David rapped the counter.

"Funny you call that 'lucky.' "

"In my job, that is lucky. But—"

He hesitated.

"Yes?"

He turned to her. "Someone called in with that information. Perfect information for me, to get me to to go there, to walk into what could have been a meat grinder. Someone did that . . ."

"And the call was untraceable?"

"Totally."

"You think someone wanted . . . you to go there?"

"Crazy, hm? Why would anyone want me to go there, lay me up in the hospital, so that . . . when I went back to work, I'd go back to this—"

He held up the cane.

"Probably just paranoia."

Mari smiled. "Probably."

She didn't say that with everything they didn't know about these killings, wasn't anything impossible? Could anything really just be labeled paranoia?

She doubted it.

MEN on the boat.

Light from a small cabin catching their faces.

Someone dark, Latin. Then the other man, thin hair blowing in the wind, steadying himself as the boat bounced up and down, the rhythm picking up.

And someone—in the dream—Linda couldn't see.

Just around the side of the small cabin at the bow.

Could she move?

Of course she could. You can always move in a dream. You can go anywhere you want to.

That is . . . if the dream will let you.

She moved forward, the other two men somehow fading

past her, like ghost people or smoke people, dissipating into nothing.

Until she saw the third man.

Small, a dwarf, she thought.

But no, not a dwarf—curled in on himself, something wrong with his body.

His arms looking powerful, oversized—as they held onto the railing, the ship bobbing up and down.

Then—and in the dream Linda thought she gasped.

Gasped.

Sucked in air . . . in a dream?

Can one do that?

He looked at her—right at her from somewhere out on the cold dark sea . . . and smiled.

STARN cut the engine back, moving the throttle into lower revs.

"Luis—the anchor!"

Shit, Finney thought, looking up. No rain yet, but the wind had picked up even more, and the boat—with the propeller barely turning—now rocked left and right.

Finney looked at the customer, Mr. Owen.

He had to say something.

"You sure you're okay with this, Mr. Owen? Kinda rougher than we thought."

Hoping that he'd say . . . Yeah, we'd better turn back. Get the hell off the water.

But instead, the man turned, the light from the cabin catching his face.

"It's the ocean, isn't it? Supposed to be—"

The boat tipped up and slapped down hard.

"Rough, isn't it?"

Finney nodded.

Most people would have tossed their cookies a long time ago. But this guy seemed completely cool.

Luis lowered the aft anchor down. Sometimes Starn would get two in the water—one in the bow, one in the stern—to keep the boat still.

But not tonight.

If he'd tried to keep the boat that still, it would have made the boat rock between the anchors like an out-of-control cradle.

"Finney, radar shows fish down there. Let's get Mr. Owen catching 'em!"

And get the hell out of here.

Finney took one of the rods out of its sheath.

"I'll get you all set up with this, Mr. Owen. Some nice squid for bait. Blues love squid. We can get one line down, then another for you."

The man nodded, hands tight on the rail, and Finney fought to keep his footing while the ship rocked.

MARI stopped and didn't go up the steps to the apartment entrance. Instead, she turned to David.

"What's up?" Mari said.

"What do you mean?"

"You've been a little quiet, preoccupied. Thinking. And my guess is you're thinking about this case."

David laughed. "Case? Is that what it is? A case?"

"But you got something else? Something you haven't shared?"

"No. Not really. Unless a doodle is something."

Mari laighed. "Could be. Come on—tell me."

David laughed. "Right. Okay. I wrote the names down. Before I met you. But—I don't know why—for some reason I put them in a circle. Made lines connecting them."

"If only . . ."

"Exactly. I have no connections. Zippo. But when I finished, you know what I had?"

"A sheet of paper with a lot of lines on it."

"Yeah, that. And something else. It looked like a web. The five people, the lines. Like we're trying to figure out the connections, the pattern—only—know what? What if there isn't any?"

"So this elaborate serial killer has no pattern? Hard to swallow that."

"That's just it. What if it's not a pattern but something meant to suck us in?"

"Like—a trap?"

"Yeah. And all that looking for connections, looking for ways this guy might do the same thing—it's all wrong."

"Interesting. And pretty damn scary."

"You think?"

"Yes. To think . . . it's a trap? For something—and no one knows what." She turned and looked at David. "Because if there is no pattern . . . if it's not about pattern and ritual, then—anything could happen."

"Exactly," David said, looking out at the street.

And neither of them said anything for a long time.

THEY got to Mari's street, and their talk had drifted into questions about her work . . . What's it like to be a journalist? Where did you go to school?

Life in the city.

The talk came easy, and laughs too.

Mari didn't want it to end.

She took his hands.

"Want to come up for a bit?"

David looked away, as though the question was something he was unprepared for.

Then back to her, eyes on her. "I'd love to. I mean—but my leg is killing me. Gets worse the more I'm on it. And tomorrow . . . got an early start."

"Okay, I'll let you off the hook." She smiled broadly. "This time."

But then he turned his hands around and squeezed her hands gently.

"No. I would love to. When I can relax, when—"

"A rain check then?"

He smiled back. "That would be my hope."

"Presumptuous."

He pulled her close, and it didn't feel awkward.

It felt perfect, she thought.

"Yes. A rain check. Maybe tomorrow night?"

Tighter, and then, equally as natural, he kissed her.

Thank god, she thought. A good kisser. Strong, steady . . .

When he pulled away, she knew that if he did come up, he would most definitely get "lucky."

"Okay. Tomorrow."

"Dinner, even, hm?"

"An early dinner."

He laughed at that, both of them on the same page.

He released her hands and she walked up to her building door.

For a moment, the thing that had brought them together had vanished.

And neither of them thought that was odd.

Neither thought there was anything strange in that.

And both of them walked away thinking . . . believing . . . that they really had plans for the next night.

THE strands—

From the cottage by the lake, to the sea, to someone turning and tossing in her bed, to all of them.

Each vision fueling and strengthening the connections, the hold on each of them.

Until the strands—so invisible—were incredibly strong.

And *so* ready.

For what it was really . . . all about.

34

LINDA hovered there, somehow able to see the man with fine blond hair wrapping a big piece of white meat—squid—onto a hook.

The line itself danced in the man's hands, responding to the crazy rocking, the to-and-froing that had him wobbling close to inches of hooks dangling from his hands.

But then he was done.

Nobody fishes like this, Linda thought.

In the dark, on a sea that's out of control.

Nobody does that.

The man with the hooks, a crewman, turned. It was as if he could see right past her. Deep blue eyes catching the light.

She saw something then.

The man is scared.

He's scared.

Scared of the storm, the water, Linda thought.

But was that all?

She tried to turn away from the scene, to turn from the bow and jump into another dreamscape, a dream with bars and eligible men and—

But that move suddenly seemed impossible.

She could only look forward, riveted to the spot.

FINNEY arched back and let the sheer filament go flying into the black, choppy water.

"There you go, sir. That should get you some fish."

The man looked up at Finney, catching the glaring light from the small cabin. "You think so. Should get me something, hm?"

He grabbed the rod from him, and Finney felt the man's large hands brush against his.

The freak, Finney thought.

Bad enough being out here in a fucking storm, but to deal with this freak . . .

"I'll get the other rod ready for you," Finney said. He grabbed more squid, slimy and slippery between his fingers, and quickly wrapped it around another dangle of hooks, hooks of different sizes.

If one doesn't get you, the other will . . .

"Going to drop this one closer," Finney said. "That way you got two spots . . ."

Finney just eased the line a little off the bow, then released the latch that let the sinker bring it down.

"Now we just—"

He was about to say wait, but immediately the first rod, held by Mr. Owen, started squealing.

"Whoa, you've got something."

Finney reached over and clicked the reel, and the line stopped playing out. He looked at the end of the rod to see how much the fish was pulling, seeing the rod ending in a big curved C.

"Got something big there," Finney said. "Now start reeling it in, Mr. Owen. Nice and easy."

The boat keeled starboard, and Finney tumbled right into the railing hard, nearly falling to the ground.

Stupid fucking weather to be fishing. He turned to see Starn by the wheel. Never gets his hands dirty with the actual fishing, Old Captain Ahab up there, watching the choppy sea, watching the sonar—

Starn shouted down.

"Got something?"

Finney gave him a nod, and then turned back to the man reeling in the fish.

"Got one hell of a blue there, Mr. Owen. Gotta be a blue, from the weight on the rod."

And Mr. Owen grinned at him, a goofy grin as if he had some secret that he just couldn't wait to spring on Finney.

Goddamn freak.

The fish popped out of the churning sea.

And it was one hell of a giant blue.

"Damn," Finney said. "Look at that fish. Bring it on and—" Finney turned around. "Luis. Get over here."

And Luis appeared with a bucket, and wearing gloves to pry the fish off the hook.

"Not bad," Mr. Owen said.

Finney nodded as the giant blue—had to be twenty, thirty pounds—flapped and kicked, making it hard for the practiced Luis to grab it.

Then the other line in its sleeve started singing the message of a new catch, the line flying out to the deep.

"Hell—damn, you got another one!" Finney said.

He went to grab the rod, and the boat slapped down into a trough, and this time Finney did slip and smacked his head against the railing, his chin landing hard.

"You okay?" Mr. Owen said. "Nasty slip."

Finney hurried. The line still flying out. He scrambled to his feet and threw the latch and the line stopped. Again the end of the rod bent into a C.

If anything it was bigger.

Finney took the rod out of its holder and gave it to the customer.

Luis had meanwhile gotten the giant blue off the hooks and—barely—into the big bucket, tail out, kicking and flapping as though it might be able to get out.

"Doesn't like it up here, does he, Derrick?"

Derrick . . . ?

How the hell does this freak know I'm fucking Derrick? Everyone calls me Finney.

Finney shook his head as Mr. Owen started to crank the reel. Luis had moved to the other rod and started baiting it.

Finney turned to Mr. Owen. "Throw it in whenever you want to. They're biting, so let's catch 'em . . ."

And then let's go the hell home.

Mr. Owen cranked faster and faster, and then another fish broke the surface, another monster blue, a prizewinner if there was a ship's pool.

But you didn't have a ship's pool when you only had one customer.

"*Madre dío—*" Luis said.

Luis gave the rod to Finney, and hurried to what could be an even bigger blue.

"They're really biting tonight," Owen said. "Oh, yes."

His eyes seemed to flash. And Finney could have sworn that he had emphasized the word *biting*.

Biting . . .

Like the guy had some secret . . .

Finney gave him the other rod.

But as he did, he felt the first few drops of rain, about to make this hellish night . . . even more fun.

THE flecks of rain brought no sense of wetness to her dream. Linda could see the drops fall, a few at first, then more steady, turning into a gauzelike curtain.

She felt none of it; but in the dream she could see . . . she could *watch* those monster fish pop out of the sea, almost funny the way they came out of the water, how they kept putting the lines back in, only to get more . . .

Even as the ship tossed them left and right.

She looked at the man.

And how he seemed to stare at the one crewman. Stare at him, watching everything he did.

No, Linda thought—gaining a bit of clarity in her dream.

Not just watching.

But savoring . . .

And Linda knew that—in this dream—something bad was going to happen. And she was connected to it.

She again wished it would end.

But that trick wasn't working tonight.

FINNEY rubbed the water off his face, his right hand locked on the handrail, rising on his toes to cushion the now repetitive slaps of the boat.

He shouted to be heard over the wind.

"Want to call it a night, sir? Got a lot of fish."

The water streamed down Mr. Owen's face.

"What? We must be just above a giant school of blue fish. Right above them! We can't leave yet."

"But the storm—"

He looked to Luis, but the other crewman shrugged. All he had in mind was his tip.

Finney turned to Starn, who also gave a shake of his head.

Starn gave him both hands open, fingers splayed, signaling . . .

Ten more minutes.

Ten more minutes in this storm, pulling out the absurdly large blue fish, ten more—

The boat keeled port, Finney again thrown against the railing.

And while Luis re-baited the two rods, he could see Mr. Owen move closer, hand over hand, holding the railing, sliding closer to Finney.

He had something to say.

Something just for Finney.

Finney pushed the hair out of his face and waited.

35

DAVID felt so tired . . .

Hadn't been that tough a day, he thought . . .

But all he could think of was sleep. Getting into bed. Falling asleep. Letting the day's events just fade away.

So that's what he did.

MARI kicked off her shoes.

The feel of the kiss still on her lips. This bit of romance seemed to come out of nowhere.

She wished he had come up with her. Probably too bold for her to have suggested it. Would he think less of her?

But . . . *what a good guy.*

Either that, or he's not interested.

No. She didn't believe that.

She thought of writing up her notes from the day. Not that she could start thinking about an article yet.

That would come later. A three-part series maybe. A behind-the-scenes—all for after they'd caught the killer.

The notes could wait till tomorrow.

Even though she was hitting bed alone . . . it still seemed like a great idea.

LINDA hovered there, somehow able to see the man, watching the two men talk as the sea raged around them, the sky now completely dark.

I'm there, Linda thought.

Then another thought . . .

To see, to witness.

And so she did.

* * *

FINNEY keeled back, his hand flying to the railing. It was time to end this, get the goddamn boat back to the dock, and forget this horrible night, this weird guy.

But Mr. Owen looked at one of the rods.

"Got another bite, Finney. Pretty good, hm? What do you think?"

The ship rose again, and Finney's hand landed on the railing, clutching as hard as he could. He noticed that the man seemed to maintain his hold so much easier, his massive arms keeping him locked on.

"This is getting to be to much," Finney said. "Captain should bring us in—"

Again, the line from one of the rods started flying out to sea, whistling above the wind. The rain turned from a heavy mist to solid drops hitting him.

When Finney looked up at Starn, he could see the captain fighting to keep the boat steady, rocking on its single anchor line.

"Something's biting again, Finney."

A quick nod, and Finney grabbed the line.

"Want to reel it in?" Finney shouted above the wind.

And then the man took a step, a crablike step closer to Finney hunched over the railing, holding the rod.

"Oh, I think I'll leave the bites to you."

The words—a threatening tone.

He turned to the man.

"What? What do you—"

"Like the bear. Those bites. Remember them, Finney? Watching that poor lady, when the bear had her pinned. Remember that?"

The man's voice soared over the whistle of the wind, the heavy splash of the surf.

Finny looked right at the man.

Thinking . . .

He knows about the bear? Knows about the dream?

Then:

Is this a fucking dream?

Had to be. The only way to explain anything like that. But this didn't feel at all like a dream.

The man's arm grasped Finney's left forearm, and squeezed.

The grip tight, the pain searing.

"You watched it, Finney. The maw of the bear ripping her open, how long it took, her screams all the time."

Then a grin—

"You were there. And now—you're here. But don't worry—you're not alone."

IN those last few seconds, Finney turned and saw Luis rocking, wobbling as he made his way to the bow . . . probably to get the anchor, probably to say that they were leaving.

Finney saw that—but as the viselike grip of the man tightened, he somehow knew . . . it wouldn't be in time.

Finney yanked his left arm back, fighting the tremendous strength of the arm. In a surprise move, the man had loosened his fingers . . .

Loosened his fingers . . .

So Finney's arm sprung free. He stumbled back, his right hand now also slipping off the wet railing.

So that Finney stood at an odd angle, unsupported, loose, free . . .

The man watching—

When the boat dipped down, tilted down, right into the open mouth of a massive swell, down into what had to be the beginning of the hurricane swells. Luis was only a few feet away.

But then the *Marlin III* rode up the other side of the giant swell, a bucking bronco.

And Finney—free, loose—felt himself ride up with the boat, his light frame no match for the upward thrust, his feet rising up, off the deck.

His hands reaching for the wet, slippery railing, but reaching too late, as now the ship dipped down again—fast—in time with his flight upward.

Dipped down, and cantilevered to the left, and suddenly Finney was in the air, in the fucking air!

Coming down from his short journey, down, on his own, right into the waiting mouth of another swell.

LINDA moaned in her sleep.

She felt the icy rain. The chilly wet air hitting the man's body. She felt that, and then the terrible oily feeling as the man plunged into the raging water itself.

Into the mouth of the swell, and then under.

The connection to her dream strong, unbreakable.

FINNEY could swim.

Not a great swimmer, but he was certainly good enough.

He didn't panic.

He just had to fight to the surface, and then stay afloat as they started to search for him.

Probably only take a few minutes for them to get the lights on the water, search for him.

Something hit his body. Once, then again.

A dull smack. Finney, legs kicking, put his hand down, wondering, What the hell is hitting my body?

His fingers brushed something smooth—

Then he felt another one of the things—as something *bit* into the soft flesh just below his thumb. A good-sized bite, the thing biting, tearing, then moving on.

The blues . . .

I landed in the school of bluefish, big blues all around, hitting me.

No matter. The plan still worked—kick up, and get to the surface. Get pulled out.

Maybe throw that short fuck over the side.

Let the blues ram him.

Another fish rocketed at Finney, and the man's words came back to him.

They're really biting tonight.

This time one hit his leg and nipped through his clothes.

Kicking, flailing, the surface only feet away—if that.

When he felt something else.

Something surrounding him, on his arms, then his face, then his neck, something like wire, like—

Fishing line.

The more he kicked, the more he twisted, the more he bound himself on the line, his struggling sending him farther down, deeper, away from the surface.

He tried to grab at it, while all the time the fish smashed into his chest, then hit his face, hit his groin with a sharp pain there that made him gulp.

Gulp, and swallow water.

His lungs already burning, on fire from the oxygen debt.

And Finney, with his plan, had the thought . . .

A revision to his plan.

A slight change.

I'm not going to get to the surface.

No. I'm trapped in . . . this web made by the fishing line, surrounded by a school of fat bluefish, and—with that gulp of water, my lungs had no way of holding on anymore.

Finney looked up.

Was it up, or was he looking down into some Atlantic Ocean abyss?

One more second of holding his breath.

Then, madly, mouth open, gasping, ready to suck in the saltwater that would kill him.

The line wrapped so tight. The fish hammering his body, pecking at his skin at will.

He opened, breathed, and felt the unique sting of water filling his lungs.

PART FIVE

All
Dreams
End

36

LINDA bolted up in bed.

She tried to look around the room, and then remembered that she had an eye mask on. She slipped it off, and then the small pockets of light—her clock radio, the glow of the microwave from the kitchen—appeared and she could see that she was in her room.

Not the sea.

No water, no rain, no—

No, there *was* rain.

She could see the flecks of rain hitting her window. Tiny drops, the storm that they'd predicted just beginning.

Linda looked at the clock. Just a little after nine. She'd just had little more than a nap.

But she realized that there was no way she could go back to sleep. Not with her heart racing, and breathing so deeply, so awake now.

She reached out, and turned on her bedside lamp.

The quiet, safe apartment filled with light.

She turned on the TV and then padded into the kitchen to put a kettle on the stove.

Thinking: Another screwed-up night in the life of Linda Kyle.

NIGHT in the city.

People work, people sleep, people party.

Some make love, reveling in those sweet few moments when everything else vanishes.

For that's the moment, no?

When there is only this *one* thing, only these kisses, this passion, this desire.

And lovemaking—or maybe sex—is one way to feel that . . . *escape.*

But for all those ways to escape, there may be one few know.

Most not understanding, not even coming close to comprehending, that there are other ways to escape.

Not having the slightest idea.

How beautifully built, orchestrated. The anticipation, the teasing, leading to this moment, to this . . . escape.

For that's what it is.

What it always has been. The time had come.

DAVID woke up.

No, he thought. I'm not awake. He sniffed the air. Something foul, the smell of something rotten, decaying.

Another deep sniff, and the air felt thick with dust, the smell mixing with particles, floating dirt and dust in—

A warehouse.

He looked up to see the few overhead lights making small, pale yellow pools on the floor.

He stood in the darkness. How did I get here? Where is this place?

He rubbed his arms, the air cold, damp. Rubbing, while looking around the giant room.

Finally, amid the stench, the smell of the place that teetered on nauseating, he heard a sound.

A moan.

Low, distant, almost inaudible.

Except the sound didn't come from very far.

It was low, so quiet, because whatever made it—
Whoever
—made it . . . that was all the sound they could make.

Then David saw where the sound came from. Just ahead, in a little sea of light on the empty stone floor. He took a step.

Now marveling at the fact that he didn't need a cane.

No cane needed here. This world, this dream, was a special place. A place where canes could be forgotten. A place where one could smell something vile, something dangerous, and still simply stand there. A place where you could hear such a terrible near-death sound and feel only . . . an odd curiosity.

He walked toward the pool of light.

Seeing: something hanging from a giant hook in the ceiling, something that swayed a bit, dangling, suspended—

From the neck.

Step . . . step . . . step.

David kept walking, and in answer, the shape slowly swung around to him.

Looked at him.

Made that moaning sound again. One of what David knew . . . had to be the last sounds the hanging person could make. Dangling, the thing standing on its toes, trying to stop the wire from cutting into the neck.

Slicing off the air.

Cutting through veins.

It moaned.

And David, walking *so* well without his cane.

Came face to face with his partner, with James—on the cusp of death.

The dream James, the nearly dead James, opened his mouth to speak.

To do something more, to say something.

He mouthed the words, but the hanging thing was too close to death. He could only make the shape of the words.

Two words.

The first . . .

Now . . . Not . . . No . . . Needs.

Could be any of them.

Then—the second, the death eyes boring into David.

Yet . . . Yes . . . You.

In his dream. David tried to put the shape-words together.

The warning. Because it was so clear that it was a warning. Two words together—when—

DAVID awoke in the darkness.

His bedroom quiet, the warehouse gone, the word puzzle . . . disappearing in the pale light let in by the tight blinds.

A nightmare. That's all.
He turned over and went back to sleep.

AN hour passes.
The rain, harder, the wind building. A young detective sits watching the New York Yankees play the Orioles. His half-finished beer now warm, neglected.
He sits.
And then—
A phone rings.

JAMES Corcoran wiped his eyes. Had he dozed off? The game was pretty much a snoozer, the Orioles lying down to the amazing and overwhelming Yankee bullpen.
He looked for the phone. Wireless, it could be hiding anywhere. Then he spotted it over on his bureau.
Damn, got to get up, he thought.
He reached the phone by the third ring, and hit the talk button.
"Hello?"
"James, David here."
"Evening, Detective. Still working? Kinda late, isn't it?"
"Listen—I think I've found something, And Christ—it's important."
James blinked, trying to get his mind awake, up to speed.
"Shoot."
"A place in Bushwick. 'Nowhereland,' Brooklyn. Some old warehouse. Think it may have been used by our guy."
It gave James the creeps the way Rodriguez said . . . *our guy.* As if they had responsibility for him.
Our guy.
"Check it out in the morning?"
"No. I'm here now. But with my leg, there are some places hard to get to. I'll give you the address."
Shit, James thought. He wants me to come now. Get dressed, drive to Bushwick—and where the hell is Bushwick? Walk around some rat-filled factory.

He debated trying to dodge it.

But you don't move up in the department by dodging things.

"Okay. Tell me the address, gimme five to get some clothes on. Did you let dispatch know where you are?"

"What do you think?"

Right, thought James.

Stupid damn question to ask of an old pro like David Rodriguez.

He scrawled down the address.

"No buzzer, and no cell service inside. Just come in, all right?"

"'Kay. I'm there. Hang tight. Won't be much traffic this time of night."

"See you," David said.

James put down the phone.

He stretched, and then grabbed his pants from the back of the chair where he'd tossed them.

He heard the light scratches of rain hitting the window.

As if a switch had been thrown, those sounds came on.

Raining, he thought.

God, even better.

Rain . . .

HE didn't think . . .

How did David get this lead?

How did he find this place?

James hurried out of his apartment.

HE parked his car across the street from the warehouse building, avoiding a pile of broken glass strewn in front of the entrance. He saw steps leading up, and a single lightbulb under an old metal shade. The street filled with papers, broken glass, and plastic bags now being whipped around by the wind and the rain.

"Better be good," James said to himself. "Dragging my ass to this forsaken bit of Brooklyn."

He didn't see David's car, but the other detective could

have parked around the corner, avoiding the tire hazard that
was this street.

James looked in his backseat to see if maybe he had put
his umbrella there.

But no such luck. The backseat only held piles of reports,
papers, and a half dozen empty coffee cups.

He was going to have to get wet.

Great night for this, he thought.

He popped open the door and ran across the street.

THE door that led inside the warehouse was already open a
crack. David was right—no buzzer, and probably no cell service within the walls of the fortresslike building.

He should just go up.

Up, and see what David had found.

He pushed open the heavy metal door, and it issued a
loud squeak.

A squeak immediately answered by something inside.
Lots of squeaks.

Fucking rat trap, James thought.

Another light spilled a pale glow onto the broad stone steps
leading up. James wondered whether he should run back to the
car; he had to have a flashlight in the trunk. Standard cop issue
in every cop car. Flashlight, flares, handy crime scene tape.

Yeah, and get soaked some more?

Already he felt as if he had run through a gauntlet made
of showers.

He called out: "David?"

His voice echoed; more squeaks.

James hated rats. Seeing them emerge in the late night
streets of New York, the true citizens of the city outnumber-
ing the humans by millions. The rats, desperate to find and
eat all the garbage left behind by the thousands of sloppy
and careless residents, even invading the very restaurants
themselves. Chewing, gnawing, relentless in their nearly
blind passion to eat, and reproduce, and—

He heard another noise.

Something being moved one flight above. David was

probably there, moving something around, maybe behind another door.

Instinctively James's hand went down to his gun. There was no reason he should take it out. David hadn't given him any reason to enter the building with the gun at the ready.

Might look pretty wimpy to walk up with a gun out.

Nervous Nellie.

Okay, no gun, he thought as he started up the stone steps.

A massive handrail ran up the side wall, the metal polished to a burnished smoothness by a century of workers going up inside this building to do—what?

Make shirts?

Grind chunks of iron into doorknobs, coat hooks?

What happened in this grim castlelike building, and how many souls worked their entire lives, day-in, day-out behind these cold walls?

Halfway up, a screech from below. The wind making the metal door shut.

Bitch of a night.

Coming out of a hurricane.

Continuing up, thinking again about taking out his gun.

Looking up, he saw something dark scurry across the top landing.

Fuck. How many of them are up here?

"David? You here, buddy?"

Buddy. They were far from buddies. But James wouldn't have minded the sound of a human voice.

Then, still distant, the sound of something being dragged across the stone, something heavy.

He was here all right, but out of range, deep within the bowels of the building.

James took the last few steps to the landing, and saw the open door, a sliding metal door leading into a giant room. More lights inside.

Al least someone's been paying the electric bill.

Home sweet home.

James slid that door open further, pushing it to the right. He pushed, the door making a grinding noise.

"Nice place you got here," James said loudly as he pushed.

Door open—he entered.

37

LINDA Kyle sipped the cup of tea, sweetened with just a half pack of Splenda. Her feet buried in slippers, her robe on.

The rain now did more than simply splatter her windows that faced west, out to the now-invisible Hudson and Jersey and the rest of the world beyond.

Now her windows looked as though someone had let rows of spigots open just above them, the windows blurry from the constant stream of water.

The wind made them rattle, and she wondered just how bad this storm would get.

The weather would update soon.

Just a few more minutes of news.

Then some grinning crack meteorologist would tell her whether this mess would continue until tomorrow.

But then—

The news was interrupted.

Breaking news.

A banner at the bottom of the screen. Then a reporter standing by the water, a dock, the wind and rain whipping around the reporter wearing a hooded blue rain slicker, microphone in hand.

Linda raised the volume . . .

"Hours ago, this boat, the *Marlin III,* returned after losing a crewman overboard in heavy seas . . ."

Then taped footage. A man wearing a captain's cap, an Hispanic crewman, surrounded by police.

"Police have interviewed the captain, who says that the man was washed overboard during the hurricane-like swells. That man . . ."

A still image.

A man with blond hair, a goofy smile, blue eyes. A face that looked as though someone had told him a joke.

A big grin, blue eyes shining.

Drowned, trapped underwater, gulping the seawater as a massive school of fish rammed his trapped body.

I have seen it all . . .

"Police are now looking for the man who hired this strange night charter . . ."

Linda hit the mute button.

She picked up the phone.

Funny . . .

How the phone was there, on the small end table. Not in its cradle, but sitting there, waiting. And just below it, her purse.

She dug in her purse, pulled out a card, and then pressed the digits for the number.

For Mari Kinsella's number.

Linda looked at her hand holding the phone.

Shaking, wobbling.

And she was so scared, she didn't let herself think things . . . like . . . *how* . . . or *why* . . . or any of those questions now impossible to answer.

MARI took a step.

A creak, the slow whine of dry wood, an ancient hallway.

But where?

She'd never lived in a place like this, couldn't even recall ever staying at a hotel or an inn with a long dark hallway like *this*.

Weren't dreams supposed to come from somewhere?

They didn't just appear.

She took another step in her dream.

She didn't recall actually deciding to walk farther down this long, dark hallway, but here she was. Taking step after creaky step.

The hallway was lined on one side with a pair of doors; on the other, with blank spaces where it looked as though paintings once hung, paintings now gone.

She came to the first door. And again without the sense
that she was making a conscious decision, she turned to it
and grabbed the doorknob.

Hesitating . . .

Because she heard a noise. Something wet, something . . .
a sound she might call *mushy*. Like someone was taking a
great wooden ladle and *smacking* it down into a bowl of
sticky oatmeal. Smacking it hard and then digging around,
playing with it.

She pushed open the door.

All shadows inside.

Impossible to see anything, to see what made that wet
sound—

Until, like the slow rise of lights being turned on by some
sluggish rheostat, she began to see *something*. A shape. No,
two shapes. Something on the floor, not moving unless the
other thing above it nudged it, digging into it. . . .

More light. Now she could see—the shape—not a human
body; the thing digging into the body on the floor, not human. More like—

A bear.

And with that recognition, it turned and looked at her.

Looked right at Mari. She'd imagined that it would have
that long bear snout, perhaps even sniffing the air.

But no. It had a human head, a man with deep crevices on
his face, the red blood on the lips looking dark in the half-
light, and that small light making the teeth glow.

She backed up as if someone had yanked her on a giant
tether. Out of the room, pulling the door closed behind
her.

Into the hallway, the missing paintings still gone. But
more doors beckoned, and somehow she knew she had to
keep walking, keep opening them.

TO the second door.

So much like a game show. The hallway of horror.

Again, first the sounds. Water. Splashing. Gulping.

She opened the door, and right at the edge of the doorway,

a churning sea. White spits shooting into the air, splashing her. A dark night sea, impossible to see.

But then—a figure broke the surface. His eyes looked right at Mari, pleading, begging. She could see indentations on his cheek, a big open gash on his neck. Bloody holes ripped open by . . . what must swim below.

The water seemed to act like a great set of chaotic teeth, mashing, munching, chomping until—it started to pull the man down again.

But in one desperate lunge the man reached out for Mari.

She flew back against the wall, flat against the dry brown wood wall, the wood creaking as her body slammed against it.

Only one door left in the hallway.

Wake up, she thought.

Whispering. If one can whisper in one's mind.

The whisper, the plea . . . *Wake up.*

A useless plea from this trap of dreams and nightmares and reality.

THE third door.

No noise. Total silence on the other side. Mari could only hear her steady, increasing pace of breathing. In, out, sucking the air in as if the air itself was a limited quantity in this windowless hallway.

The third door. The last door. A good thing.

She opened the door.

To an empty room.

No sound, because there was nothing here.

She looked around, awaiting the surprise, something that would jump out and startle her, having lured her by the quiet and emptiness.

But—no there wasn't anything here.

Then—taps. Something hitting the floor. A repetitive . . . *tapping,* closer, louder.

And then a different noise.

A click.

From behind her. But not in this room.

She looked down at the floor. This room—now with a stone floor, and filled with smells now, foul smells that made her stomach tighten. Bile rose in her throat.

She turned to an old clock ticking seconds away on the wall.

A painting hung in the hallway.

The painting showing someone pointing a gun right at her.

The gun in the painting *moved*, rising from some shot aimed at her midsection, until she knew it was squarely pointed at her head.

She couldn't see who aimed the gun at her.

She thought: Please, let there be more light, let me see who it is.

But all she could clearly make out was the gun, the barrel aimed squarely between her eyes, and now a finger tightening, a practiced finger taking so much time to pull the trigger and send a bullet crashing into her skull.

She shook her head; she moaned.

The first sound from within this third room.

And before the blast, the explosion of a bullet racing toward her, something made it all fade into . . . something else completely.

LINDA waited.

Was it too late? Too late to call? Mari might be asleep, and maybe this should wait until the morning.

(But Linda knew that she couldn't wait. She had to talk to someone, tell her what had happened.)

Another human voice might help.

On the fifth ring, Mari answered.

"Mari, Linda Kyle. I . . . I . . ."

How to tell her what had just happened? Tell her, explain it so she didn't seem mad?

All she could do was describe everything—the dream, the details, the images—how she had *been* there.

Then the reality . . . that it really happened.

Nearly done, Mari interrupted.

"Listen, Linda. I couldn't tell you before. But all the people who were killed . . . they dreamed of each other. And remember what you said today?"

Linda's hand still shook.

"No. What did I say?"

"How he could *know* about us. Me. Maybe you. And now you just dreamed about someone real, someone dying who you never knew."

"God . . ."

"Linda—"

The voice was strong, and suddenly Linda felt that she had done the right thing when she called Mari.

"I found something, with one of the detectives. In a building in Bushwick."

"Bushwick? Where is—"

"I'll tell you. But I think you should see it. You need to see this. It could help, could be a breakthrough. It might tell us about the killer. And Linda—"

"Yes."

A strong gust rattled the giant picture window. Linda felt as though she was being assaulted here, the rain trying to break into the apartment.

"I don't think you should stay alone. Somehow he's been able to connect to you. Come to this place. It might help. But at least you won't be alone."

"Go there . . . now?"

"Grab a cab. If you had this dream tonight, it might mean—"

The reporter's voice stopped.

"What were you going to say?"

"It might mean that you're in danger now. Tonight."

Linda felt like crying. Suddenly her secure world of teaching, of the academic discussion of serial murder, had somehow turned . . . real, now close to her.

She tried to breathe deeply.

Again, Mari repeated the words.

"You shouldn't be alone."

"Right. Tell me the address. I have a car service I can call."

Linda started to write down the address.

Then she disconnected, and called the number of the car service, a number she had memorized.

AND if . . . Linda had looked at the phone log of recent calls . . . if she had pressed the little button that could scroll down past all the recent incoming numbers, the outgoing numbers, why then . . . she would have been very surprised.

But she didn't do that.

38

INTO the warehouse room—

James took a step, following the trail of lights. Hearing noises from inside, coming from the back of the dimly lit room.

Guy must be deaf, he thought. Not hearing me. Lame, and deaf, and—

He had moved out of one small pool of light, following the trail to the next light, just ahead, across a small puddle of shadow and darkness—

When he felt something brush his legs.

First thought: A rat moved down there. But then he felt a tightening, something closing on his legs, tightening, closing, then biting into his skin.

He bent down to look.

"What the fu—"

Which is when the second thing happened.

The second thing, of a two-part event.

First the legs, then, when he tilted down to look at his legs standing into the pool of shadow, the second part.

As something closed around his neck.

Closed.

Tightened.

He gagged, as quickly he felt his neck yanked up, the metal tightening around his throat, but not tightening so much that breathing was impossible.

No, he could with the greatest of efforts, suck in a small bubble of air, then force it out, the windpipe closed to such a narrow diameter.

A quick few thoughts . . .

On the stone floor, the decayed walls barely catching any of the light.

Where's David? Had he been trapped too? Is that why he didn't answer? Is that why he didn't respond to any of James's calls?

Speech was impossible. James Corcoran felt lucky he could still get air past the metal garrote around his neck.

Another thought:

Whoever was doing this was permitting him that small opening, allowing James to breathe.

He was an expert. He knew just how tight to make it.

Not enough to kill him.

Just enough to inflict agonizing pain.

And bizarrely, James felt grateful.

He knows what he's doing.

Grateful . . .

Then he felt the wire around his neck start to go taut. It didn't tighten any further. But somehow it was being pulled from above, slowly yanking his head up.

Until James had to start to go on his tiptoes.

To the very end of his toes, using the hard leather of his cop shoes, the toe end, to keep himself up.

And balance too.

Had to balance, waving around, trying not to topple, which would only make the metal noose dig deeper into his neck.

The yanking stopped.

The only sound James could make was the almost inaudible gasp, a hollow wheeze that someone could really only hear if he stood right next to James, strung up, suspended, waiting.

Because the thought that James then had—

The most terrible thought was . . .

I'm waiting, *he's waiting* . . . for the others . . .

Gasp. Wheeze.

Wait.

THE driver had shaken his head when Linda gave him the address.

"Gonna cost you extra, lady. This time of night, this

weather. And going there. Why you go to Bushwick anyway?"

Linda just felt relieved to be with another human, to not be alone. But she'd feel a lot better when she got to Mari, and the detective.

Amazing how quickly her apartment had turned scary.

As if the idea of staying there was crazy.

The wind made the trees bend, and the driver had to dodge branches that fell to the ground. His wipers worked overtime, slapping at the rain.

The driver had music on, Indian music, a high-pitched warble, a woman's voice wailing up and down an octave.

Crazy. Surreal.

Across the Williamsburg Bridge, they came to a neighborhood with the lights out. Cars stopped at the now-eerie corners without traffic lights; they hesitated, waiting for some invisible sign that it was their turn to go.

Linda wanted to tell the man to hurry.

She wanted out of the car.

But the driver didn't seem to want to be out in this weather any more than she did, gunning the town car through a series of dark intersections before heading down Metropolitan Avenue . . . and to where the lights magically returned.

"Such a bad night out. And you go all the way out here?"

He grunted.

Down Metropolitan, then a turn at Bushwick.

Another turn.

Until the car stopped.

"HERE?" she said.

"This is the address you give me, lady. Of course here."

Linda looked out the rain-smeared window. She saw the steps, the light—just as Mari described.

They—Mari, the detective—were inside, up a flight. No cell service there, she said. Linda would just have to go in.

The driver turned around.

"And listen. I won't wait."

"No, no. They will bring me back."

(Mari had said that.)

"Right. So good night then."

Something made Linda hold back for just a second. But then she grabbed her umbrella and then, with her other hand, the door handle.

"Thanks . . . ," she said.

Another grunt.

She popped open the door, and simultaneously hit the button to make the umbrella unfurl, the wind quickly ripping at its spine, trying to turn it inside out.

She ran up the stone steps . . .

39

MARI had dozed off in front of the television, the sound low, drifting away.

The phone rang, the sound jarring.

She woke up and could see that the rain had turned worse, the storm fully over the city.

She looked around.

Where the hell was the phone? She tried to wake up and locate where she had put the phone, always slipping between the pillows of the sofa, or hiding somewhere in the kitchen, under papers, magazines.

Then she saw it on the built-in shelves by the small kitchen. She sprung up from her chair and got to it by the third ring.

David.

She tried to make herself snap to wakefulness.

"No. It's okay. Not too. I'm fine—"

She listened.

David and his partner had stumbled upon something, something really important—thanks to her ideas.

Mari thought about that for a second. Had she really done much? What had she told them?

The wind made her windows rattle. They needed replacement, probably original to the building . . . prewar, pre-everything—

She heard him say . . .

"Maybe you want to be in on this . . . ?"

"Now," she said. "Go—where?"

Then the address—and Mari looked out the window. A horrible night to go out. The worst. Could she even get a cab to take her there? David said don't bring her car.

He'd get her home.

Not to worry.

And she knew that, as a reporter covering this thing, if he had something to show her—

Something big . . . something important . . .

She had no choice.

No choice at all.

She held the piece of paper, a pad from an Aruba resort that she'd visited a year ago. A little link to warm nights and gentle breezes as a storm raged outside.

She said:

"I'll go there. I'm coming now."

She hung up, and got ready to leave.

LINDA pushed her way into the loft, following the pools of light leading up the stone stairs.

And of course she called Mari's name.

The sound echoing in the building.

"Mari? Mari, you up there?"

But the reporter had told her that she would be inside the building, to just come in.

Linda Kyle felt no nervousness, not really. She had been alone, trapped in her apartment after watching that man drown, die miles away in the choppy Atlantic.

To talk to Mari, even here, would be a tiny piece of sanity.

She heard noise upstairs.

Mari, probably with some other people, maybe the detectives.

Linda quickened her pace.

TO . . . the door into a big storeroom.

A single rat darted up to the dark floors above, floors without those warm pools of light.

She wondered if the rat had lingered on the steps, watching her as she went inside.

Inside. Hearing noises, steps, sounds, not a voice exactly.

The overhead bulbs, faint, pathetic bulbs that made only

small islands of light, left most of the big room in darkness and shadows.

She tried calling again. This time Mari would hear her.

"Mari—you back there?"

Because:

Back, in the distance, there had to be giant spaces, maybe other rooms, doors, tall shelves that went to the ceiling, to store things.

She thought: Is this where the killer hid? Did they find his hiding place? Was he already gone, and this place ripe with clues?

Noises, to the side.

Past one light, deeper into the warehouse. Scratching sounds, and something—almost like a grunt.

A gulping noise.

She rubbed her arms.

Her desire to tell Mari, to be with someone else, began to quickly, sickeningly fade.

A betrayal.

The reality of the moment was, suddenly, clear to her.

Where she was.

The strangeness of this place.

Then, from somewhere, the thought that had been banished. A thought that any sensible person would have had.

That Linda certainly should have had.

Yet—didn't.

Till now.

Until it was too late for that thought to have any value at all.

SOMEONE there.

A little farther, Linda thought.

Just a little farther, and she'd see.

And she did see.

A shadow, swinging from something, the shadow looking human, swinging, alive.

And those gulping noises? Those desperate sucking sounds?

Clearly coming from the top of the shadow.

A weird thought then: It has a head.

This thing before me, dangling, swinging, has a head.

And—it's *alive*.

In her mind doors of every shape and substance began closing, as logic somehow returned.

As she became aware of where she was, and then—the penultimate thought—what *this* might be.

The tears she started crying were silent.

She turned and took a step, knowing full well—especially her, especially with all she knew—that it was already too late, and had been from the moment she entered.

Gulp . . . gulp . . . wheeze . . .

The thing so close by produced such a terrible small sound.

(Gasping for air.)

She turned. Took a step.

As planned, as thought, as orchestrated—

SHE felt something metal on the ground in front of her.

Had it always been there or had it slid into position when she was mesmerized by the thing hanging in the shadows?

(The person in the shadows, the hanging person.)

The step down hard, as she pivoted, turned, and then a heavy *click*.

A strong metallic sound as something became released, as something became freed—

She looked down, but much too late to do anything but observe what happened.

And what she saw was this:

Two rows of jagged metal teeth, each metal fang inches long, with a pointed end. A metal smile made up of metal teeth. The heavy grinning teeth, surely designed for something far larger than her, closed.

Snapped shut!

The sound filling the room.

Linda howled as the teeth neatly cut into skin, chomped on bone, and trapped her leg.

She screamed, the warehouse now filled with her screaming.

But there was only one person to hear, and for the moment, he paid it no notice.

THE screaming could not last.

She heard another noise, quickly identified as the rattling of chains. A chain being pulled, dragging across the stone floor, then—

A yank!

And Linda was pulled to the ground, roughly dragged to the ground by the steel trap, reeled in.

(Like a fish.)

Reeled in, pulled across the floor.

Her screams turned to moans, shouted words. Things people say. So familiar, so predictable.

As if words have any power.

Words like "no," and "god," and the least effective of all . . . "please."

Pulled, dragged across the floor.

Close now to the shadow thing, the hanging man.

Because she could see that the gulping thing was still alive, only able to make that slight sound trying to force air in, his eyes bugged out, watching her.

Linda opened her mouth again.

But there had been enough screaming.

Heavy tape went across her mouth, leaving her nostrils free to breathe.

There was work to be done . . .

40

DAVID Rodriguez, a good man, a thoughtful man, gave in to the temptation to let himself fall back on his couch.

So tired. The tension, the stress of working this case when he knew that physically he wasn't up to it.

That thought . . . his last as he grabbed the overstuffed sofa pillow and let his eyes close.

Not up to it.

Should leave it to James.

Take a desk job.

Then:

What the fuck . . .

Why do I care?

A thoughtful man.

In this sense . . .

He observed. Noted. Watched. A source of pride for him.

In the Bronx his amigos could just miss things, do stupid things, let things slide.

It could cost them their lives.

Not David.

He'd see, think, remember.

The phone rang.

DAVID'S eyes popped open. He looked at the clock. Just past midnight.

He swung around and stood up.

His cell was on the bureau, sitting in a sea of coins, scraps of paper, and his wallet fat—not with money, but with all the junk that modern living still somehow produces.

And—

He got up. He stood up. He walked over to the phone.

To hear Mari Kinsella, excited, breathless. She had found *something* relating to the young girl, to dead Caroline Brzow, something that led to an abandoned warehouse in Brooklyn.

She asked him to come.

"Sure. Of course. I mean, are you okay? Everything all right?"

And everything was fine, Mari said. Just hurry. Get here fast. Then, to add urgency . . . *He may have been here.*

And even in the midst of that call, David had the presence to ask:

"I can get a squad car there. Just till I arrive."

But no, that wasn't necessary. The place had been abandoned, and if other cops showed up Mari would be quickly removed from the scene.

Which was true.

"Okay."

David wrote down the address. Bushwick. Some grim spots there. Grim, dangerous.

He hung up.

HE slipped his cell into his pocket and turned to the couch which only a few minutes ago had provided a soft island, a sanctuary where he could ignore the rain outside, ignore his work.

He walked back to the couch, his shoes on the floor, lying on their sides.

And next to them, his cane, on the floor beside them. Probably had slipped down while he tossed and slept.

The cane had slipped down to the floor.

A quick thought, because he had to hurry, Mari was waiting:

I got up and walked here.

Walked back.

Without my cane.

Maybe I'm getting better. Had to be getting better to get up, walk over there and back.

He tried to stand up.

The pain was quick, immediate. A sharp spike that hit his thigh. The leg protested at that much weight being put on it.

He reached down for the cane, his constant companion.

How had he done that?

But there was no time to think about it. He put on his shoes, grabbed a cheap rain poncho from his closet, and with his friend the cane close at hand, he started down to his car.

HAVE I ever been to Bushwick? Mari wondered.

Does anybody ever come here?

She ran up the stairs, her dark hair plastered to the sides of her face by the rain, leaving wet spatters on the stones.

She saw other wet spots on the ground, probably from when David had come here. Amazing that he had such confidence in her to share this.

Amazing, unbelievable.

Her cell was indeed dead here. She glanced down as she ran up—no bars, no signal.

Probably all that stone.

"David!"

Her voice echoed, though he had told her to just come up to the main storeroom of the warehouse.

Follow the lights, he had said.

Still, she felt the need to call him. "David, you up here?"

In answer, she heard some faint noises.

He must be inside, looking at things.

Mari picked up her pace.

MARI entered the room, a massive warehouse dotted with lightbulbs that did little to chase the darkness and shadows.

She stopped.

Some bit of instinct was allowed to emerge, an instinct that said:

This isn't right.

But as soon as she had that thought, she heard the door to the warehouse room slide shut.

More lights came on.

So many more lights here.

Not just the ones on when she came in.

Her fist went to her mouth, an impulsive gesture. To stifle a moan, to somehow keep from making a sound.

She saw the young detective, so clearly in the light now, on his toes, weaving, wobbling. His red face a balloon of skin and bone, his mouth open wide, gulping at the air.

Mari's stomach turned.

She took a step back.

Then—Linda.

The woman, also suspended, but upside down, a heavy chain arched over pipes, water pipes, or pipes to the sewer, the metal chain holding up a metal trap—

(A bear trap.)

Linda Kyle's foot trapped there, hanging her upside down. Her free leg kicked, and as she kicked she spun around to see Mari.

Pleading, begging, but both of them knowing—

Having to know at this point . . .

That it was too late.

Another step back.

And she felt someone touch her.

THE man before her seemed curved in on himself, as though he had been injured—and now his back wasn't at all shaped right. His arms were oversized, massive, nearly ape-like, ending in hands that Mari could see matched the giant arms.

A creature wounded, twisted, damaged from years of—what?

He looked at her.

The background noise: the sounds made by the rattling chain, the detective's shoes desperately scraping the floor.

Mari's eyes darted left and right, looking for a possible way to escape. He couldn't be that fast, this troll-like human; she could outrun him.

Her right foot moved just a bit.

The man smiled.

Suddenly one hand held a syringe and, with amazing speed, it went flying toward Mari. She pulled back, but not nearly fast enough as the needle landed in her side.

The man cocked his head as if intensely interested in what would happen next, as if he wasn't at all sure what would happen.

Mari's hand went to where the syringe still lay buried in her side. She yanked it out and threw it to the ground.

She now took a big step toward to the door . . .

(Slammed, locked . . . she did not know.)

One big step, then another, waiting, expecting that whatever the man had jabbed her with would knock her out.

But she was wrong there.

41

ANOTHER step, and Mari's leg seemed to give way, as if the bone had been sucked out of it, leaving only rubbery flesh. She collapsed on her own legs, and made another discovery.

She should have groaned when she landed.

But instead she heard a grunt as the air was forced out of her body.

She opened her mouth.

To speak.

But though she could open her mouth, whatever he had injected into her had left the muscles of her tongue, her lips immobile. She couldn't speak.

No words, no cries.

She also felt that her arms were lifeless things.

Her head had smacked against the floor hard, and blood from that gash now stained the stone. Her head tilted and pointed back where she had come from.

Back to the man.

Mari watched as he came to her, his wavering, wobbly walk almost not human. Crablike, as if he'd had to learn to walk in some new way with this damaged body.

He came close to her, his head oversized, and she could see that the man was old. Powerful, but the face lined; deep, ancient crevices on his face.

He leaned close to her.

"You were so good . . . Doing everything the way you should. All of you. So helpful, so—"

His arms dug under her, and he scooped her up, a rag doll, held by him.

"—easily lured."

She could feel him wobble. Walking alone was difficult for this man—

(This creature.)

But holding her, every step tended to make him keel over. Still, going slowly, he made progress.

Her head turned the wrong way, and with—as she now knew—no muscle control, she couldn't see where he was taking her . . . except it was back, farther, deeper into the warehouse.

Until, with a grunt; he shifted her weight a bit, getting ready to release her, place her—

And she saw a wooden chair.

Like a chair from some ancient school, the chair of the principal. Heavy, wooden, with thick legs.

He lowered Mari into the chair and her head tilted backward. But as soon as she was in place, he cradled her head and craned her head forward, so her chin pressed down on her chest, her eyes looking ahead with a good view of the entrance and—peripherally—the other two captives.

The man hobbled away.

Into shadows, away from Mari's line of sight.

Then she heard him coming back, heard him dragging something.

Again, no sound possible for her, no head movement. Just the awareness that he was returning, dragging . . . something.

Until he stood in front of her.

HIS hand carefully held what looked like wire.

But in a moment Mari knew that it wasn't wire.

My thoughts are clear.

I can't move—but my thinking . . . *totally clear.*

He shot me with something to weaken . . . disable my muscles.

The wire had hundreds of twisty spikes, sharp, curved hooks through its entire length.

What do they call it?

Razor ribbon.

Her captor, the man that trapped her, started to separate the pieces. She saw some of the hooks catch on his hands, digging in. Little bloody bull's-eyes bloomed on the massive hands. He didn't seem to care.

When he had the wire spread out, he turned to her.

Held up his hands.

"It digs in so fast. The slightest bit of movement. These"—he examined one of his own wounds—"they're nothing. Not compared to when . . . it's around your whole body, when you have to move—"

Mari's breath caught.

When I move?

Did he have something he was going to give her, to make her move, struggle, while he watched?

The man took a step closer to the chair, holding the wire up to Mari's face.

"It's time. I've been patient. Planned so hard. But the time for planning is over . . . It's been time for me to change. So overdue. And he will be perfect."

Mari wondered . . . What is he talking about?

He held up his arms, brandishing the wire like a trophy. "And you will play such an important part in making it happen. Don't worry, by the time you need to scream, you will be able to. The drug will wear off soon."

He loosened the metal coils more, and began to wrap them around Mari.

As he did, he whistled.

He whistled . . .

As he completely surrounded her body with the wire, from her head to her feet, the hooks just barely touching her skin.

And when it was done, he walked over to a far wall of the warehouse.

Mari heard a click, and the room became filled with bright light, everything in the room became bathed in new brilliant lights from the ceiling.

42

DAVID stopped the car, and felt the wheels slide with the sudden breaking.

He looked up at the building, a blackish-gray hulk rendered blurry by the rain.

And there was no way he couldn't think about it—

The *last* time he'd walked into a building after a call.

How all that turned out.

He picked up his cell phone from his shirt pocket and, scrolling to recent numbers, selected Mari's cell.

It immediately went to voice mail.

As she'd said—no service inside.

He put his hand on the door handle—but then—hesitated.

INSTINCT.

The reason he became a detective.

He always had this feeling that he could read people, even as a kid.

Always knew when his father was lying about working late, and when it came out that his father had some young Chiquita mistress in Manhattan . . . David was not surprised.

Or when his older brother lied about being involved with the robbery of a local bodega, a place recently taken over by Koreans.

Knew that his brother was lying as soon as his mother asked his brother the question . . .

You have anything to do with this . . . you, your friends?

David stood there, and could see the truth.

Some people can sing, some can write, some are great with numbers, some can hit a fucking baseball a mile.

We all have our talents.
And now—

HIS hand rested on the door handle.

Thinking: How did Mari get here? Why would she come here alone, if she was alone? To follow some lead? And look at the goddamn weather. Who would come out on a night like this, and, and—

A voice in his head.

Belated.

You're here, aren't you? Go find out . . .

Right, and only now was he questioning it.

And there was this: something else bothered him, something that didn't make sense.

But it was elusive, floating around, just out of the grasp of his mind.

He felt down to his side, to the gun strapped across his chest.

Good thing putting on that gun was automatic. Something he didn't have to think about.

Because he knew, quite clearly now, that he hadn't been thinking when he came here. Not *really* . . . thinking. His instincts ignored.

Ignored . . .

Or maybe something else.

Lightning flashed, close, quickly followed by a clap of thunder. In the glow the street, filled with debris, lit up, showing the wet pools of water building in the heavy downpour.

He grabbed his cane.

Only one hand free, he noted.

Just a bit of information.

One hand.

And with that hand, he popped open the door.

DAVID walked through the metal door, then up the broad steps—a rhythm from the steady click of his cane landing as he walked, up the stone steps.

The steady *tap* . . . *tap* . . . *tap* . . . such a clear signal.

No chance of a surprise here.

But then he heard noises just ahead, just beyond the last row of steps, into the big room, with a bright spear of light escaping from the door, open only an inch or so.

Strange. Why wouldn't she have left the door open all the way?

Why shut it, with just that tantalizing little crack?

And as he walked, David realized something else. He was fighting to awaken his instincts, to recover something turned numb, sleeping.

He reached the door. Stopped. Listened to the sounds.

Noises he couldn't identify. Breathing sounds, scraping, and then—rising above it—

A whimpering. So terribly sad; a trapped, pitiful sound.

His hand reached for the door.

He stopped.

His free hand reaching for the damn door, his other holding the cane.

No. That's not the way it would be.

His left hand dug out his gun. He took the safety off, checked it. Then the hand holding the cane reached out and grabbed the big sliding metal door.

Thinking, with a tiny burst of clarity . . . Seen this kind of door before, haven't we?

Then—the dream he'd had. The nightmare. That wasn't such a different place, was it? In fact, it could have been—

Right here . . .

And with the gun out, thinking himself ready . . . prepared . . . David entered the warehouse room.

TO see:

A brilliantly lit room, a stage filled with bright light, the gray walls fully lit showing their gouges; the towering metal shelves, all backdrop to the prisoners.

David's finger tightened on the trigger.

The lights made sweat bloom on his forehead, mixing with the rain still dripping off him.

He licked his lips. He tried to force himself to be aware, ready to react, but knew already that he was far behind, years behind, hopelessly behind . . . any reaction.

He saw:

James, a dangling puppet that might already be dead, having danced on his toes as long as he could to protect his neck.

Just like in the dream . . .

Another woman, upside down, unrecognizable from the stream of blood that trailed down from the trap holding her leg, the trap digging in and causing the blood to flow, the white of the bone exposed by the bright lights.

Then, to . . .

Mari, sitting in an old-fashioned wooden chair, surrounded, engulfed with razor ribbon, a spider with a cocoon of metal around her, a cocoon of metal barbs.

But she could speak.

"Behind you," she said, her voice raspy, hollow.

David started to turn, and the metal door slammed shut.

And he knew . . . it was all ready to begin.

43

DAVID turned, and the lights now blinded him and he could only see what was a shape, walking to him, a loping, rocking walk.

Then, from behind him.

"Shoot him, David. You *have* to shoot him!"

Mari's voice, from inside her metal trap.

"Stop there," David said. The gun pointed at the shadow, the scene surreal with so much brilliant light.

The shadow thing seemed to tilt its head, and take another step.

"For god's sake David—kill him!"

The voice behind him. A few thoughts as David pointed the gun to where he imagined the head to be, where this twisted man moving toward him had to have a head.

Thinking . . . *All the planning* . . .

The five people killed, drawing us together. And now, like a game, like bugs responding to a lure, to these . . . bright lights . . . and here we were.

But why? For more torture, more death?

So careful, so perfect.

Each of the other three trapped, hopelessly torturously, and yet—

I stand here with a gun.

Another step, the man's feet making a hard sound on the stone.

I need to shoot now, David thought.

"Kill him!" Mari screamed.

So well planned, and yet I stand here, gun in hand, about to kill—

David turned quickly back, then moved to the side.

His cane kicking at the stone to help him turn.

Until then he'd had a view of only the arena.

Because that's what it was, *a torture arena.*

Now he could see the three of them, and *now* the man in the shadows.

The man stopped, waiting. David turned to Mari, closer to him now. Maybe closer than planned. Because David had forced himself to move.

David looked at her; she kept repeating the words, a bleating appeal to *shoot the man, kill him.*

All this . . . in mere seconds. No time to think, no time to really question it.

He looked at her eyes.

The eyes. They tell so much.

Mari's eyes.

He felt his stomach tighten.

Her words ignored, the sound of her pleading ignored. Anyone else would have blasted the shadow. But something had been wrong, something bothered David.

The eyes. They were wrong. Dark empty dots in her head. Black bullets staring at him as she screamed for him to shoot, to kill, and—

He remembered.

It came, with an icy chill that made gooseflesh rise on his arm.

A mistake.

Everyone makes mistakes. Everything makes mistakes.

The call.

He had gotten up and walked to the phone. He walked back to the phone.

In his apartment.

And he did it all . . . without his cane.

Because it wasn't real, that call . . . how could it be?

And the dream . . .

And the words the dream James tried to say . . . *Not* . . . *Now* . . . *No* . . .

Needs.

And the other word mouthed in the dream . . . *Yet* . . . *Yes* . . .

You.

He could get up without his cane because it wasn't real. There was no call. Like the dreamers, something simply put it into his mind, what it wanted to put there, what it needed . . .

To have me here, to do this.

(And why?)

Not knowing that in a dream turned real, a doomed James could try to tell him something so important.

The reason.

But David had no time to think about that, looking at those eyes. The eyes widening, seeing a shift in David, seeing that something might now be going awry.

He heard the steps behind him.

If he was wrong, in seconds he'd become another prisoner, fallen into his own horror trap.

But David knew that this wasn't about . . . that. Not really about prisoners. Torture. Agony. Death.

Not this time.

Maybe even starting with the original five slaughters, it never was.

This . . . was about something else.

James's silent words.

One last mouthed entreaty from Mari . . . the voice finally slipping out of recognizability with David's awareness . . .

"Kill . . . him . . ."

And David turned, his gun raised, and pointed it at Mari.

SECONDS seemed like lifetimes.

David's right hand supported himself on the cane. So pathetically weak. His breathing coming so fast now. If he was wrong, if he had read this madness wrong, then the true horror would claim him and own him forever.

Needs . . . you . . .

He kept his eyes locked on Mari.

Those black empty pools, the face now contorting as it saw what he was going to do, what he understood.

He whispered an apology.

James close by—still alive!—looking over, the nearly dead doll watching this, gasping.

David pulled the trigger.

HE had aimed at the shoulder, and hit Mari just a bit lower, just below the shoulder blade.

She screamed.

But then she stood up.

The razor ribbon vanished.

Vanished!

Never there.

Sounds from behind David, mumbling from the shadows. A whimpering sound. A female voice.

The person in the chair stood up, unencumbered by the razor-sharp spikes. Stood up, and grinned.

If I am wrong . . . David thought.

He aimed at the right leg, near the pelvis, and pulled the trigger again. The gunshot—a thunderclap in the room. Blue smoke caught the brilliant light.

The target fell forward.

Only, in falling forward, it was no longer Mari at all—as two leglike arms, arms built like beefy thighs, went forward to break the fall.

Mari was *gone.*

And now the man looked up at him.

He said nothing, but started to crawl toward David, his massive hands stretched out like pincers.

David lowered the gun to the man's head. He debated firing.

But then—We'd never know all his secrets. How he did all this.

There was life, even speed left in the crawling man. David fired a third shot, this time squarely hitting the collarbone. The man moaned, gurgled.

A pool of blood bloomed around him.

He stopped moving.

And David turned around.

* * *

AND when he did turn around, there was Mari.

Alive, sitting in the chair—this time real. Her mouth making sounds, as if struggling to speak again.

The wire completely surrounded her.

David looked at her. "It's okay," he whispered. "It's over."

He reached down and looked at the razor wire.

"The others," she mumbled, slurred, ". . . get them down."

He nodded, and quickly went over and undid the wrapped coil of wire strapped to a wall fixture that held James up. He loosened the coil around his neck.

"Can you breathe?" David said.

James managed the smallest possible nod, then gestured to the woman.

David hurried there. The woman didn't move. David grabbed a hand. Felt for a pulse.

Nothing.

He turned to Mari, and walked back.

"I'm sorry—was she . . . ?"

"Linda Kyle. David, I . . . I . . ."

Mari started to cry, heaving tears making her shake, dangerous with all the wire.

"Hold on."

He found where the trail of razor ribbon began, and started slowly, carefully uncoiling it.

He stood directly in front of her.

The man was behind him.

Nothing else held Mari, just the wire—and the slightest movement would make it cut into her.

David removed the last coil that circled around her legs.

"There!" he said.

When something grabbed the ankle of his bad leg.

DAVID felt himself quickly jerked back, his gun flying away, into the air . . . then his body was yanked backward as though he weighed nothing.

"You were the one," the man on the floor hissed. "All you

had to do was kill her, and you would have been ready for me. For me to become you." Another yank, smacking David's head hard against the ground. "Years and years, beyond your imagination, and you would have been *next!*"

The man raised his meaty hand. "Centuries—and you stopped it."

The wounded man then started to smash down his hand onto David's bleeding head, ready to—David could see—crush his head against the stone.

When he heard a shot.

MARI had never fired a gun. But the principle seemed simple enough. Aim, hold it steady. And pull the trigger.

For a moment she felt this small cloud of doubt float into her mind.

Shoot? Shoot . . . which one?

Could she be sure?

She aimed at the man's head, his hand starting to fly down like a mallet on David's head.

Another explosion; blood flying like a ghoulish circus act. The mallet hand flipping away due to the recoil.

David looked up at her.

And with that look, she knew she had done the right thing.

Epilogue

CAPTAIN Biondi put a hand on David's shoulder.

"You're gonna take some time off, Detective?"

David looked up at his boss, Captain Hicks. He could tell from Hicks's expression that Biondi's question . . . wasn't a question at all.

"Yeah. Think so."

"Good idea." Biondi looked at Hicks, and David had been a detective for too long not to sense some secret deal between the two of them. "And when you come back, we'll have a new desk for you. Your own office."

A smile bloomed on Hicks's face.

"They're going to set up a new division, David. Something you'll head. For all those homicides that just don't—"

David finished the thought—

"Fit the pattern?"

"Exactly. Interested?"

David nodded, a large bandage covering the side of his head. "Yes. When I get back. I'll be very interested."

They hadn't talked much about the unreality of what had happened. *There will be time,* Hicks said.

When you're better.

There will be time . . . to understand how each dreamer, each strand, all led to David.

And David had to wonder—What would that have been like? If he had shot Mari? What would have happened next?

The office door opened, and a young Hispanic detective, someone who'd come on board the same time as James, looked at each of them, from one to the other.

"Um, Detective Corcoran's parents are here. Does—"

Hicks slid off his desktop.

"I'll take this."

But David grabbed his cane and, with surprising quickness, was on his feet.

"No. I think I want to do this."

Hicks stood beside him. "You don't have to. Not after—"

"Okay, I know I don't *have* to. But I want to, all right?"

He turned and followed the young detective, a kid.

Like me once, David thought. Back when there weren't many Hispanic detectives.

All so different now.

TWENTY minutes later, David walked out.

He felt the eyes of the secretaries, the street cops, and some detectives—all on him.

All thinking . . .

How was it? How did it go?

All of them knowing that there was no way he could have told the two people, parents, both a little over fifty, both now facing decades of whatever horror pictures their minds would conjure.

David had walked the narrow line between telling the truth and protecting them.

He emphasized their son's bravery. How they worked this case together.

How James Corcoran was one of the smartest young detectives David ever met.

But eventually he had to get around to his death.

The details, and more importantly . . . how long?

James's mother looked up at him during the meeting, her eyes begging not for the truth, but for some believable fantasy that she could hold on to . . . along with the pictures on the mantelpiece—graduation photos, baby pictures—all that was now left of her son.

"It happened fast. It was all over so quickly."

David had looked her right in the eye, knowing that the woman's husband's knowing gaze was also on him.

"James didn't suffer."

Now, standing in the office, he felt everyone's eyes on him, all of them knowing the difficult course he had just navigated.

It was time for him to go.

To go, so that someday he could come back.

And do the only thing that he knew he could do so well . . .

NONE of this ever made the official reports . . .

Nothing about the dreams, nothing about how they were all lured there.

Nothing about the visions each had, and how it all played into some plan.

And nothing about how David almost killed someone innocent, a killing that would have allowed the killer to escape.

An escape that, when David and Mari spoke of it at all, they knew had probably been going on for centuries.

He would have become me, David said.

And Mari would say nothing.

They stopped him. And that was good enough.

Except . . .

MARI turned in her bed.

The dream tonight cutting across time, and locations.

In the glistening sun of the desert seeing someone dressed in a tunic, torturing dozens of people, all of them begging in an incomprehensible language.

Then—in dark forest, a camp where travelers stand tied up while someone readies implements of torture, long spikes and hot pokers, blades that could split a hair, and so many teethed clamps designed to crush all different parts of the body.

The man goes from person to person, doing his work.

Then a foggy street, lamplight, and the sound of a girlish voice, giggles, sweet, alluring, until those giggles turn into gasps, moans, shrieks, screams—before finally ending.

Mari's at the foggy corner.

And a man in a back cape turns, and it is a face . . . she knows.

Mari cries out in the dream.

And she opens her eyes.

THE room is dark.

She turns to her right, to the person sharing her bed. She reaches out and wraps her left arm around him.

He stirs, pressing his back against her, reassuring.

A tighter hug.

"You okay?" David mumbles.

It is months later.

Months.

But it doesn't matter.

"Yes. The dream again."

Now David turns to her. His arm goes around her. He brings his face close to hers so that even in the dull light of the dark room she can see his eyes, his lips.

"I'm here," he says. "And this time—it was only a dream."

Funny, she thinks. That he could say that. *Only a dream . . .*

"I know. I know that."

"Want to get up? Some tea. Let the light chase the phantoms away?"

She shakes her head.

"No. Just hold me close. Tight."

He turns and pulls her close.

As he does, she feels the blessed warmth of his skin, and Mari finds his lips . . . and kisses him hard.

And they know that on this night, like other nights, it will be a long while before they both fell asleep again.